W9-CJO-041

I AM THE LIGHT OF THIS WORLD

ALSO BY MICHAEL PARKER

Hello Down There

The Geographical Cure

Towns Without Rivers

Virginia Lovers

If You Want Me to Stay

Don't Make Me Stop Now

The Watery Part of the World

All I Have in This World

Everything, Then and Since

Prairie Fever

I AM THE LIGHT OF THIS WORLD

a novel by

Michael Parker

ALGONQUIN BOOKS OF CHAPEL HILL 2022

Published by
ALGONQUIN BOOKS OF CHAPEL HILL
Post Office Box 2225
Chapel Hill, North Carolina 27515-2225

an imprint of Workman Publishing Co., Inc.
a subsidiary of Hachette Book Group, Inc.
1290 Avenue of the Americas
New York, NY 10104

Printed in the United States of America.
Design by Steve Godwin.

Library of Congress Cataloging-in-Publication Data

Names: Parker, Michael, [date]– author.
Title: I am the light of this world / a novel by Michael Parker.
Description: First edition. | Chapel Hill, North Carolina : Algonquin Books of Chapel Hill, 2022. | Summary: "The story of Earl, a 17-year-old boy who goes to prison for a crime he didn't commit"— Provided by publisher.
Identifiers: LCCN 2022025655 | ISBN 9781643751795 (hardcover) | ISBN 9781643753454 (ebook)
Subjects: LCGFT: Novels.
Classification: LCC PS3566.A683 I32 2022 | DDC 813/.54—dc23/eng/20220602
LC record available at https://lccn.loc.gov/2022025655

10 9 8 7 6 5 4 3 2 1
First Edition

For Maud Casey

A sense of destiny is a terrible thing.

—JIM HARRISON

I AM
THE
LIGHT
OF
THIS
WORLD

PART ONE

Stovall, Texas, 1973

I.

BECAUSE EARL'S CLOTHES were line-dried, they smelled of sun, grass, earth. But the girls on the bus said he smelled like creek mud. The girls were even meaner in the winter when he wore parkas donated by the Kiwanis Club coats-for-kids drive, easily recognized by the fake fur collars, which reeked of the kerosene used to heat their house.

At home, his family treated him like a second cousin much removed. "Oh, look, Earl," they'd say after he'd been sitting quietly in a room for a half hour. He was seventeen and did not mind being unseen, but he knew he was creek mud to them, too. And so he refused their offer of a snack of celery filled with peanut butter and dotted with raisins, because, seriously? Ants on a log?

Into the smoke from neighbors burning their trash in rusty barrels slipped Earl, on the lookout for someone to whom he might define himself. But he always ended up in the woods, listening to the transistor radio his father had given him, or reading aloud from the biography of Lead Belly he carried with him always.

His people were proud Louisianans who'd moved, for reasons unknown to Earl, across the border to Stovall, Texas. His father was vaguely around. His mother talked all the time to her sisters in Bossier City, installing a twenty-foot cord on the telephone so she could sit outside on the front stoop and smoke and ask her sisters about the fates of various men she might have married instead.

Prison, preacherman, gay, career military, Port Arthur were the answers Earl imagined coming across the line. "Shoo now, Earl," said his mother when she caught him snooping.

Earl had two brothers, two years older: Cary and Larry, identical twins. They were sly and slow-eyed. When they were young, all three boys wore striped T-shirts and crew cuts. Therein ended the likeness. Now, his brothers rode their banana bikes cock-legged, hips jutting as they looped surly circles down the street, talking sideways to each other in a language both unique and precociously foul. They spent most of their time heckling Cedric Drawhorn, who had been beat in the head with a tommy gun during the Korean War and thereafter walked the streets shooing imaginary swarms of gnats from his head.

Earl liked to believe his family were not bad people. Nobody ever beat him with a garden hose. His brothers were technically juvenile delinquents—they put out the eye of a neighborhood boy with a slingshot and dropped bricks from overpasses onto only Winnebagos—but aspects of their choices could be intriguing. They wore cutoff blue jeans year-round. They sheared off the pant legs in a zigzagged pattern that impressed Earl, even as he struggled to understand it.

His father, when he worked, laid pipe or worked in the oilfields. He claimed to be Acadian but his mother said he was out of Lawton, Oklahoma. She once told Earl that their last name was "assumed," adding that this didn't bother her because Boudreaux sounded better than Miller, which she'd spent her first seventeen years hating. Wherever his father was from, his brothers and cousins soon arrived in Stovall and a compound of trailers and vehicles sanded down to primer or missing bumpers or outright wrecked beyond repair sprung up in the piney woods on the outskirts of town. Earl's father once took him on a walk through the woods to a pond, where he taught him the words to "I'm So Lonesome I Could Cry." Even when his father disappeared for weeks, Earl had his transistor radio, on which his father claimed to have listened to stations out of Fort Wayne, Indiana, and Matamoros, Mexico, when he was a boy in his bed at night. Was there anything in the world more romantic than listening to radio stations from other countries illicitly after lights-out?

Yes there sure was, and Earl came one day to hear it on some old forty-five of his father's. Earl couldn't even remember who was singing or about what. He just remembered lying on the floor watching the warped vinyl hiccup and here came an ample solo of what he would learn was pure pedal steel. Earl felt draped by a blanket and shocked by a cattle prod. The pedal steel both softened and sharpened. Say you were a river. Say there was no wind. Still river equaled words set to music written out flat on a page. Now add pedal steel. Wing it in on a westerly breeze. Hear the plaintive shiver of leaves through trees lining the bank.

Pedal steel could turn a song into what, Earl didn't know, your heart struggling to stay in rhythm and burst out of you at the same time? Trying to define it made Earl feel foolish and that is how he knew it was true. He would die trying and that is how he knew it was true.

Earl walked the outskirts of town, past tire shops that sold only retreads, stores that claimed to repair sewing machines. The air smelled of bacon grease, gasoline, and pine resin. Paths snaked off into the piney woods, beer cans and cast-away underpants lining the trail instead of the breadcrumbs of phony fables.

On his walks he often ran into street lurkers: Moonwalk, Sleepy T., Burnt Cheese.

"Hey, ho, Earl, what's the good word?"

"The blue light was my baby, the red light was my mind," said Earl, a line he'd heard his father sing while shaving.

Often he would see these same men later in his backyard on nights his daddy was in town. They gathered there to listen to music by their shed, its wormy chestnut walls painted by the day's last slant of yellow. They favored what Earl dubbed the negative adjectival: if a man did not have a light, he was one no-pack-of-matches-having sapsucker. Earl liked to listen to them argue over what was worse. He never heard them argue about what was better. On into the night they would argue, while the world turned black and white and branches in shadow clawed at the walls of the shed, though only Earl seemed to notice.

Was he put on earth to notice? He saw a Band-Aid stuck to

the bottom of a swimming pool. Once he'd seen it, he couldn't not. He saw it in the sky while floating on his back, watching grackles chase each other from the limbs of a live oak to the top of a telephone pole. Between the live oak and the telephone pole, a Band-Aid the size of a jumbo jet, wavy in the manner of items on the bottoms of pools. He saw a grocery cart come not to rest at the bottom of a roadside culvert and its eternal restlessness did not unnerve him. It was no blight, unlike the music played on the radio, 97 percent garbage food from a chain store. Nor did the lone shoe in the median bring on a bout of melancholy. Most would consign to this sight only loss; Earl saw independence, freedom, escape.

On his walks he collected scraps of sun-dyed paper dancing leaflike across lawns. Grocery lists; receipts from the gas station; on a lucky day, love notes. All he had to do was bend to pluck the paper and sometimes scrape dried mud to read the words. Sometimes the paper was stiff from having been soaked by what Earl believed to be tears. Here came the sun to dry off and preserve the better part of it, send it on to Earl. *Baby why you do me like you do me? Darling are you really only fifteen? Meet me at the fiddler's convention outside Alexandria.* As he read them he heard his aunts recounting the fates of his mother's might-have-marrieds.

Other people's messages: on index cards filed in a plastic box, he wrote them down, along with other phrases, some he'd found in books he checked out from the Stovall library and some he overheard on his walks. As for other people themselves, well: he welcomed their company, but he preferred to talk to himself.

"I am the light of this world," he told himself, because he had heard it said in a song. "I am good at stripes. I can recognize the four basic face shapes, I can hum the minor-key melodies that accompany movie credits playing in my head."

"Well, let me ask you this, Earl," replied a voice celestial but garbled by a passing logging truck. "Can you be not good at No and not terribly good at Yes?"

"But of course you can if you want to please everybody by going along for the ride. Just pat your pockets for your forgotten wallet when the car rolls up to the gas pump."

2.

DAYS AFTER THEY met, Tina would say to Earl: "I always think of when in school we studied various origin stories. From many cultures worldwide. I don't know what month it was but maybe November because there was rain and leaves falling out of the sky, and I was somehow able to stare outside at the wet leaves sticking to the sidewalk waiting to be carried away on the bottom of somebody's shoe and listen to how a certain Native American tribe believed an eagle dropped the first two of them—their Adam and Eve—into this sacred valley. The valley was in the desert, but it was also blue or maybe turquoise with some streaks of silver. I was really into it until this girl Sharon raised her hand and said, 'How's that different from the whole stork thing?' And the teacher said, 'What stork thing?' And Sharon said her mother told her that a stork delivered her and her brother and sister and the teacher said, 'That's not really an origin story as much as it is a euphemism.' And then Sharon's mouth fell open in a slack 'Say what?' position that was pretty much its normal position and the teacher took pity on her and said—instead of, 'Your mother does not think you are mature enough to know how to get down'—'Does your mother believe our civilization arose out of stork deliveries?' By civilization she meant the white people of Texas because she was a racist bitch, her idea of created equal was to let a Black or brown kid beat the erasers clean on a tree once a semester, and Sharon said, 'Um, yeah, she does?'"

Earl and Tina were in the woods not far from where they had first come upon each other. Deep silence alternated with the gunshots of offseason poachers and the buzzing of illegal sawmills. Tina did not need to spell out what all this had to do with Earl. Earl knew she would not mind switching out their origin story.

But Earl treasured the way they found each other because it was so normal as to be unbelievable. One day Earl was sitting on a log in the woods reading *Lead Belly: His Life and Times* when Tina appeared.

She was freckly and appeared tall, though it was true Earl was sitting low on a log. Her hair might have made it to her shoulders had it not twisted away in curlicues that made Earl think of ribbon and also smoke. She was bony. He thought of a line from his other favorite book, *Satchmo*, the authorized biography of Louis Armstrong, wherein Satchmo described a slender woman as being "raggedy as a bowl of cole slaw." And yet Tina glowed with a rare pale energy.

"Read me some of that book," she said by way of greeting.

Earl read from the section where Lead Belly was freed from prison due to his astonishing musical ability. When he was done, Tina said, "I know this guy from Brazil. Soccer player, only he calls it football."

Earl did not see why, if a famous folklorist discovering raw genius in the cotton fields of Angola evoked a memory of a Brazilian soccer player, he ought not to be able to skip the interminably awkward chitchat he knew was up next and go straight not just to necking but love. He was planning his move when Tina started telling him about going to see Leon Russell in Houston.

"There were so many thousands gathered, of all walks of life, singing 'Delta Lady.' I guess you could say it was really something."

She sang into the silence of the woods, between gunshots and chainsaws, "'Please don't ask how many times I found you / standing wet and naked in the garden.'"

Earl said he would never ask such a question. He did ask her, in an attempt at chitchat, or rather a land speed record at getting such chitchat out of the way, what scared her.

"School nurses. Cuckoo clocks."

Not the most original primal fears but at least not cave crickets or spelunking. She sat down beside him on the log and told him to keep on reading and he did, but the words were delivered as if by stork, for he was discovering what he would always love about Tina: he could be with her and also elsewhere. For instance: in a sunken field he once passed on the way down to the gulf. Late winter and cloudy. Standing water in the furrows of roadside fields. A tractor disking black earth, a string of gulls in tow. All Tina had to do was be Tina for Earl to remember a booth he favored in a diner at the edge of town. Duct tape covered a rip in the Naugahyde. The seat cushion was so worn, the springs so long shot, that the space between it and the back of the booth nipped sweetly at Earl's buttocks.

Earl shared with Tina his love of pedal steel. Tina said she favored a Hammond organ. Why, he asked, and she was ready with the answer: Because I like to roller skate backwards.

Only later did Earl learn she was from Navasota. Her father had sent her to live with his sister in Stovall after her mother got committed to the state hospital in Austin. That was all he knew about her for the longest time. Talk fell off when they went to kissing. Earl thought, while kissing Tina, of pressure washers powered by air compressors. And he thought of snowflakes, and sought a compromise, with his lips, between the two.

Turtles sunned themselves on shore. Their indifference to budding love was annoying and noteworthy.

Earl took Tina night swimming. Her skin felt like velvet, but in an oil slick.

"What do you see yourself doing in five years?" Tina asked Earl as he held her in the dark water.

The question put Earl in the mind of mathematics, of outer space. Yet he had some idea of where he would not be at age twenty-two. When he was still in grade school he had decided that, much as he loved the country, and maybe *because* he loved the country, the country was no good for him. If you tended toward melancholy, the country—its cornfields raspy in the autumn wind, and its line of woods in the distance beyond the fields, the shadowy mouths of those woods as bloodred as the mouths of love singers he had watched on television, contorting with microphones, their love wracking their bodies with seizures, wacko love about to strike them dead on stage—the country whispered secrets. According to the country, love was dark and wet and deceitful.

"You first," he said, thinking of the far future, the last of his days, which he would spend in some city high-rise reserved for elderly swimmers, with a view of water and of afternoon storms rolling in from the west and lights blinking on at dusk.

"My friend Alicia goes out with one of the roadies from ZZ Top," said Tina. She said she was going to go to Houston and get her GED and live in an apartment with Alicia, who didn't have to work because the roadie floated her from his roadie money plus what he made selling pot to high school students, which is how he met Alicia.

"I guess I'll get work at a water park," said Tina, but Earl hardly heard her because he had a vision of the future. A ferry crossed a river. It docked at an abandoned shipyard. Tugboats rusted at a tilt, as if listing in surf, in waist-high sea oat. Only Earl knew how to get there, by back road.

"You can come with us," Tina was saying. "Alicia goes on the road with the band sometimes."

In the future Earl would have no body at all. He would hear the voice of his beloved everywhere—in sirens, the cries of seagulls circling the abandoned shipyard—and he would be without vertebra or even cartilage. He would be a note slurred by a trumpet muted with a balled-up pair of tube socks. But who was this beloved?

"My father told me *Tres Hombres* was recorded just up the road in Tyler," said Earl.

"I think not," said Tina.

"Maybe not, then," said Earl, though he was pretty sure his father would not lie about ZZ Top. He might lie if he had another family in Arkansas, but not about *Tres Hombres.*

"I'm glad I'm not scared of things I can't see in the water in the night," said Tina.

She pushed herself out of his embrace and swam away from him. She wanted him to follow and he did, underwater, his arms extended, pretending to be a school nurse holding a cuckoo clock.

Tina needed to get home to her aunt. Her aunt was respectable and Methodist and probably lesbian according to Tina.

"At the very least a thirty-eight-year-old virgin," Tina said. They had dried off and were lying in the sun on a bedspread by the water. "My life would open up in astounding ways if only she would take a secret lover. I don't care male or female, just so long as she had something to do besides me."

"Why does the lover need to be a secret?" Earl asked.

"She couldn't just up and start dating at her ancient age. He would have to be married or a she."

"My mother can't stand her," said Tina. "She never cared for any of my father's people. My mother is from Houston and she eloped with my father against the wishes of her family. Now where are they? He's gone and locked my mother up in the bin."

"Maybe we can go see her," said Earl.

"Oh really, Earl, can we?" Tina said, scooting close. She spoke in the theatrical manner of an actress in a grainy movie from the forties you could only see on a television when you were home sick from school and there was a lull in game shows. Though his mother loved these movies. The women in them all wore boxy-shouldered dresses and wavy hair and they made his mother cry when they said things at once desperate and vulnerable.

"Oh can we please?" Tina was saying. "Would you do that, would you do that for *me*?"

"I can borrow a car from a cousin. I have about twenty-three, give or take. Between them they have enough vehicles to put the Stovall Christmas parade to shame."

The first time Earl brought Tina around to the shed where the lurkers sat passing bottles and joints, Burnt Cheese said, "Hold up now, there goes our boy Earl, stepping out and stepping *up!*"

There had followed elaborate introductions from each, ranging from *Hey Little Mama I am pleased to acquaint myself to yourself, they call me Sleepy T but you can call my hotline anytime* to *Earl is our special one and only pearl so go easy now Tiger Lily, treat him royal,* etc.

To escape the scrutiny (which Tina did not seem to mind) Earl led her away from the shed and into the house, down the back hallway, where he pulled down the folding stairs to the attic. He wanted her to see his safest place: his treasured eaves. Because the attic darkened at its sloped edges and those edges in their endless shadow suggested to Earl not only the world beyond his world but the very curve of the earth, he had spent hours here, having strange thoughts: that he would spend his last days in a city high-rise watching the plumes of passing airplanes imitate clouds; that, should he live where it snowed and it snowed, he wanted only to think, well, it's snowing, just that, without wondering or caring whether it was a good thing or not, snow.

"Are there any dressmaker's dummies up here?" Tina asked. "In movies, old attics like these are full of dressmaker's dummies. Oh man I forgot to tell you Alicia told me about going to this ranch with her roadie boyfriend, some filthy rich guy who hired the band to play his private pool party for like thousands and they all got high and rich dude took them all up to the top floor of this barn where you're supposed to store hay bales and it was filled with piñatas hanging from the rafters and the piñatas were filled with pills."

"No way," said Earl, staring at the hypotenuse extending into infinity. He used to come here hunting silence. If it was not to be found—if his mother was outside yelling into the phone at one of her sisters so loudly it was coming through the vents for the attic fan, if his brothers were downstairs bragging, if the noise of the record player terrorized his quiet—if phone ring, if floorboard creak, if bird song—he waited. And when silence came, it was a showering of cotton balls come to bury him. He lay himself down to sleep in it.

But now he wanted Tina to see what he saw in the sloping shadows.

"It's hot up here," said Tina.

Earl pointed to the corners, and explained, as best he could, his mysterious eaves.

Tina put her fingers in his belt loops and pulled him to her.

"Are we about to slow dance?" said Earl.

"Better," said Tina, and she kissed his neck and said, "You see everything, don't you, Earl. That is why I can't stand it when you go away. I just sit around and look out a window and think, what would Earl see that I don't? And how does he see all that when's he not even high?"

Sometimes they did get high on the dirt weed his brothers hid, badly, beneath a brickbat out by the shed. He watched them hide it, from the woods one day. His crazy-mean brothers: they would kill him if they saw him spying from the woods when they stashed the baggies they carried in their underwear, certain that no cop would pat down their crotch. He was careful to pinch only enough to roll a scrawny joint. Earl could only feel it if he put his head under some pond water and breathed bubbles, but Tina got all glassy-eyed and laughed into hiccups at a twig tangled up in Earl's hair. Either she wanted to be high so bad the very ritual of it got her off, or the grass worked on parts of her that Earl did not have.

He fell hard in love with those parts. They were inexhaustible and Earl believed they would always be, for his love was high hope as much as lie down and die. Sometimes, though, he felt more of the latter when she was over at her aunt's looking out the window trying to see what he might see.

One day after he'd brought Tina home several times, his mother found him sitting under a tree with *Lead Belly: His Life and Times*.

"So where did y'all meet?"

"In the pines," said Earl.

His mother sighed her once-I-had-aspirations sigh. "I guess that's just what happens when forced to raise children in the wild," she said.

"Where did you meet dad?"

"He's just always been there."

"You knew him when you were little?"

"We were little when we got together if little means how old y'all are now which by the way that is exactly what little means."

"She's eighteen."

"I like her hair," said Earl's mother. "What she's up to with it and all."

"She doesn't believe in those blow dryers. Something about carcinogenic."

"She seems a little odd? Baby, I know I can say that to you. I know you won't hate me for it like your brothers would if I were to say something about the trash they string around with, which why bother? I like her, Earl, but have you noticed that when she speaks it's like she's all of a sudden been given the lead in some musical? Except she can't sing?"

Earl said no, but he meant, well, yes. Or he meant, actually, she can sing, just off key and a little too loud.

His mother said, "I wouldn't know her people because I am not from this godforsaken town but who is she?"

"She's from Navasota. She came here to stay with her aunt."

"Her parents sent her off? What did she do?"

"She didn't do anything. Her mother is in the hospital."

"Oh dear. Poor girl. I take it all back. Except about the hair."

"The hospital is in Austin. I want to take Tina to see her."

"That's nice. Your father seems to like to go to Austin instead of to the oilfields where he is meant to go. I have no idea what he does there and I don't think I care anymore."

"Are you going to leave him?"

"Oh, Earl," his mother said. "Put down your book for once."

Earl held *Lead Belly: His Life and Times* tightly to his chest. It was open to a favorite passage, and he did not want to lose his place.

"Listen," his mother said.

But she didn't say anything. They sat listening. At first to nothing, and then to trees falling in forests. The thrum of traffic on Interstate 20, an hour north. The faint drumbeat of marching band practice in a Dallas suburb, the squawk of badly played horns ricocheting off buildings and cars.

The silence became symphonic. What they heard together was everything in the world, beyond the terrifying thump of blood in their hearts.

"Did you hear?"

"Yes."

"Just remember, Earl."

3.

YOU DID NOT need a license to drive in the black-mouthed country so long as you observed the etiquette of Texas back roads: pull to the shoulder when a vehicle comes up on you traveling at a higher rate of speed. Do the same for an ambulance. Always stick up an index finger in greeting to all pickups and never fail to keep to the right of a passing lane unless passing.

So long as your feet could reach the pedals and you could steer enough to keep it between the ditches, Johnny Law would not waste time on your no-driver's-license-possessing self, at least in the country. But what about the city? Earl had never even been to one, and he'd certainly never driven in one.

For all he knew there was a gate around Austin. High fence topped with barbed wire, or at least the low enclosures of the ranchettes they passed as they cut down Texas 31 toward Corsicana. The ranchettes were humble but proud, each marked by its own ornate wrought iron gate framing the rutted two-track that led off into pasture or piney woods. When houses and outbuildings were visible, they were studded with rusty tin Lone Stars the size of wagon wheels. The Texas flag adorned entire sides of every other barn they passed.

They had packed sandwiches, which they ate an hour outside of town at a roadside picnic area by the Trinity River. Earl wanted to strip down and fling himself into the water, which was black and still and, being liquid, inherently dangerous and sexy, but Tina had not stopped talking since Earl picked her up in the Galaxie 500 he borrowed from his cousin Leif (not his real name, stolen from a teen idol who stole it from a Viking) and was talking about some Western she'd seen. Maybe it was two Westerns? Earl came up from the bottom of the river to hear Tina recounting the plot of *They Call Me Trinity,* but when he submerged himself and popped up again, she was on to *Trinity Is Still My Name.*

Neither seemed her type of movie. Certainly they weren't his. Earl favored movies featuring the blind. *The Miracle Worker, A Patch of Blue.* When he was in the first grade his father had loaded them all up in a station wagon and taken them to the drive-in to see a double feature of *Help!* and *A Hard Day's Night.* Even then he knew that he preferred the Stones to the Beatles, though he'd yet to hear the Stones. He just knew things he'd never heard or seen and when he saw them, heard them? Let's say they existed only for him to encounter them and when he did—when he heard for the first time "Ruby Tuesday" or saw in a library book a reproduction of *Christina's World,* he was all like, Well, yeah.

Tina talked on, free-associating about Westerns that shared a name with the river Earl floated down in his mind. The river emptied into the gulf where Earl got a job on an oil derrick cooking for roustabouts too dissolute to make it in the oil fields, or anywhere on dry land. Barbarous souls, pirates essentially, who used their shifts at sea to dry out, though they were always popping White Crosses or Black Beauties so that they might stay up all night to see the sun rise from the ocean where they were convinced it slept.

The question in Earl's head at the moment, however, aside from how to drive in Austin proper, was: Was Tina the sort of person whom one might call complicated? She ate everything you put in front of her and remained mostly bone. Was this the result of the famously revved-up teenage metabolism or some deep and hopefully conflicting desires raging in her soul, requiring 24/7 fueling? Earl was slow to eat his sandwich, so preoccupied was he by the river, and when he looked down he saw that she'd eaten half of it, plus a can of Pringles and some grapes. Also it was barely nine in the morning and they'd already stopped for lunch.

Of course she was nervous about seeing her mother, who was locked up in the Texas state asylum. Your daddy's rich and your mother's good looking but crazy. Hush little baby, don't you cry.

Back on the highway, Tina was talking about donut holes, which she saw as a symbol of greed and also stupidity because the whole point of a donut as opposed to a kolach was that it had a hole in the middle, as did, she said, most adults—especially her aunt, which she could easily fill with a secret lover—but back to donuts, it made no sense at all to sell the holes cut from donuts as it rendered the concept . . .

Earl had to quit listening and pay attention to his driving since he was without a license. The speed limit was seventy until you came to one of the hamlets that appeared every five to ten miles. Earl was especially careful not to speed in these backwaters because Moonwalk had told him that all these busted, no-revenue-earning towns could only fund their Fourth of July fireworks show if they pulled people over for going a mile over the limit. Earl mostly coasted, which was difficult in East Texas. You could only coast for a few yards before pumping the gas.

"You are a very staccato driver," Tina said, which made Earl beam, as it seemed proof of her complexity.

"Why don't you have your license?" Earl asked Tina once, and she blamed it on her aunt, which Earl could have predicted. She blamed everything on her aunt, her father being rich and her mother good looking but maybe insane, which was somehow also her aunt's fault.

Earl saw a sign for Navasota. He thought to point it out, but he was at that moment in a helicopter above the brownish Gulf of Mexico, which is how he got to work at his job in the galley of the oil rig.

The radio played forgotten songs.

"See can you find any Roy Orbison," said Tina.

"You like Roy Orbison?" He'd only heard her talk about ZZ Top.

"My mother's favorite singer," she said.

And so he twisted the dial, lingering a bit on the preaching, which he had a thing for. It was the rhythm of their testimony—chicken-fried incantatory if they were white, hot-buttered gospel if they were Black—that carried the message. Hell, it *was* the message. But Tina wasn't about to put up with the preaching, and so he twisted the knob past the raucous accordions of a Tejano station; brash advertisements for ambulance-chasing personal injury lawyers, which made Earl sad as he pictured them busting out of their cheap, shiny suits, fat off the proceeds of someone losing a lung from working in an asbestos plant; rock and roll of the stripe he would live to later hear called "classic"—searching for Roy Orbison but encountering only thunderous static.

Tina was talking about the Houston water park where she would get a job while attaining her GED. The apartment where Earl could stay with her (you might have to pay some rent, she said) would have a balcony. Who doesn't love a balcony? She wouldn't be draping any wet beach towels and bathing suits over it, even though come to think of it she would probably have to wear a bathing suit to work.

"It would be my uniform," she said. "Think of me in a bathing suit with a name tag."

Try as he might, Earl couldn't quite picture the name tag.

Around Waco the trees thinned. Slight hills appeared, covered in blonde grass and clumps of cattle. Cacti clumped together also, often around mailboxes. Earl, who had never been west or south of Stovall, wondered if this was a strategic move to keep folks from stealing mail, putting a mailbox upside a bunch of cacti.

"When we get to Austin we should go by and see my friend Richie," Tina was saying.

"Don't you want to go see your mother first?"

She had not said a word all morning about her mother. But why would she? Surely she was terrified to see her and maybe even more terrified to see her in a place she could not leave.

"Richie works at Tower Records. He gets a crazy discount. You should see his collection. Well, you're about to."

"How do you know this Richie?"

"*This* Richie? You sound like my aunt. Already you don't like him."

"Already I don't know him. I am not your Methodist upright possibly lesbian aunt." The traffic was thickening. They were suddenly on the sort of highway called super. Back home it was called a four-lane and avoided for back roads. Earl longed for a back road into the city, one that exposed, like the tracks that carried trains, the backs of things: factories, foundries, banks, houses. What might you see from the window of a train? The part not meant for public viewing. Backyards littered with toys. Some teenagers sleeping on a trampoline. A man cutting another man's hair on a back porch. Maybe lovers in their glorious apex. An entire family dancing to "Fun," by Sly and the Family Stone.

"So many dang trucks," said Earl. He clutched the steering wheel hard as if the Galaxie might get sucked by passing trucks into another galaxy, in the manner of his thoughts and especially his thoughts when he was with and simultaneously *not* with Tina.

"What do you have against Richie anyway," Tina was saying.

"I don't have anything against Richie," he said. "Maybe he can tell us how to get to the hospital."

"Get off here," said Tina, pointing to an upcoming exit, which Earl had to cross two lanes to make. They passed a massive football stadium where Tina said she'd seen Emerson, Lake and Palmer. The piano player, you wouldn't believe it, his piano rose up in the air and started doing somersaults and he was playing it the whole time.

Earl wondered how he defied gravity, but he was too busy driving to ask, plus Tina had pointed out the tower where the sniper shot and killed all those people some years back.

"I believe he shot a pregnant lady and her baby maybe lived? Imagine that kid's life."

Earl was happy to be invited to imagine anyone's life, but he was, he realized, too busy imagining his own. Plus, so many people! It was warm out and everyone drove with their windows down, sending stray guitar and even drum solos out into the street, as well as clouds of smoke. It was not unlike tuning a radio, driving down this street, which Tina referred to as "the Drag." On one side a strip of pizza and beer joints and T-shirt stops and on the other the orderly quads of campus. All the roofs were tiled in the Spanish manner and the bricks were yellowish as they were in Earl's part of Texas, which was essentially Louisiana once removed.

"Turn right," said Tina. She seemed awfully familiar with the neighborhood, but her mysterious knowledge was sexy to Earl. They passed blocks of houses with grassless yards and ratty couches pulled close to porch railings.

"Here," she said, pointing at a house with a turret where a party, it seemed, was in progress. As soon as Earl put the car in park, Tina was out the door and up the sidewalk and into the grassless yard and up on the porch.

He found her in the kitchen, having passed many people sitting around listening to some sort of jazz fusion, if that was the term for it. Jazz fusion had not reached Stovall, which made Earl both wary and insecure. The kitchen was packed with slit-eyed people who looked as if they came with the house, like a stove. Wandering the house in search of Tina, Earl saw records and posters, musical instruments, a lamp made from the bottom half of a female mannequin. Also a paper-mache llama, which Earl suspected was filled with pills.

"Richie, this is Earl. Earl, Richie," said Tina. They were wedged in a corner hard by the fridge. Richie wore his hair pulled back in a ponytail and his mustache extended to the edges of his jaw. There was a name for this, but Earl did not remember things like the names of mustache styles. It seeped in some part of his brain that absorbed information of no real use to him now or later. He was never going to say to Richie, "I really like your [insert name of style of mustache here]." Nor would he ask Tina why her friend Richie favored [insert name of style of mustache here].

Anyway, in a few minutes they would be on their way to the hospital.

Richie slid his hand along Earl's outstretched palm and gripped his fingers in what seemed to be a weak modification of the elaborate handshakes favored by the likes of Moonwalk, Sleepy T, Burnt Cheese.

Earl said, "Are you from Navasota?"

"From where?"

"Where she's from," said Earl, but Tina was pulling Richie by the hand to another side of the kitchen where she whispered into his ear something long and breathless, which made Richie shake his head in a manner that made Earl realize that Tina was right, he did not care for Richie at all. But then they came back over and Richie pulled a joint out of the pocket of his T-shirt and lit it with a flick of a zippo and passed it to Earl and said, "Welcome to Austin, Tina was just telling me you've never been here so please allow me to be your ambassador and your emissary not to mention I can get you anything you want, whatever you desire, say the word, boss man."

Earl was used to the tiny-buzz-and-big-headache weed he stole from his brothers. Richie's grass was of a quality that allowed him to pick out a bass line in the faraway jazz fusion and pronounce it profound.

After a half dozen hits Earl was striking up conversations with strangers. He introduced himself as Clothesline, the nickname Moonwalk and them gave him because, they said, he could hang. Someone handed him a beer and it seemed to still be in his hand an hour later, half full. He had embarked upon a long lecture on the proper uses of what he had dubbed, after studying it during many late-night drinking sessions by his father's shed, the negative adjectival. His audience was a philosophy major named Eric, who quoted some Germans and introduced everyone who passed by to Clothesline, Master of the Negative Adjectival. Earl was called upon to demonstrate the unknown construction for every new person and no one minded when he called a fellow a no-mustache-growing-look-like-a-hairy-wind-blew-out-the-barbershop-window-and-grazed-you-lightly-above-your-lip son of a something or another. Well, maybe the fellow minded, but the laughter was so general he was forced to join in.

"Wherefore art thou, Tina?"

Wherefore doesn't mean where, said Eric the philosophy major, and Earl understood he had spoken aloud.

"You check Richie's room? Upstairs. You have to go through the bathroom to get to it. Richie lives in a walk-in closet."

Why would Tina be in a closet with Richie asked the part of Earl diligently mindful of their errand, which was to visit Tina's mother in the Texas state mental asylum, to which she had been committed wrongfully by Tina's father. Remembering his purpose made him feel deeply ashamed for impersonating someone named Clothesline and the shame deepened into anxiety, quickening his breath and then nearly robbing him of it. Once Moonwalk told him that a cat would suck the breath out of a baby.

"Never leave a baby alone with a cat," he said.

"You are one strange dude, Clothesline," said Eric.

Off he ran in search of Tina. The stairs were hard to climb, crowded as they were with people who sat staring down at the landing as if it were a stage. The jazz fusion had thankfully been replaced by *Workingman's Dead*, a record that Earl admired for its unabashed and seemingly pure embrace of country music, especially the pedal steel and the high, sweet, lonesome harmonies.

High and lonesome is what you are in this world, said the no-driver's-license-possessing part of Earl.

Upstairs were many rooms with mattresses on the floor and on the mattresses passed-out people and in one room a naked couple making unself-conscious love in a shaft of sunlight. They would have been beautiful if they had not appeared to be wrestling. But light hit the hair of the woman, isolating its wild strands, emphasizing its resemblance to a thicket, and Earl said, Oh. Unlike his "wherefore," he spoke to himself, which was a good thing as it made his departure from the room and from the house far easier.

4.

"NICE TO MEET you, Earl. How you feeling?"

Had he felt like talking to a cop, Earl would have said he felt like creek mud. He had been up for three days and his belly felt like a trash-burner wood stove of the stripe he'd seen in country churches. He was thirsty enough to drink dew off poison ivy.

"Whenever your lawyer gets here, I'm going to ask you some questions and I want you to answer me honest Injun, okay?"

Honest Injun, was this guy for real? Earl was seventeen not six. Plus, the racist fuck, what if Earl *was* Injun?

"How old are you, Earl?"

Well now that depended. Earl was there but not there, which messed with time, making murky even the number of his years on earth.

"It's not a question requires a lot of thought put into it, Earl."

"Seventeen and a half."

The door opened and a big man in a small suit arrived. "Don't tell him anything," the man said, which led Earl to assume, from watching Perry Mason once or twice with his mother, that he was the lawyer.

The lawyer looked at the tape recorder and said to the cop, "That thing rolling?" and the cop said, "Of course not, you're late as per usual, Arthur," and the lawyer leaned over and said into the machine, as if it were recording, "Let the record show that counsel is only five minutes late" and the cop played along with the tape-recorder-switched-on game and said, "Let the record show that counsel was waiting in line at Sunrise Biscuit when he should have been in this room and also while we are showing, let's show that counsel did not bring me nor his client jack to eat or drink though he himself is sipping on a large iced tea and has in hand a bag so greasy it's got to be a chicken biscuit."

"I didn't know what kind of biscuit you favored, Phil." The lawyer looked at Earl. "You neither, though you ought to be out of here in a half hour tops and I'll buy you a biscuit on the house. Well, your mother's paying for this, so it's not exactly on the house. I just mean I won't charge her extra."

The cop pushed Play on the machine. He said his name and that he was a detective for the Stovall Police Department and then he said the lawyer's name, which was Arthur something, Earl didn't catch the last name, and that he was also present.

"How did my mother find you?" asked Earl, who would have figured his father more familiar with the law, unless his mother didn't pay her phone bill.

"It was a family friend brought me to your mother's attention," the lawyer said. "I believe you might know him by his nickname. Sleepy T. he goes by."

"Lord in Heaven," said the cop.

"That smacks of prejudice, Phil. You might be familiar with the fellow, but his character is irrelevant in the here and now. "

The cop sighed and asked Earl to state his full name and his date of birth.

"You know the boy's name and you don't need his date of birth," said the lawyer. He was about to bust out of his slick suit. He looked to have walked out of one of those radio advertisements that promise to procure folks with incurable cancer fat settlements from asbestos plants. But he was not unlikeable. He seemed like the type to wink at everything without actually winking.

"It's procedure," said the cop.

"Proceed right on with the charges, then," said the lawyer, opening the bag and pulling out a chicken biscuit and taking a big bite and rudely chewing.

"He's already been charged. Auto theft and driving without a license. You knew that or you would be sitting in your booth at Sunrise, cussing over editorials of the Stovall *Daily Advance*, as is your daily habit. But there's the question of this missing girl and your boy here being the last person seen in her company."

"I don't see what his driving without a license has to do with this missing girl. He's old enough to drive."

"That's your defense?" said the cop.

The lawyer turned to Earl.

"Why don't you have your license?"

"It's on the list," said Earl, which was something he had always wanted to say.

"Are you going to shut up and let me interview this little peckerwood?"

The lawyer smiled sidelong at Earl and said, "We got that on tape, him telling counsel to shut up."

The lawyer didn't seem to mind Earl being called a peckerwood.

The cop was bulky. He was wearing a light green dress shirt too tight about the neck. Something about him suggested to Earl he had been turned down by all branches of the armed forces including the Coast Guard, which took in Burnt Cheese until they found out what he was made of, which was burnt cheese.

"Let's start with Adelaide Morgan."

"Start with who now?" Earl said.

"The young lady last seen in the passenger seat of the car you stole."

"I never stole it. I borrowed it from Leif. And are you talking about Tina?"

"You were driving a car that was reported stolen. Without a license, to boot. But let's talk about this young lady that's not been seen since she left town with you in that same vehicle going on three days now. Where and when did you and Adelaide Morgan first meet?"

"In the woods. Not sure when." *Farmers were burning their fields. Her hair smelled of smoke.*

"What woods?"

"Behind the gravel pit."

"What were you doing in the woods?"

"Sitting on a log reading a book."

"Doing your lessons, were you? What book?"

"What does it matter what he was reading?" said the lawyer to the cop. He turned to Earl. "Just out of curiosity, though, what were you reading?"

"*Lead Belly, His Life and Times.*"

"Not a great role model," said the lawyer.

"Who is Lead Belly?" said the cop.

"Are you culturally illiterate as well?"

"As well as what?" said the cop.

Sometimes Earl lived in the country. Sometimes he got a notion. He wondered what did old Huddie Ledbetter mean he would get Irene in her dreams? Was he saying, Girl, catch you later in dreamland or was it more like, You can't escape me, even when you're lying up in your bed sweet-dreaming? Which? What makes it a good song Earl guessed was the not-quite-sure-could-go-either-way, but sometimes there is one answer, like for instance, now: He had never stolen anyone's car and last time he saw Tina she was with some asshole named Richie up in Austin. Earl had nothing to do with whatever they thought he did which they would not even tell him what that was.

"Hasn't it been a half hour?" Earl asked the lawyer.

"I just need to ask you a few more questions," said the cop.

"Okay then, fucking ask," Earl said.

"You best watch your mouth, son," the cop said.

"I am not your son."

"There's no call for that kind of talk, Earl," said the lawyer. "Though I never did like it when a man not my father referred to me as 'son' neither."

"You were in the woods reading a book called *Lead Belly* and this Adelaide Morgan all of a sudden just shows up?"

"Yes sir."

"And what was she doing walking around in Beamon's woods?"

"She never said. It's not the kind of question I tend to ask, why someone's walking around in the woods."

"You sure you didn't meet her in town and take her down into those woods? I know that's how y'all boys do, I know what all goes on in those woods."

"You know this how?" said the lawyer.

"It's my business to know everything goes on in this town."

"Oh, so this is a business you're running? The harassment-of-innocent-kids business?"

"It would be good of you, Arthur, to back the hell off and let me ascertain why this girl was in those woods like your boy is claiming."

Ascertain, said the cop. He wasn't just trying to find things out.

"I've managed to find out a bit about this Adelaide Morgan," the lawyer said. "From what I have learned, she might just be the type to go walking around in woods like that."

"I wouldn't go blaming the victim," said the cop.

"Victim of what? All y'all got is her family raising hell and claiming my client abducted her in a stolen vehicle which in fact was lent him by his cousin."

"He told us he borrowed the car from a fellow named Leif. I checked and there is not a soul in this county named Leif."

"Leif is not his real name," said Earl. "He stole it off the radio, but it came originally from a famous Viking."

"He's not talking about the football team out of Minnesota," the lawyer explained to the cop.

"Your boy Earl here lied when the arresting officer asked him whose car he was driving. As I said, there is no one in this county or likely the state of Texas name of Leif. And I know what a goddamn Viking is, Arthur, so I'm going to choose to ignore you. Sort of like everyone did in high school when you ran for student body president. Put up all those corny-ass signs in the halls above the lockers. 'Have a heart, vote for Art.'"

"I won," the lawyer said sidelong to Earl. "Landslide," he whispered.

"So you met her in the woods. What happened then?"

"I read aloud from *His Life and Times*. The part where he gets freed from Angola. When I was done, she said she knew a boy from Brazil who played soccer only he called it football."

The lawyer leaned over to Earl and whispered, just for his edification apparently, "That's what they call soccer everywhere but in America. In South American it is spelled F-U-T-B-O-L."

"Hold up just a minute," said the cop.

"I thought you were all about moving forward so we can get out of here," said the lawyer.

"I am just trying to understand this bit. He reads to her

about some convict, and she starts telling him about some guy from Brazil and soccer or football or what have you?"

"Yeah, well," said Arthur, "as I was saying earlier, my research into this young lady has revealed a long history of—"

"There you go blaming the victim again."

"What is she a victim of, exactly?"

"She has disappeared. She was last seen with this boy. I am trying to figure out where she is. Sooner you let me ask my questions, sooner you can get over to Rosa's for your meat and three."

The lawyer put his hand up, all "please ma'am after you."

"So you continued to see this girl, Adelaide Morgan, over time?"

Over time they kissed alongside lakes, indifferent turtles their witnesses. Likely you won't get word one out of them. In the night they floated in the velveteen oil-slick water while the Naugahyde nipped Earl or maybe it was minnows. Over time he was there but also not.

"Yep."

"And how come you stole your cousin's car and run off to Austin with her?"

"Leif's just mad because I was a little late getting the car back to him."

"Two days late is what the cousin claimed."

The lawyer turned to Earl. "Did you wreck it?"

"No, sir."

"Spill Pepsi on the windshield? It's a bitch to get off, man, makes you wonder what they put in there."

"I didn't spill anything on it. I was on my way to return it to him full of gas when they pulled me over. I had even checked the oil."

"Quart low I bet," said the lawyer.

"Quart and a half," said Earl. "Though I only had money for one."

The cop turned to Arthur and said, "So I'm supposed to believe that my man here borrows a car, essentially performed maintenance on it and it took a bit longer than he originally expected. Let me ask you Arthur how many times you have taken your car into the dealer and he claimed it'd be ready by noon and you're still waiting for him to call you when you get off work?"

"It's not about the car. His cousin's not the most reliable source, I admit."

"Well at least he has taken the name of a valiant Norseman," said the lawyer.

"I think he got it from the singer," said Earl.

The cop said to the lawyer, "Ask your boy here for his driver's license."

"Why would I? You already arrested him for driving without one," the lawyer said. "That's how come I'm here. Earl's mother hired me to make sure y'all didn't try to pull something sneaky like, for instance, pinning the disappearance of this Adelaide Morgan on him."

"How did you even know about Adelaide Morgan anyway?"

"It's my business to know what goes on in this town. It doesn't make much sense, you calling him in for questioning before he's even been charged. I figured you must have had something other than this bullshit."

"I am glad you are staying busy, Arthur. We pulled the boy over because he was driving a car that had been reported stolen. And it turned out he didn't have his license. That last part I might be willing to talk to the DA about dropping. I am also willing to talk to the DA about what the boy is claiming was just a misunderstanding with the cousin if Earl here will tell us about the girl."

The lawyer looked at Earl. "You get all that?"

"He wants me to tell him about Tina." Earl said into the tape machine. "She's scared of school nurses and cuckoo clocks. She loves a Hammond organ. I never saw her roller skate backwards, but I don't believe she'd lie about such a thing. Also, she is awfully fond of Leon Russell and ZZ Top."

"Leon Russell's the best thing to ever come out of Tulsa," said the lawyer.

"You don't like J.J. Cale?" Earl asked him.

"Goddamn it, we ain't here to talk about y'all's record collections. What led you and Adelaide to take a trip down to Austin?"

"She kept talking about wanting to see her mother, who is locked up in the state hospital down there."

The lawyer studied Earl a little too long. Then he studied the cop to see what he was thinking. He was a studier.

"Her mother's been in my office twice in the last four hours," the cop said finally. "She lives down in Houston. Real estate agent. Drives a LeSabre."

"What was her girl doing in Stovall, then?" said Arthur.

The cop appeared reluctant to divulge this info. But the

lawyer was smiling at him like he already knew everything and so he said, "She was staying with her aunt for a while."

"And why is that?"

"I guess you know why, seeing as how you done all this research."

"I get the sense my client is in the dark."

The cop said to Earl, "How well would you say you know this girl?"

What does it mean to know someone well enough to be with them and elsewhere at the same time? To Earl it meant in bone and blood. She was pedal steel. If wind was desire, he'd be blown out the jail-house wall and all the way to the black-mouthed woods.

"She told me her name was Tina," Earl said.

"Proving my point," said the lawyer.

"What point would that be?"

"We have a girl can't leave her house without getting in trouble back down in Houston. Truancy, shoplifting, underage drinking, simple possession. Her daddy's a big cancer doctor at MD Anderson and her mother's one of those real estate ladies who handles mansions up in River Oaks. The girl's messing up their image, so they ship her to the father's sister in Stovall, thinking, Piney woods backwater, no big-city temptation. Thinking she could stay with her aunt for a while and get her grades up and . . ."

"Are you about done?"

"Not about. She meets my client, and she lies first of all about her name and then she trots out some sad story about her mama being locked up in the bin and could they please go see her, and my client, smitten, believes every lie she breathes."

The lawyer leaned back. He rested his hands on his ample stomach. He rested his case.

"So this peckerwood got took," said the cop, pointing at Earl. He'd never been called a peckerwood before, and he had to switch around to see who they were talking about.

"You know as much about this girl as I do," Arthur said to the cop.

"I know she ain't no choirgirl and I also know I'd be hard pressed to find a teenager in this town, or hell, up in Tulsa, since y'all love to talk about Tulsa, that hasn't messed up some. The other thing I know is that she's missing. So maybe she told little Earl here some fibs. He's still the last one to see her."

"No I'm not," said Earl.

"Who is?"

"Richie."

"Who would Richie be?"

"Insert type of mustache here," said Earl.

"Say again?" said the cop.

So Earl told them what happened when they got to Austin, leaving out certain facts such as the quality of the herb and its effect on his personality, i.e., turning him into someone named Clothesline. He left out his lecture on the negative adjectival to the philosophy major and other interested parties. He told the lawyer and the cop how he lost Tina in the kitchen and found her upstairs in bed with Richie. How he walked out of the house and left her there.

"You never said anything to her?"

"What's he going to say, Phil?"

"If she was mine, I'd of said get your clothes back on and I'd of took this Richie . . ."

"Really, Phil? We're going to put on tape what you would have done had you been in my client's shoes?"

"I'm just saying."

"You're always just saying. All y'all are just saying. My job would be a lot easier if y'all just stop going around saying stuff."

"She wasn't mine," said Earl.

"Say what now, son?" the cop said.

"You said what you would do if she were yours. She was never mine. She was just something I knew and then she wasn't anyone."

The cop leaned over the table. Earl could feel the lawyer sizing him up sidelong, like he'd said something wrong.

"What do you mean she's just 'something?' And while we're at it, what do you mean when you say she was not anyone"?

"Not anyone to me," said Earl, which was his first and maybe his only conscious lie of the day.

Both men looked long at Earl. Finally the cop said, "Let's say your story is true. This fake-named cousin of yours reported his car stolen because you were two days late returning it. So my question to you is, if you left the girl with this Richie fellow not long after y'all got to Austin, where were you the last two days?"

The lawyer watched Earl, as if he was just fine with the

question. He appeared at the moment hungry and annoyed. Not only did he *appear* hungry, but beneath his hands, resting on his stomach, came a volcanic rumbling.

Earl said he couldn't say.

"Can't say or won't?" said the cop.

"Let me have a minute alone with my client," the lawyer said.

"About time you did some actual lawyering."

"Justice academy let you double-major in law?" Arthur said. "I thought they had their hands full teaching y'all illegal choke holds."

"I'm going to bring your client a Pepsi. Since you're too selfish to have brung us a biscuit from Sunrise."

The lawyer pulled a roll of bills from his pocket. He unpeeled a dollar.

"Buy yourself one too. And turn this tape off before you leave."

The cop reached over and pushed Pause. He made his exasperation known by chair scrape and door slam.

"Be better to push Stop than Pause, wouldn't you say, Earl?"

Earl looked down at the desk. It was scrawled with what appeared to be the Phoenician alphabet. If he had time and means to leave his mark, he'd say, I am the light of this world. He'd say, Tell everybody in this world.

"Okay look, you're right," Arthur finally said. "I hear you about J.J. Cale. He plays a mean slide. But he's the quiet type. Smart, though. You can hear how smart he is in the way that first record is mixed. It's all muddy. You know what I mean? He buries his vocals and the lyrics are not much more than whispered to start. You can see him thinking a muddy sound is best because the guitar comes out so crisp it's like a 'ring in a bell' to quote another dubious musical role model. But Cale, seems like he made a lot of other people famous. Eric Clapton, Lynyrd Skynyrd. People heard his songs and went looking for his album and discovered his versions were superior to the covers. But he didn't care. He was content to sit back. Let someone else take the credit. It's not un-admirable. You seem like that type to me, Earl."

"I don't write songs," said Earl. "Only thing I know how to play is my dad's radio."

"Where were you the last two days?"

"Did you know it's mostly ocean, this world? And the human body, if you were to wring it out like a sponge, there'd be about a third of you left."

The lawyer sighed over his stomach rumble. "Okay, I'm going to share something personal with you and then you can reciprocate. So old Phillip here"—he pointed across the table at the cop's empty chair—"used to go with my younger sister. They were together all through high school. And then she went off to Sam Houston State and he decided he wanted to be a cop and even though it's not that far down to Huntsville, she got tired of coming home on the weekends just to hear him go on about his police training, so she dumped him for some old boy from Plano who to tell the truth has not turned out to be an improvement over Phillip. This is a small town, Earl. Phillip is not fond of my sister and even though it's going on twenty years or more since they split, I get the sense I remind him of her."

"Do y'all favor?" Earl asked.

"Naw, Earl. Un-unh. Nope. Your turn to talk."

But Earl couldn't say where he'd been. He would have if he could have.

"You do something down in Austin you're not proud of? Hell, that's what Austin is for. All I need to know is where you were so we can get it corroborated and get you out of here and Phillip and them can find someone else to blame for that girl taking you for a cab ride."

"It wasn't like that," said Earl.

"What was it like?"

But then the door opened. The cop who used to go out with the lawyer's little sister came in with two other men: one in a uniform, one in a suit.

"Where's his Pepsi? Or else, where is my money?"

"Earl's going to have to come with us now."

"Earl's already *with* y'all, it seems to me."

"I'm talking a cell, Arthur, until we can get in to see the judge."

"You just sat here and told me you were willing to speak to the DA on the operating-without-a-license charge and if the cousin didn't press charges on the late return of his vehicle . . ."

"We asked his cousin to bring in the vehicle. Earl might have changed the oil, but he forgot to clean out the trunk. It's a goddamn mess in there. Blood everywhere."

The lawyer looked at Earl. Earl looked at the floor. Gauzy

was the memory of being pulled over in the parking lot of a Holiness church the night before and another cop, a uniformed boy not much older than Earl, reading him his rights. There seemed to be some rights he'd left out, like the right to have his hands cuffed, and the right to be yanked by his shoulders around the table. Yet another was the right to look back and see his lawyer in a way that Earl had not seem him previously, a way that made Earl like him: he looked shocked. Given what they were claiming about him, Earl guessed the lawyer had every right to be shocked.

5.

"YOU'D BE HURTING right now if you weren't down with Moon and Sleepy and them," Earl's cellmate told him. He was skinny and long-haired and white, but like Moon and Sleepy and Cheese, he talked like a Black dude. "They put word out on you. How come you to run with those bottom-feeding motherfuckers?"

To be but mostly not be in that smelly cell, Earl recalled things he had noticed: a melancholy stack of newspapers by a storefront, soaked by overnight rain.

"I mean, you don't look the type to string with those off-brand bitches."

The rain bled ink from the papers, all the news of the town, the county, the world. Birth announcements and obituaries. The court docket and the For Rent notices, all of it ran down the sidewalk and dripped into the grated gutter.

"You a no-talking-little-hands-off bitch too. Another thing

that don't line up with those dudes. Sleepy T especially talks all the time."

Earl thought of his box of index cards. One time he found a loose card under his bed on which he had written only "Winnipeg." Earl had forgotten why Winnipeg but it did not bother him in the least.

Writing a thing down on a card to remember it made Earl remember it without looking at it, so he didn't really miss or need the box of index cards. What he did need was *His Life and Times* and his father's radio and for Tina to show up because he knew she was not dead.

"How old are you anyway?"

"Seventeen and a half."

"Hold up! Words can come out that mouth?" his cellmate said.

Earl asked his cellmate what his name was.

"I got a name in here and I got a name the C.O's call me. The one you need to know is what they call me in here."

"What do they call you in here?"

"T-Bone."

Earl told T-Bone to call him Winnipeg.

"Winnie-who?"

Lead Belly, radio, Tina come show your face so I can walk again in my beloved outskirts, past the windowless strip clubs, the cinderblock tavern with the *It's Miller Time* clock blinking through the barred window, the car lot with a half dozen sad vehicles and a sign that says NO CREDIT NO PROBLEM in English and Español, all the tawdry concerns pushed to the perimeter in order to emphasize town giving way finally to farm, pasture, forest.

"You best choose another name. Even your crew can't protect you if you go calling yourself Winnipeg. But it don't matter. Nobody in here's going to ask you your name anyhow."

"What if they want to talk to me?"

"You better hope they don't. And they won't, because everybody knows your crew."

"I met them on my walks through the streets."

"Streets is their office."

Earl never saw any of them doing any sort of business besides standing on various corners. Shuffling about smoking and talking trash. He did notice that they did not seem to care about the weather. If it was hot they were out there mopping sweat off their heads with rags. Winter they'd puff up in long jackets and Sleepy and Moon would be wearing a Saints toboggan with a ball on top, and Burnt Cheese, a Cowboy's toboggan with no ball. If it was sprinkling or misting or even raining, there they were on the street.

Why did they even like Earl? They'd come around to the house nights to listen to music and cut up with Earl's father and brothers by the wormy chestnut barn, but even to Earl's face they talked trash about his father, as did everyone. Earl assumed they were amused by his father. He said things to them that he thought were normal responses to life and they fell out in the median by the corners, clutching their stomachs, slapping each other on the shoulder. It was because of them that Arthur was representing him, or whatever it was Arthur was doing. Did they have money to burn on biscuits, Coke, and Arthur doing research into the previous life of Tina not her real name? Maybe Sleepy T and them took care of him because they liked his mama, who got off the phone to cook for them when they came around and also because Earl's daddy was no-count even to his so-called posse.

For a long time Earl sat up on his bunk, staring at the water stain on the ceiling.

"I have to go to the bathroom," he said finally. There was a commode in the corner of the cell, not ten inches from T-Bone's head.

"Well fucking do your business."

"Can you not look?"

T-Bone said, "You are one lucky bitch to have the friends you got."

That first night he did not sleep. He thought about crawl spaces. He loved attics for their mysterious and infinite eaves, but he hated basements and especially crawl spaces. Once his father had made Earl and his twin brothers crawl under a double-wide they were renting to spread sheets of plastic over the dirt. Insulation, his father said. Redneck insulation is what he'd heard others call the plastic stapled over leaky windows in the old bungalows and trailer houses they stayed in. He was terrified the whole time he was under the house. He had to hold a tiny flashlight between his teeth. It made him gag. With one hand he dragged his body forward and with the other he pulled the roll of plastic. He butted his head on pipes that gurgled with flushed toilets. And here he was in another crawlspace, but why? Why was he here? All he did was leave Tina in a nasty-looking embrace with Richie.

In the afternoon his lawyer came to see him. He was wearing a V-neck sweater and a shirt with wide, leafy collars spreading out from the V almost to his shoulders. To Earl it was a look that said, I might be a professional, but I am also a man of leisure. It also said, I'm trying too hard.

They sat in a small room, facing each other across a metal desk, but there was a window and from the window sunlight and in the sunlight dancing motes of dust that Earl studied after taking note of the lawyer's get-up.

"Man oh man, Earl. I went out to visit your people. Quite a compound out there. From what I gather after talking to your people and also just general observation from our previous interactions I judge you to be the dreamy sort. Half-here. Am I right? You don't have to answer, Earl. I get it, see? I'm the same, man. Always floating around in my head. Your mama told me you like music. I already knew this after our discussion of the Tulsa Sound, but she drove it home. Said you were always listening to something, always had a radio up to your ear. I get that too. You can be anywhere listening to music. You can be in line at Arby's and a song's playing and all of a sudden here comes the bridge. You lean over the side of it and a good ways down flows the river over some rocks and you are all of a sudden caught up in that current. Am I right so far, Earl?"

"Somewhat."

For he was somewhat right. He left out pedal steel, which was wind. Wind was desire. *Pedal steel is wind, and wind, desire*, Earl wrote out on a blackboard in a ravaged classroom in an abandoned schoolhouse he came upon deep in the piney woods where beer cans and underpants stood in for the bread-crumbs of phony fables. Near where he once sat on a log reading *His Life and Times* and along came Tina whose name was not Tina. Not from Navasota either. Most but not all of what she told him were lies. The thing that mattered, how she made him feel: Was that a lie?

"Somewhat, you say? Well, I'll take that, even though I don't know what is some and which is what, but I'm thinking I'm never going to get certain things out of you Earl. But that's okay, in fact it proves my point."

"You make a lot of points," said Earl.

"That disproves my point."

"Which is what?"

"That you are kind of half-here. And half not. I think you are going to find out, Earl—and it's going to be a cold-ass plunge into a frozen ocean when you do—that when you get a little older, let's say old enough to join the workforce and take on a profession in which it is expected of you to show up both in body and in mind, what is now tolerable if not kind of amusing to people—I'm talking the half-here-ness—that's liable to going to be um, misconstrued, or let's say misunderstood. People are likely to see you as being a little off."

"Off?"

"Odd, then."

He'd rather odd than off. Also it was not really true.

"But it was Tina," he said.

"You mean Adelaide Morgan?"

"Tina is the one who made me feel . . ."

"Feel what?"

"That I could be with her and also at the same time somewhere else."

"For reasons I don't have time to go into right now, I'm going to have to ask you to never ever repeat that. Especially should you be called to testify under oath."

"When I swear to tell the truth and nothing but, you are saying for me to lie?"

"I swear, Earl. Most of my clients lose their sharpness after a couple jailhouse meals. Lying around in their bunks. Sleepy said he'd seen to it you'd be safe in here. I trust no one's messing with you?"

"You want me to stand up in court and lie?"

"Okay, look. What I'm saying here is that it would be best if you did not articulate to a courtroom of what in this county is never going to be a jury of your peers, no matter who you are, that's just the way the system is set up, what you just told me about Adelaide Morgan making you feel the way you said she made you feel."

"Why?"

"Why? Because it suggests what a shrink would call dissociative behavior and that's not a good thing to suggest when you were the last person to see her."

"So you want me to act like I'm off?"

"First of all, Earl, let's go with odd. It's not exactly a stretch. Second, I don't think you are going to want to explain anything to the jury about how you feel. I think you are better off *being* it than articulating it. Because the thing is, it has become apparent that you and this Adelaide known to you as Tina got on pretty good. Honestly, I don't believe you laid a hand on her. What I'm saying is, I have been around to see your people and spent some time talking to them about you and what I heard from them—and all this was said with the utmost love and support—is that you are kind of, to use your brother's words, a space cadet."

"That would be Larry?"

"Those two boys favor."

"That's because they're twins."

"Well there you go."

"Every time I come in the room Larry starts singing 'Ground control to Major Tom.' I fucking hate outer space."

"You don't care anything for stars?"

"I like the moon. If there are bare branches brushing upside it."

Arthur smiled. "You are truly fascinating, Earl. I could listen to you talk all day long. But I have business to take care of, I'm afraid. And it's getting on toward lunchtime. I could chin wag with you for hours. But they only give me a half hour with you and we've got just a couple minutes left, so let's review here: it's not a bad thing, this sense that other people have of you of being . . ."

"Off?" Earl said. "Or odd?"

"Those are just words that come straight to mind. My own perspective on it and again it takes one to know one is that you are, let's say, unto yourself. Or dreamy."

"Was my daddy there?"

"He was not. Your mother could not seem to locate

him. Apparently, he was not at the job site where he said he would be."

"One of my aunts lives at the Shreveport Country Club."

"Your mother is beside herself. She is trying everything she can think of to get you out of here. But the bail is high, Earl. I'm not going to lie. It's more than your friends Sleepy and Moon, who paid my retainer, can come up with, and they are in a lucrative business as you know. And just so you know, I don't approve of the business they're in, I just believe that everyone needs representation, especially in East Texas."

"Sleepy told me once when I was little that he worked as a crossing guard."

"He's got his own corner he looks after, if that's what he meant."

"But he also told me one time that he had a lawnmower blade-sharpening business."

"I believe that is what is known as a side hustle."

"Meaning crossing guard is his main gig?"

"Lawnmower blade-sharpening and cross-guarding is not going to keep a fellow in jet skis."

"I don't think Sleepy can even swim."

"Either you miss my point, Earl, or you are deliberately messing with me, and I know which one it is. I hate to get us back on track, but I got to tell you, the bail? It's crazy high given they don't have a body."

"That's because she's still alive."

"You heard from her?"

Not in the way Arthur meant. Not by phone. If there was a post card it might read, *Dear Earl, me and Richie went to see*

Commander Cody plus New Riders of the Purple Sage. New Riders did like a twenty-minute version of "Panama Red" for an encore. Richie's just an old friend. We were just catching up is all. Please don't hate me, Earl. Please come back and get me. I'm ready to come home and "catch up" with you. Love 4 ever, Tina.

"No," said Earl. "I just know."

"What we have to do next is find this Richie fellow. Can you tell me where he lives?"

"Not exactly. Somewhere up near the college. Kind of in this neighborhood that's mostly students living in big old houses and also some apartments. I could find my way back there. You'd have to get me out of here though."

"I'm working on it."

"We parked right up beside the place when we got to town. But then when I got back, the car wasn't parked where we left it. I walked around awhile and finally found it a couple streets away."

"Wait once," said Arthur. "When you got back from where?"

The C.O. opened the door.

"Are you saying you left the car there and went somewhere?"

The C.O. said, "Time's up."

"Where were you those two days, Earl?"

"Let's go, chief," said the C.O. He said to Arthur, "This one's got to get back to class, bossman."

"I need to know where you were," Arthur was saying as the C.O. cuffed him.

6.

EARL WAS OUT of breath as he pushed downstairs, past the statues sitting on steps watching the landing.

"Hey Clothesline, come here a minute," the philosophy major called to him as he negotiated the crowd in the living room. He was swimming toward a pier in high chop. The pier was in reach; waves rose and pulled him backwards, then forward. He dove under, closed his eyes and frog-kicked.

Near the front door he knocked a drink out of someone's hand. "Hey man, that's not cool," said the guy whose drink was all over Earl's T-shirt. It smelled of spiked Hawaiian punch and stained his T-shirt bloody.

Outside he ran right by the Galaxie. The keys were under the driver's-seat mat. Tina would need a way to get home. He wasn't going to wait on her, though. She did not love Richie. Earl could tell from the way they went at each other. It was athletic and desperate. It was not love me tender. More like the sort of sex his brothers had shown him, grainy videos in which a couple went at it in a laundry room. Why was it always a laundry room? Mostly he and Tina had sex on blankets in the woods, or in the black lake at night. Their love rippled outward like a skipped stone. *Concentric* was the word for it. Outward into the world, like radio waves, like sound itself.

Earl, if asked to describe it, might refer to it as grown-up married-folk love. The love of folks who knew they were going to get another crack at it, tomorrow and the next day, so why try to fit it all into one session in the back seat of a car parked in the woods or in your Methodist, possibly lesbian aunt's bed while she was at work? That was for kids. That kind of love was stamped with an expiration date. It belonged to kids who would grow up and grow out of each other as quickly as they grew out of their clothes or shoes. Earl and Tina had time. What greater luxury are we given?

Tina needed some time with her friend. With whom she was having ungainly sex. Horrifying to watch, really. Like a catfight in a back alley. Almost made Earl want to bet on one or the other of them.

She knew real love, Earl thought as he walked past the large houses cut up into apartments for students. Bicycles rusted against trees. Music blared from windows propped open by speakers. There was much bathing by students in the now full-on rays of the sun.

He did not hate Tina at all. She was upset about going to see her mother. Why would she not be? He'd heard it called "acting out." The term had been applied to him by a guidance counselor when he opted not to come to school in favor of a log in the woods and *His Life and Times*. Earl would've preferred Tina acting out with him, but maybe it was better acting out with a guy she did not love. It meant nothing, it was just her nervous energy. Had she acted out with Earl, she might've ended up crying.

Someone at the party had told Earl about a magnificent swimming hole. They said it was and was not a pool. They had Earl at "was and was not." He asked as many questions as his muddled mind could summon. Were there lifeguards? Yes, and they blew whistles and hollered at you if you ran on the sidewalk, but it wasn't like a regular pool because, instead of concrete on the bottom with lines painted on it to which band-aids sometimes got stuck, there was dirt. Vegetation would get in your hair. You might get out looking like the Creature from the Black Lagoon, said the person, he could not even remember if it was a girl or a guy, telling him about the pool. Also there were fish in it. Fish! In a swimming pool.

It wasn't hard to find the pool. He stopped the first freak he saw and described it as it had been described to him and the freak said, Yeah, man, Barton Springs, and Earl said, Can I walk there and the freak said it would take about an hour or longer and drew him a map on the back of a flyer he was attaching to a telephone pole announcing the upcoming gig of his band, to which Earl was invited.

He passed campus and entered into what seemed, from the boxy architecture, the business of the state government. These awful buildings flanked the capitol, which was gold-tipped and handsome if a little preposterous-looking in the manner of oft-photographed landmarks. Then a good half hour of businesses and men in suits on the streets before he reached a river.

"What river is that?" He asked a fellow leaning over the side of the bridge, which was rumbling with steady traffic.

"That's Town Lake," said the man, looking at Earl with impatience before spitting into the water.

A river was a lake, a pond was a pool: Earl was growing fond of Austin, though it was hot out, hotter than East Texas somehow, even though it was less humid. He was glad when he got to the pool and paid his fifty cents and pushed through a turnstile.

Earl was good at turnstiles. Tell everybody in this world.

Below him stretched what seemed to be a lake, not a river or a pond or a pool. It was enclosed on three sides by sidewalk; one side was high cliffs. It lay in a ravine—though in Austin it was likely called a valley—and there were more people there than Earl had ever seen at one time in Stovall, even at the Christmas parade or the Fourth of July fireworks. Most wore bathing suits, but some walked around only in their underwear, men and women, and here and there he spotted a woman wearing only her underpants or bathing suit bottom, it was hard to tell from up on the hill. He thought he better get down there and see.

Walking in, he had seen a list of prohibited items, including radios, but from the hills came the clash of competing radios. Garbage songs from chain stores mostly, but he was high still and any music sounded complex. Earl isolated two songs from the din—"Ride Captain Ride" and "Brandy." Brandy's eyes would steal a sailor from the sea. The captain was riding his mystery ship on his way to a world that others might have missed. It was not lost on Earl that only nautically themed songs were playing on prohibited radios.

Earl made his way down the stairs to the poolside. He found an empty spot on the far hill beside a sleeping couple. The girl's bikini straps were undone and laid out in the grass like the tendrils of a jellyfish. In sleep her boyfriend shuddered. Earl was a little self-conscious about stripping down to his underwear, but no one knew him, and he had arrived at a world others might have missed.

He folded his clothes neatly and laid them atop his shoes, where he had hidden his money, though if he were looking for money, the first thing he would do was shake a shoe. He had the sense that he did not have to go to Tina, that she would arrive here soon, that they would meet in the water and he could hold her as he did in the black ponds of the piney woods, and her skin would feel like velvet not in an oil slick.

And if she did not show up, he could bring her here after they visited her mother.

He walked down to the sidewalk and stood on the lip. He dipped a toe in the water. Shockingly frigid compared to the pissy-warm ponds to which Earl was accustomed.

"None of that," said a girl sitting next to where he stood. She was with two other girls, and they were all dangling their legs in the water and they all had long, wet hair clinging to their shoulders and seemed not a little high.

"None of what?"

"Just fling yourself in," said one of the girls.

"Are y'all like the pool cops?"

The way they giggled confirmed their highness. It allowed Earl to name them Your Highnesses.

"She's for sure a narc," said the second Highness, pointing her finger at the crown of Highness Number One.

"You're about to get busted if you don't fling yourself in that water," said Highness Number Three.

"What would be the charge?"

"Cowardice," said Number One.

"Foolishness and also total uncoolness," said Number Two.

Earl wasn't sufficiently moved by being afraid or a fool or even not cool, but when the third Highness said "acting like a little pussy," he jumped. After all he was still a teenage boy and to have a college girl refer to him as a little pussy was an affront to his adolescent male psyche.

He didn't have to think about it because for the first time in his life he had cause to use the word *bracing*. But the shock of the cold was brief and it was exhilarating. The water was so clean he wanted to eat it; he felt that he could survive off of it for the rest of his days. This water and a little pedal steel. His copy of *His Life and Times*. Maybe his daddy's radio, though maybe he had grown out of that radio and grown out of his attachment to his absent daddy.

He felt cleansed in a ridiculously religious way. Was this holy water?

He sculled around on the bottom, his eyes open, everything visible unlike the murky waters of the ponds back home. He searched for fish but saw only grasses and algae and rocks and sand and pebbles. Well, he had Time.

When he popped back up to the surface the three highnesses applauded.

"Well?"

What words were there for this world that others had missed? Earl was aware that he was still high enough to feel self-conscious about the words he chose, their efficacy, their specificity. And so he smiled his answer and his smile spread into a grin and the highnesses read in it his pleasure and giggled. He might have still appeared like a little pussy to them, but he didn't care because he dove down again to discover more.

Above him the serious swimmers passed, their bodies aligned with the surface of the water in a way he envied, as he was a sinker. Their rotating arms reached and sliced down to graze their hips before emerging, high-elbowed, to reach again. Their flutter kicks looked mechanized. Earl would learn to swim like that.

He and Tina would work here! What water park could compare? They could get their GEDs here surely. Then transfer to the university.

He swam over to His Highnesses.

"How do you get a job here?"

"Get in line?" Three said.

"The back of the line she means," said One.

"Do you have your certificate?" asked Two.

"I have a certificate from the 4-H. I won their hundred-yard dash."

The girls collapsed against each other in giggles. They resembled a house of cards in the act of disintegration. He thought they might fall in, they were so boneless.

"What kind of certificate do I need?" Earl asked.

"Life-saving, duh."

But he was already a life-saver. He thought he might be saving Tina's life right now. Allowing her to act out before he reunited her with her mother. Getting her away from her aunt. Earl had only seen the aunt from the street. Tina had never invited him in. He was her secret. Secrets were inevitable and contrary to public opinion they weren't bad. Though it was true that Earl's father had many secrets. You could see it by studying the dashboard of his pickup. A man without secrets carries everything on the dash of his vehicle. Receipts, a spare gimme cap, lighters, half empty packs of cigarettes, pocketknives, other people's objects borrowed but probably stolen, Styrofoam cups stained with gas station coffee, powdered creamer, a tape measure. His father's dash was clean as was his glove compartment. Guess what he had in his glove compartment. Gloves!

"Do y'all believe secrets are bad?" Earl asked the highnesses.

"I think Secret Agent Men are hot," said Two, and started singing a song on the subject.

"Are you a Secret Agent?" said One.

"I'm Earl."

"He's a spy," said Three. "Isn't there a book about a spy who got out of the cold or something? You better get out of the cold."

But Earl's underwear was wet and droopy because it was handed down from not one but two brothers. Also he was sure it was see-through. And of course he did not have a towel. Why would he have brought along a towel to visit Tina's mother in the state asylum? How did he end up here, anyway?

"I'm good," said Earl, yet his teeth were chattering, his body shivering.

One of the girls got up and went up the hill and came back with a beach towel. It was vibrantly colored with a pattern of playing cards across it. It made no sense to Earl and he was grateful for it.

He pulled himself out of the water and quickly wrapped himself in the towel. He sat beside the highnesses on the wall, and they told him their names: Teresa, Brenda, and Marcia.

"What's your major," Marcia asked him.

He thought of *His Life and Times.*

"Music," said Earl.

"Wow. I hear that's hard. All that practicing. What instrument?"

Earl said, "Pedal steel."

"Isn't that, like, bluegrass music?"

"It's more like wind."

"They have a major in pedal steel?"

"Technically I major in guitar."

"Marcia plays guitar and sings," said Brenda. "She's done the open mike at Threadgill's, just like Janis."

"Okay," said Earl.

Earl asked the girls where they were from and what was their major and the answers went into his brain and lodged there along with telephone numbers missing half their digits and foggy memories of childhood trips to visit relatives in smelly houses outside Shreveport.

"I'm from Shreveport originally," said Earl. "But now we stay in Stovall."

"You don't live in Austin?" said Brenda.

"I mean my people."

"He means his people," said Marcia and the rest of them giggled.

"Well, lookit, Earl," said Teresa. "Do you want to go get high with us?"

Earl looked around the pool. So many people and none of them were Tina. He thought of the ungainly sex he had witnessed. He wondered who had won. Tina never saw him looking. If she had seen him, she would have ceased her wrangling about. She would be missing him. She might be beside herself, whatever that meant. Or she might still be bouncing on top of old Insert-name-of-moustache-type-here.

"Sure," said Earl. "I need to change."

They pointed out the locker room on the far side of the hill and said they'd meet him in the parking lot. He carried his clothes up the stairs to the locker room, which was open to the elements and filled with naked men, some beneath showers placed like trees in the middle of the open space, others just sitting around talking. Some of the men watched him in a way that seemed to awaken some dormant part of him and also creep him out. He shed his saggy underpants and put them in a trash can. He was struggling into his jeans when a guy appeared beside him and asked him how his swim was.

Earl said it was great.

The guy had long, wavy brown hair to his shoulders and was wearing only sunglasses. He stood close to Earl and talked about how nice a day it was, as if talking about how pretty it was out while sporting only shades and a semi-hard-on was normal. He didn't look down but he didn't have to look down to notice that the guy's cock was growing as he talked.

"Want to hang out?" the guy asked.

Earl did not think it would be easy for him to be friendly when jaybird naked. Therefore he was a little amazed at how amiable this fellow was.

"I'm with Marcia, Brenda, and Teresa," he said, as if everyone in Austin were on a first-name basis.

"A foursome, wow. You must have a lot of jam, man."

"I mean, I guess?"

The guy laughed and said his name was Tom. Earl shook his hand even though it felt a little weird shaking the hand of a man wearing only sunglasses and a semi-hard-on.

"Richie," said Earl.

"Right on, Richie. Y'all need a fifth wheel? I'm looking to party today, and I got the goods."

"The goods?"

Tom leaned in closer to whisper into his ear. "Crystal. Also coke. Also hash oil and some killer weed."

"Okay," said Earl. Tom pulled on his hip-hugger jeans and a David Bowie T-shirt, the one with his face painted with a lightning bolt. They walked out together.

"Hold on a minute," Earl said and he found the girls in the crowded parking lot sitting on the bumper of a beat Dodge Dart.

"I met this guy Tom and he says he wants to party with us."

"Where is he?"

Earl pointed him out.

"He's pretty cute," said Marcia, and Brenda said he seemed

kind of into himself and Teresa said she liked his T-shirt. She stared a little longer and said, "Also his pants."

"He says he's got the goods."

"What goods?"

"Coke, crystal, hash oil."

"Well why didn't you fucking lead with that, Early," said Marcia. "Go get your boy and let's roll on out."

Marcia drove and Brenda rode shotgun. Teresa sat between Earl and Tom.

"So how do y'all know Richie?" Tom asked the highnesses.

"Who?"

Tom looked over at Earl. Earl looked out the window.

"Man I'm sorry, I'm terrible with names," said Tom. He turned to Earl. "What was your name again?"

"He's Earl. His people come from Shreveport," said Marcia.

"Bossier City, to be exact," said Earl.

"He's a secret agent man," said Brenda.

"They're all cops," said Earl, pointing to the front seat.

"Not really," the girls said in unison.

"Well that's good to hear," said Tom. Teresa, Earl noticed, leaned into Tom on the curves. Tom didn't seem to mind. In fact he seemed into her, though he looked over at Earl like they shared a secret and the secret had to do with more than just the fake name Earl had given him.

"Where to?" Marcia asked and Tom gave the name of his neighborhood, which seemed to give even Teresa, at this point suctioned to Tom like a barnacle, some pause.

"My block's safe," said Tom. "And my roommates are gone so we'll have the place to ourselves."

The neighborhood looked fine to Earl, but he was used to Stovall, its unfurling outskirts, its shotgun shacks and trailer houses giving shade to mangy dogs, its children with sunken eye sockets and scabby knees. Inside the small bungalow, two giant speakers flanked a wall of records. A cat that lay on the windowsill looked up indignantly before slinking away. Tom disappeared into a back room and came back with a small mirror and a razor blade.

The girls got excited. Earl could smell their excitement. It smelled like the pool that was actually a pond exposing their natural odors, which were mixed but not unpleasant. Earl wondered did he smell like creek mud? Would these girls turn out to be just like the ones who rode number 78 bus in Stovall?

"Crystal," said Tom, pouring powder on the mirror. He opened another baggie and poured out a pile of what must have been coke.

"So, um, we don't have any money," Brenda said.

"That's cool," said Tom. "On me today. I'll give you my number. I can hook you up most of the time. Occasionally I get reds and trees. Sometimes 'ludes. Occasionally Eskatrol. That shit is wicked. I buy it straight off a pharmacist. I don't touch smack, but I know where you can score. Oh, and I got a guy out in Kerrville who gets mushrooms. He's got a farm out there."

The girls got on their knees and snorted their lines through plastic straws sitting in a cup on the coffee table.

"Try the crystal," Tom said to Earl, who was sitting next to him on the couch. "It's a little better quality than the coke."

And then Earl, after snorting a few lines of crystal, was standing in front of all four of them, who had clumped up on the couch, and he was Clothesline again, reciting from memory long passages from *His Life and Times*. The girls were passing a joint and giggling. He launched into a lecture of the negative adjectival for the second time that day. Tom was making out with Teresa. Brenda was making out with Marcia. Earl went into the kitchen for a beer and encountered strangers. He told them he was good at turnstiles. He told them about his friends back home: Moonwalk, Sleepy T, Burnt Cheese. What else are you good at Earl? someone asked, and Earl said he was the light of the world. He said, Tell everyone in this world. Tom was beside him, laughing. Play "Crystal Ship," he told Tom. You got it, boss. *Before I slip into unconsciousness I'd like to have another kiss,* sang Earl into a plastic spatula he found in a drawer. It got dark out. Earl went outside to commune with the dusk and saw people standing in the edges of the woods, frozen, as still as deer.

Earl tried the coke. He did and did not care for the dripping at the back of his throat, but he believed Tom when he said it was not as high quality as the crystal for almost immediately he needed more of it, and then some.

Tom and Teresa disappeared. Earl talked nonstop to Marcia about the steel guitar.

"But isn't it like a Hawaiian thing? Like my father's really into Don Ho and I feel like I've heard . . ." but Earl cut her off and said pedal steel was actually not a thing but a sphere you could enter if the conditions were just so and only when they were just so. Then Teresa was standing beside him dressed in only a David Bowie T-shirt. She said she and Tom wanted to talk to him and to follow her.

"Who's Tom?" Earl said.

"Your new best friend, Earl. You know, the guy with the goods. Our gracious host."

Teresa took his hand and Earl grabbed his beer and followed her down the hallway to the back bedroom. Tom lay on a waterbed, a thin sheet covering him. There were mirrors on the walls and a poster of Angela Davis. Earl had read about her in *Look* magazine. He might have seen her picture on the wall of the post office in Stovall.

"Come smoke a joint with us Earl," said Tom. "You need to knock it back a notch, little buddy."

Teresa took off her shirt. Tom got up to lock the door. He was naked and, as before in the locker room, at half-mast. Earl must have shown his confusion for Teresa took the beer out of his hand and pulled his T-shirt over his head and then unbuckled his belt and used one end to tug him over to the waterbed, onto which she yanked him. Tom put *Let It Bleed* on the turntable. Earl had never met a drug dealer and was not familiar with their penchant for high-end audio and low-riding two-seater vehicles. To the first chords of "Gimme Shelter," he raised up so that Teresa could pull off his jeans.

"Jesus, I see why y'all asked him to come along now," said Tom.

"You should have seen him in his wet underwear pulling himself out of the springs," said Teresa.

But Earl was not really listening as Merry Clayton was working up to her celestial solo and it was coming not from the speakers but from the clouds. Earl looked out the window at the smoky last light and there was rape and there was murder and there was love a shot a kiss away. Four hands were caressing him. Tom and Teresa made out and then Teresa kissed him and then she turned Earl's head toward Tom. Tom kissed him on the neck. In his head Earl said hold up but his body said, Well, okay, then. Weird, but everything in this town is weird. Tom told Teresa to get between them and she did and the bed sagged and Tom began to lick one nipple and he moved Earl's head to the other. *Fire is sweeping our very street today.* Teresa was moaning. She wants you now, Earl. Earl felt like everything had gone away but the words out of Merry Clayton's mouth and the softness of Teresa's body. She pulled him atop her and locked her knees around him and he kissed her and Tom kissed her and he kissed Tom and Merry Clayton sang "Mad bull lost its way" as Teresa said she wanted to watch the boys. Tom went first and he had some experience as it did not take Earl very long at all to finish. Then it was Earl's turn and he held Tom's cock in his hand and Teresa ran her fingers through his hair and he took Tom into his mouth, worried about his teeth, which he knew from sometimes with Tina could get in the way. Then Teresa said she wanted Tom to finish on her and Tom pushed Earl's head away gently and rose up over Teresa like a warrior.

Teresa got up to go to the bathroom. From a shoebox beneath the bed, Tom retrieved more goods and a mirror. They did two lines each of coke. The sun was coming up. Had it been dark that long? "Gimme Shelter" was playing the same word: *away.* How long had the record been stuck?

"Did you like that, Earl?" Tom asked, and Earl said, "I caught my girlfriend fucking some guy named Richie," and

Tom said, "That's a bummer, man, some women are really bitches which is why I like to get with guys too. Some guys freak out after their first time with another guy but either this isn't your first time or . . ."

"It *is* my first time," said Earl, and Tom said he knocked it out of the park. Tom went to get them some beers and while he was gone Earl wondered what it was he knocked out of the park. While Tom was gone, Earl had pulled on his jeans, but Tom was still naked when he returned with two Lone Stars. He put on *Close to the Edge* and he sat on the foot of the bed with his eyes closed, nodding his head. Many birds were chirping loudly. Earl looked around the room and then got up and peeled back the Indian print fabric tacked up as a curtain. He stared out the window before he realized the bird chirping was coming from the speakers.

Then they went out to join the others, but the others were gone. Earl went outside and sat in a chair for a long time. A little girl played on a swing set in the next yard. Earl waved to her and she waved shyly back. He threw up pizza. When had he eaten pizza? After he threw up, he was hungry, which made sense when he thought about it. He took off his shoe and found six bucks. He went inside and brushed his teeth with his finger and a dap of toothpaste. Then he went into Tom's room to say goodbye but Tom was not there, so Earl reached under the bed and pulled out the shoebox and helped himself.

At the end of the street, he found a diner. He sat at the counter and ordered huevos rancheros and a Coke. Rough night? asked the waitress and Earl said he didn't remember there even being a night. There was a night all right, said the waitress. Earl ate everything on his plate and took a couple of halves of toast off a plate left by a diner beside him. He went to the bathroom and was sick again. What he needed was a Goody's Powder. His father swore by their healing powers. He found a store on the corner of South Congress and bought a powder and a Coke and walked down the street toward the dome of the capital, lit by mid-morning sun. He passed over the river they called a lake and then he passed the capitol and came to the university. Amazingly he recognized the street where they had parked by the telephone pole where he had encountered the freak posting flyers. That freak, if he only knew what he'd gotten Earl into.

7.

"NOW YOUR BROTHERS, see, I always expected them to end up like this," said Earl's mother when she came to see him in jail.

In fact his brothers would end up busted for running a meth lab in a Quonset hut outside of Enid, Oklahoma. But that would not be for another twenty years, during which their encounters with lawmen and the criminal element were not minor enough to fall into the category of scrapes.

"But *you*, Earl? You are the one I thought would get away from all of this, and for all of us."

Earl wanted money for some Funyuns from the vending machine. There was a hardness in his feelings toward his mother's recriminations. She ought never to have gotten an extra-long phone cord and it would have been far better if you did not have to trace the phone line from where it came out of the wall to a closed bedroom door, the porch, the bathroom if you needed to ask her something like, What is there to eat for dinner, ma?

"I had it in my mind you'd go to college and beyond."

Earl had it in his mind he would be a photographer for *National Geographic* and wear a vest with too many pockets to count, khaki in color.

"And here you are not even out of high school and locked up already."

"You think my life is over?"

"I just want to know what happened between you and that girl."

Earl remembered his mother sitting with him outside in the dusk and telling him to listen. He tried to hear what they had heard, but jail was loud and it seemed now like lazy parenting, that listen-to-the-silence trick.

"Never trusted her," his mother was saying.

"I told the lawyer everything that happened."

"The lawyer told me there were two days you could not account for. How is that, Earl?"

Earl wanted to ask his mother if she could account for the last thirty years of her life since the night she met his father in the parking lot of some hamburger joint in Bossier City. He often had the sense that she knew only that moment and the present one, with no clear notion of the in-between.

"I told the lawyer what I knew."

"You like that lawyer okay?"

"He's got pretty good taste in music. Sometimes he seems like he's in a hurry, but something about his hurry-up seems fake. One thing about him, he stays hungry."

"I should have brought you something to eat. I ought to have made you a cake or something."

"I'm not in the hospital, ma."

"Where are you? What is this place? How did this happen? What did I do wrong?"

Earl had heard her say these exact same lines numerous times to one of her sisters on the telephone. He said, "Dad told me *Tres Hombres* was recorded in Tyler, but Tina said he was lying."

"Oh, Earl. You're still gone on that girl, aren't you?"

"Where is Dad?"

"Last I heard from him he was down in Beaumont. But he might have crossed a line. A state line or some other kind. You know how he is."

"Is he coming to see me?"

"Not to side with Tina, because I would like to wring her little neck, which I ought not to say because somebody might have already done it and I know you would never do anything like that Earl, but truthfully? I have been to Tyler and I'm inclined to be skeptical myself about his story of a recording studio in a dry county with a church for every three houses. I mean, it doesn't add up."

"You want everything to add up?"

"I wish I could get the money to get you out of here. Your father's friends and your friends too, it seems, generously paid the lawyer a retainer, but they told me that they cannot afford to pay bail."

"What about Aunt Lucy?"

"That stuck-up bitch? She and Wally just bought a new golf cart, and she claims she's stretched because of that."

"I guess you need a golf cart if you live on a golf course."

"Neither of them know how to play Putt-Putt. She just got

it because her neighbors have one. All she uses it for is to drive her uppity girls to swim practice at the pool."

"Good thing we don't have any neighbors or a pool," said Earl.

He thought of the pool that was a pond. He remembered the river that everyone called a lake. The is and is-not of Austin came back to him. Sitting in Tom's backyard. The little girl in the next yard over playing on a swing set. He waved at her and she waved back in the manner of a fat-legged baby in a grocery cart, though she was old enough to play by herself. After he waved, he leaned over and threw up. When he looked back at the girl (he threw up for quite a while) she had not changed her expression, nor moved. Her hand was still in the air, as if it were stuck. This saddened him as it seemed the little girl routinely came out to play in her backyard only to find boys throwing up the next yard over in the morning sun. Only Earl realized it was not morning. Or maybe it was morning, but it was not the morning he thought it was. There was more than one morning at Tom's is what he remembered. Because he had forgotten all about the ride in Tom's car. They went to a place called Hamilton Pool. It was way out in the country down bumpy roads beautiful and dusty-shouldered. Earl stared out the window at the cacti and mesquite, a line of low hills in the distance. It was beautiful in an unexpected way, or maybe he was not expecting beauty.

At this place called a pool, a waterfall spilled over a ledge from far overhead. Behind the waterfall was a shallow cave. Tom told Earl to go stand under the waterfall, which Earl did because apparently this was what one did at Hamilton Pool.

The water on his head felt like needles but because he was still high it was more pleasurable than painful. How was Tom able to drive? Oh, right, they kept pulling over to sample the goods. Also they stopped off several times on their way out to the country for Tom to handle what he called transactions. This was after all the people cleared out of Tom's kitchen and after Teresa kissed Earl goodbye and told him not to be a stranger. Earl had never heard the expression and thought Teresa was referring to his here-and-also-not-ness. Or maybe she was telling him to quit being so odd? Earl didn't know how to stop being Earl, even though there was more than one of him.

He and Tom at Hamilton Pool: he'd forgotten that part. It came back to him as he stared at his mother across the metal table in the loud room: they'd hiked down to the Pedernales and stripped and swam naked in the shallow green river. On the walk back they veered onto a side path and walked a good ways into the woods and smoked a joint. Take off your shirt and lean against that tree, Tom told Earl, and Earl did and Tom unzipped his pants and went to town. Then they literally went to town, or back to town, first to a bar on a windy road high above a lake that looked like another river. Tom called the regulars at the bar "cedar choppers" and complained about the hick jukebox, but Earl loved it because it was filled with pedal steel. Almost every song on that jukebox contained a breeze of sweet pedal steel winging in from the west, bringing with it the sad truth of life.

"It's not what I came here to talk about," Earl's mother was saying. "Golf carts and swimming pools and my too-big-for-her-britches sister."

Earl did not go to Austin to end up back at Tom's place so high on hash oil and coke that he sat immobile on a couch between Tom and Teresa and Marcia, who Tom had called to come back and party with them when they got home from the bar with the heavenly jukebox. Earl asked where Brenda was and it seemed clear she was not invited, for his question hung unanswered in the air. He sat on the couch listening to side one of Lou Reed's *Rock 'N' Roll Animal.* The guitar intro to "Sweet Jane" lasted at least forty-five minutes because every note was like being shot with buckshot. The shot lodged inside Earl, agreeably. What happened after that? Oh, yeah, they were back in the bedroom and Tom was handing out something called "lewds." Earl and Teresa and Marcia and Tom, except no one was "with" anyone else. Earl wasn't with anyone because he was with Tina.

At first he and Tom watched Marcia and Teresa, then the girls watched the boys. Tom lifted his head up from Earl's lap and said he was going to fuck Earl next. Earl said no thank you sir to that. Come on Clothesline, said the girls, laughing. We'll be your clothespins.

Tom said he'd go gentle. Was it the lewds that stopped Earl from getting dressed and running into the woods and all the way back to Stovall? School nurses ought to hand out these lewds. Cuckoo clocks should dispense them on the hour. Tina would not have to be afraid of them anymore. As relaxed as he was, Earl still thought he might have said no thank you sir again, but he remembered the Highnesses kissing him and calling him Clothesline. Tom grabbed him by his legs and pulled him to the edge of the bed.

The pain was excruciating. He might have cried out for Tom to stop had Marcia not been kissing him, then Teresa. Earl believed he did cry out for Tom to stop but into their mouths. They were woods to his falling tree. He remembered trying to think of what else. He searched for a song in his head but there was only the rhythm Tom made.

Earl tried to remember what happened after that. Someone, maybe Tom, handed him a towel and Marcia and Teresa laid down and curled up alongside him. The girls held hands across his ribcage to protect him, or maybe to keep him from leaving. His clothespins. Maybe they slept a little. Earl didn't remember if he slept. Next thing he remembered was the four of them standing around in the kitchen ordering two large pizzas. When the pizza was delivered, Tom opened the door naked and the pizza guy rolled his eyes as if every other customer opened the door naked. Tom handed him a joint and a lot of money for two pizzas in Earl's opinion and the pizza guy stayed a while talking to Teresa, who was wearing Tom's David Bowie T-shirt. Teresa gave her number to the pizza guy, which made Marcia jealous. There followed a huge fight in the kitchen ending in pizza slices sailing about and lodging between appliances. Maybe give them more goods to settle them a little, said Earl, because he was ready for more goods himself, and Tom said, fuck that, they know what they need to do to get more, and so do you, Earl. Earl looked at Tom and wondered who was this naked awful person? Why was he in this man's kitchen? He put on his clothes and went outside and watched the sun come up. There were people gathered at the edge of the yard in the shadow cast by trees, standing still as deer. They'd been there the whole time Earl had been in Austin. Maybe they had been there before houses and drug dealers and poor little girls playing on swing sets. It was both still and noisy. He remembered then when his mom told him to just listen and he tried her trick and thought he heard a vacuum cleaner high in a downtown hotel and also a grain elevator being emptied into trucks in Emporia, Kansas. Cows mooed as they made their way across muddy pastures to milking sheds in Northern Alabama. He heard a fight between two girls with flying pizza slices. He heard someone's mother slicing a bell pepper. He went back in the house and into the bedroom and woke Tom.

"We've got to go get Tina now," he said.

Tom didn't want to go, and it took some time to get him out of the bed, but they drove across town in Tom's Karmann Ghia convertible. It was drizzling out now. "I'd Love to Change the World" came on the radio, then "Don't Fear the Reaper," then "Reelin' in the Years," which was a pretty fucking great set they both agreed. Probably the best commercial-free set they'd ever heard. Earl could not find the street at first and they drove around the neighborhood. Tom was getting annoyed. He said he had some transactions and was this going to take all day?

Then Earl spotted the Galaxie.

"That's your ride?"

"It's my cousin's. He goes by Leif like Leif Garrett. He's a pretty boy."

"He ought to get himself a pretty car," said Tom. "If you had wheels, why did you walk to the Springs?"

Earl told Tom again about the unruly commotion in which

he had last spotted Tina. He said he did not want to leave her there without a way home, so he put the keys up under the mat.

"I was always planning on coming back to get her, though," said Earl.

"And you did come back," said Tom. He squeezed Earl's shoulder and said, "You're a good guy, little buddy," which made Earl feel worse about himself than anything that had happened thus far in Austin. "You got to be careful, though," Tom was telling him, "because people will steal your ride in this shitty neighborhood. Which house is she in?"

Earl looked up and down the street. All the houses looked similar but none of them looked like Richie's place.

"Wait," said Earl. "Go back to that main street runs alongside the college."

"The Drag?"

"Yeah, that one. There's a poster on a telephone pole," said Earl.

They found the flyer announcing the concert of the freak Earl felt bad for missing. A couple blocks away, Earl recognized the house. The door was open and he tried the baggy screened door. It was unlocked, but Earl knew better than to enter a dwelling without knocking. He found Tina and Richie upstairs lying on their mattress on the floor, as if they had not moved since he'd seen them last. Everyone was asleep. It was his lot to wake them. He tugged at Tina's shoulder. She woke, blinking.

"I need to talk to you, get dressed and come outside with me," whispered Earl, but Richie never stirred, even when she lifted his arm off of her midriff and pulled on his jeans and a T-shirt and came outside. Tom was rocking on a porch swing the next house over. His eyes were closed but Earl knew he was listening.

"I'm not coming back with you Earl," she said as soon as they were outdoors. "I realize I owe you the up-and-up. You might think I let you down, but you have to ask yourself lots of questions."

"Like for instance?"

"I offered you opportunities you otherwise might never have experienced."

"Name some."

"Well I think it's pretty clear that I'm the more sophisticated of the two of us. I mean, I'm not sure you really understand anything about life. You see, I've been around."

"No doubt," said Tom, who was suddenly standing beside them.

"Who is this?" said Tina.

Earl introduced them and Tom asked Tina if she liked to party and she said it depends. Tom said on what. She said on the interested parties, no pun intended.

Then she said, "Wait, how old are you?"

"Twenty-eight," said Tom.

She looked at Earl a long time and then shrugged, as if to point out to Earl the obvious: You make your own choices in this world.

Tom said, "Look, are you coming? Because this neighborhood is fucking dead and my place is bumping twenty-four per day."

Tina said to Earl, "I figured you would have gone back already."

Earl was about to tell Tina he would never even think of leaving her when Tom said, "You mean the Clothesline? Go back? The Clothesline has got more hanging to do."

Tina studied Earl. He felt like he had a twig in his hair. "You don't look like you even slept since I saw you last."

"That would be because he hasn't," said Tom.

"Is this guy, like, your interpreter?" Tina said. She was looking at Earl, but Earl felt like she was really trying not to look at Tom.

"I'm talking to you in my head," said Earl, and he giggled.

"Like that's new," said Tina. "Where did y'all meet anyway?"

"At this pool that isn't really a pool."

Tina said, "If anyone else said that to me, even if they were high, I'd think: 'crazy person.' But I know how you love a swimming hole. I won't ask what it is if it isn't a swimming pool. I can look at your eyes and see that your answer would be even weirder. Look at your eyes, Earl. You ought to see your eyes."

"My man can see right into your soul," said Tom.

"I'm an X-ray machine. But I don't bother with bones."

Tina laughed, and then caught herself laughing, as if it leaked out of her, as if she didn't really think all of this was funny at first but was starting to.

"Richie's got some excellent pot," said Tina, as if this was her reason to stay.

"Excellent pot is excellent as far as it goes," Tom said.

"Did you come up here to smoke some excellent pot and go to sleep on a mattress on the floor? Because in Stovall you can sleep in the frilly bed at your aunt's house if it's sleep you need. Plus, Tina," said Earl, performing a little now that he had become an X-ray machine and could see through and past everything, especially Richie and his excellent pot, "we did not come up here to see Richie. I won't say what we came up here for because I would put it in the 'personal' category, but as long as we are here you should come meet the people who stand at the edge of the woods behind Tom's house."

"What is he on?" Tina asked Tom.

"What is he *on*? That sounds like something off of *Dragnet*," said Tom, which made Earl laugh. *Dragnet* almost always made him laugh, even though it wasn't a comedy.

"He's not *on* it, he's in it."

"He's always in his head," said Tina.

"Are we going to talk about me or are we going to level off some. That radio station plays every song I want it to and bleeds one into another. Like one long song by different bands."

"I guess I need to take whatever he's been taking to figure out what he's talking about."

"Good guess," said Tom.

"I'll go get my things, then," she said, and Earl said, "You never had any things when you arrived."

"These are his jeans," she said, and Earl said, "Fuck him," and Tom said, "Exactly."

They climbed into the Karmann Ghia but Tina had to sit on Earl's lap. He didn't mind, but she said it hurt her neck to sit like that all bent over and asked how far was it.

"How about y'all follow me in Earl's pretty-boy cousin's ugly ride?" said Tom.

"How about you are crazy if you think I can drive from here to the corner," said Earl.

"Fuck it, I'll drive," said Tina. Earl thought she did not have her license either but maybe she did. He knew next to nothing. Nothing was better than next to nothing when talking about Tina.

Tom dropped them off. He said he had a couple stops to make on the way home. Hang tight, he said. Hang five, said Earl, and Tom slid his palm out the window and Earl slapped him five.

In the Galaxie, Earl tried to find the station they were listening to on the way over, but it was all brash ads and static. Maybe it was only in his head the whole time, but he didn't care, nor did he care to explain anything else to Tina, who was concentrating hard on making the car go in the lanes. They followed Tom over the river that was called a lake and then up into some hills where all the houses had spreading lawns and large garages and some had swimming pools. He pulled over and got out of his car and went up to a house. Far below they could see the lights of the city. This is his place? Tina asked. Earl said no, he was just taking care of a transaction. A what? Earl started to explain but stopped because Tom was back and they were following him again and Earl was bent over twisting the dial. If Tina was talking, he didn't remember what she was saying. Tina never did *not* talk so he assumed she was pushing him to define the word *transaction*. Earl knew all sorts of new things but goddamn if he knew the names of any of them. Tom stopped again at a dark house with a mop in a bucket on the front porch. The mop was so dry it was no longer a mop, really. The strings were mottled and Earl could see from the street that they were stiff. It was a stick in a bucket with bad hair. Something that might chase after you in a nightmare.

Earl's mother said: "I had it in my mind we would talk about more practical things. And that I could offer you more in the way of . . ."

But she trailed off and Earl stared at her for a long time across the table and said finally, "I got so much in my mind right now."

The problem was that what was in his mind was not in any order from which, say, for instance, sense could be made. And some things—like what happened after they left Richie's house with Tina? If that was in Earl's mind, it was hiding.

8.

EARL LAY ON his bunk in the jailhouse staring at the water spot and tuning out T-Bone. T-Bone talked his way through the endless boredom of incarceration. Did he think if he talked faster he would get out quicker? He had not said what he was in for. Earl knew not to ask. Somehow he grasped jailhouse etiquette. Also he respected people's business. He could not imagine stopping an emaciated patient taking a lap around a cancer ward while supporting himself with a rolling IV stand to ask, What got hold of you, my man?

T-Bone got to go out for meals but not Earl. The C.O. brought him a tray and watched him eat.

"You best be glad for room service," said T-Bone. "Your boys might have a rep around here but there some of these jokers are out of Houston or Dallas. They'd soon fuck you up as look at you."

The C.O. came to take him to shower and stood outside the shower while the men smacked their lips but did not touch him. You were given a washcloth and some soap. Even Earl knew not to pick up the soap if you dropped it. He held on to it like it was the mane of a horse he was riding bareback through a forest pursued by banditos.

Earl had been in jail for two days when his lawyer showed up.

"When do I get out of here?"

Arthur said he was working on it. He said he had a guy up in Austin trying to track down this Richie character.

Earl had not told Arthur all that he'd remembered when his mother came to see him. He had not told him about Her Highnesses or Tom or the goods or the people who stood at the edge of the backyard where the grass ended and the woods began or anything past finding Tina and Richie all bound up in ungainly acts. He would not tell Arthur all of it. He might not want to hang himself over all that mess with Tom, but that did not mean he wanted to tell Arthur, who, for someone out of Stovall, had decent taste in music and a big vocabulary.

Also, the goods: could he not get in trouble for telling them how much he'd taken?

That was Clothesline who did those things. It was not the Earl who prowled the outskirts, who worshipped pedal steel, who memorized whole passages of *His Life and Times*.

Maybe if he told Arthur what he *could* remember, however, he would remember the rest of what happened after he and Tom took Tina back to Tom's place. Which is the wall against which his memory dead-ended, even though he had spent hours lying in his bunk trying to summon what had happened next.

So he had told the C.O. he needed to speak to his lawyer. Two days later the C.O. came to get him.

Earl thought of asking Arthur, Where were you those two days? The difference was that Arthur would say, I was busy, Earl, busy eating and hobnobbing with the treasonous bastards that run this bilge-water sinkhole of a township. He was from Stovall and talked trash about it until someone else did, at which point he defended it as if it were his mama who had been maligned.

"Well, Earl."

"Well, Arthur."

Arthur produced a greasy sausage-and-egg biscuit and a large Pepsi with crushed ice for Earl, and one for himself. They watched each other chew.

"I remembered some things," said Earl, swallowing.

"Which things?"

"Those two days."

"Well lay it on me, cowboy."

Earl started when he got to Barton Springs and the locker room and Tom. He thought he might hesitate, but he did not even slow down. He must have sped up, for after he described Tom in shades and semi-hard on and nothing else and proceeded on to the parking lot where their Highnesses awaited, Arthur held up his hand in the Hold Up position.

"This is getting complicated," he said. "Lots of characters in this horse opera. I'm going to take some notes."

He pulled a legal pad out of an ancient and creaky leather satchel that Earl understood without asking was his daddy's or maybe even his granddaddy's and that he came from a long line of lawyers.

Earl talked for another twenty minutes. He told Arthur everything he could remember. It was not easy to tell Arthur about the things he did with Tom, and it was a lot harder to tell Arthur about one thing Tom did to him, to which he believed he said no thank you sir. It seemed strange to Earl that he never thought about it at all until Tom appeared beside him in the locker room wearing only mirrored shades and a hard-on. He had thought often and in great detail about the things he had done with Tina before he did them. In fact he had been thinking of them for years. They woke him in the night, and sometimes left him a mess. What did it all mean?

"So you and Adelaide followed Tom back to his place."

"Me and Tina."

"Tina, okay. Call her what you want for now. Just keep talking. Did you go directly back to Tom's place?"

"Tom stopped for some transactions on the way. We parked on the side of the road. He didn't invite us to go inside with him."

"I don't imagine he did. Do you remember where you went?"

"One place was a mansion overlooking the city and the other one was kind of a dump."

"Well, that helps. Then what?"

"I don't know then what."

"Okay. But how is it you remembered all the stuff you just told me?"

Earl followed the phone line from his mother to the woods. The line led to hours previously hidden somewhere in his mind.

"I don't have any answer for how memory works," said Earl.

"Well look here, Earl. Maybe you are under the impression that because of the so-called "goods" you sampled and it sounds like you sampled enough to put a man twice your size in the hospital, you are lucky your stomach revolted and you got some of that poison out of your system even though I hear you about that little girl watching from her swing set, that's some sad shit to have to witness when you're just trying to climb up your slide, anyway you might think . . ."

"That we can use it as a defense? I am not slow, Arthur."

"No," said Arthur, "but your memory sure is. Also, they've got you lying on tape."

"What lie?"

"You told Phil during the initial interview that the last time you saw Adelaide was with some guy named Richie."

"Far as I knew at the time. So not technically a lie."

"Well, anyway, Phil is not the problem now. It's the DA who is going to question how you suddenly remembered all these not-insignificant details. Most of which are incriminating."

"Which are what?"

"The fact that you were on a drug binge when you and this drug dealer went and got that gal is not going to help."

"Has this DA never been to Austin?"

Arthur studied him. "Not everyone who goes to Austin ends up sleeping with members of both sexes while high on coke, speed, and did you say hash oil? Some people go up there to visit the state museum and learn about the storied history of the Republic."

"I'm from Louisiana," said Earl. "Also I didn't sleep with anyone. I didn't even sleep."

"It's a euphemism, Earl."

"Like the stork story?"

"Say what?"

"Where babies come from."

"That's not the example I would have chosen," said Arthur. "Nor would I have pegged you for it. Back to Tom. I need to find out if he's been picked up for anything, which from the way you describe him is likely. If he's got a record, we can track him down. What's his last name?"

Earl shrugged.

"Right," said Arthur. "You let him pick you up in public, but you don't know his last name."

"Tom might not even be his real first name."

"Not that I'm trying to make you feel bad for what you all did. Because what you do and with whom? That's your bidness, partner. But I'm not going to lie. Once all this comes out? You know you're in the Bible Belt, son."

"I'm not your son. You have never called me son before."

Arthur ignored this, as if Earl were trying to derail one of his precious points. "There are people who would deem that a grievous sin, what you and this Tom or whatever his real name got up to. A burn-in-hell type situation."

"All but one time, a girl was present."

"Not exactly going to change things. Probably make it all worse. To these people a threesome is when they get stood up on the golf course. So let's leave that out, okay? Because you just need to understand that people—for instance, the DA, who is a devout Southern Baptist—will think if you are capable of committing that sin, it will be no stretch to them to think you capable of hurting this Adelaide."

Earl thought about it. If it got out that he went with boys (even just one boy, who was technically a man) as well as girls, they would likely just think him a straight-up faggot because if you get with one guy, that is what you are. In which case, why would he want to harm a girl? Even a girl he had slept with, who he had caught sleeping with some other dude?

He didn't hate Tina for getting with Richie. He loved her for her ability to allow him to be with her and also not. Which Arthur had told him never to mention to anyone again.

"I need you to tell me everything you can remember about Tom. Where he lived, what kind of car he drove. And if it comes to you, where y'all stopped off for him to carry out his so-called transactions."

"He drove a rag top 'sixty-eight Karmann Ghia."

"Of course he did. What color?"

"Green."

"Good, Earl. What did he look like?"

"Long wavy hair. Dark skin. Tall. Kind of like Mick Taylor, come to think of it."

"Thank goodness they went with Taylor instead of Jeff Beck," said Arthur. "Can you imagine?"

"I think Taylor's the fingers in *Sticky Fingers*," said Earl.

"What's your favorite Taylor solo?"

"Easy," said Earl. "'Sway.'"

"I'm going to go with 'Time Waits for No One.'"

"I hear that," said Earl.

"Back to Tom. Did he share any personal information? Say where he was from, where he'd gone to school, anything like that?"

"He likes David Bowie a lot."

"'Heroes' is epic," said Arthur.

"I like 'Aladdin Sane,' said Earl.

"Too frenetic," said Arthur. "Though I'm beginning to think frenetic is your thing?"

The truth was that Earl did not know what his thing was. The scarier truth was that he wasn't bothered by this because he thought he had his whole life ahead of him to figure it out.

9.

T-BONE'S TRIAL DATE was approaching. Whatever he'd done, it did not seem to Earl that he had any real hope of getting away with it. Earl was glad he did not have to worry about whether or not he'd get away with anything since he'd done nothing wrong but take a lot of drugs and return a borrowed car to his cousin two days later than promised.

He saw himself back down home, sitting out by the shed, at the edge of the party, his face half-lit by fire, listening to the men argue over what was worse, slinging negative adjectivals, while his cousins banged out songs on their guitars. Eventually when the bottles were low, they would break out "I'm So Lonesome I Could Cry," and even Moon, who didn't care for country music, would join in. All of them loved to sing about the lonesome whippoorwill, the midnight train. All of them knew the nights so long, the moon crying behind the clouds. It's in all of us, Earl believed, it was there before we were born. We heard the silence of a star falling through a purple sky when we were in our cribs or some of us a dresser drawer cushioned with sock balls so we wouldn't bang that soft patch on our brand-new heads. We heard it and we sat right up in crib or drawer and said in our baby blubber, I *been* hearing that.

In the pokey the nights were long but instead of the solace of whippoorwill call or midnight train, he heard T-Bone. T-Bone's chatter was a dripping tap. He kept it to a whisper because you could hear everything up and down the block, the man in the next cell pleasuring himself, all night long coughing, and good God the sawmill snoring.

T-Bone's words seeped up from the space between the bed and the wall. The quantity of them, which had previously annoyed Earl, now touched him. T-Bone's talk was the equivalent of nervous sweat. He could not control it, just like you can't do a thing about how your sweat smells. When you are chopping wood or playing kickball with your brothers it smells different than when you get sent up to the drug store by your brothers to shoplift some Robitussin. Guilty sweat had a sweet odor, a little like the morning-after perspiration of a drunk but not quite as cloying.

"I never had a real job in years unless you count stealing batteries or the cars they come in or before that, stripping copper. I've got a four-year-old girl lives with my parents. Outside of Concan. Gabriele but we call her Gaby. Her mama's Mexican. She might of went back to Mexico. I met her in a hotel up in Mesquite. I guess you could say I was a customer of hers? Then she wanted out, so we went and stayed in Concan in the back of my uncle's body shop, he had a little apartment back there and she got a job at HEB. I was supposed to stay clean with her when she found out she was pregnant. We were both shooting dope. She did good because she wanted her baby to be healthy, but I kept messing up, Earl. I reckon I was scared but what does it matter now why I messed up? She said she was going to take the baby and go back to Mexico and why couldn't I at least get on at my uncle's body shop—I am a self-trained mechanic, Earl, I started fixing go-carts when I was seven, eight years old—but my uncle was already doing me a solid letting me stay there, and when his tools went missing he wasn't going to hire me after that. She had the baby and moved in with my parents and stayed six months. One night I came back from town and she said I smelled like pussy which she was correct, I stepped out on her because it had been since she was what, four or five months since we'd got down. Next day she was gone, left Gaby with my parents. I haven't heard from her since. I tried to track her down in Dallas. But nobody had seen nor heard from her. I figured she went back to her people in Mexico."

Her people. Earl remembered the highnesses laughing when he spoke of his people, as if they did not have any.

"My parents kept Gaby. What else were they going to do? They love her to pieces. She's as sweet as they come, Earl. You know what, though? She might not be mine. We don't really favor. But if my parents think she's not mine they haven't said, and I wouldn't even care. She could be mine. I was with her mother more than a few times and I didn't always pay for it and it seems to me a paying customer cannot get a woman pregnant. Also I guess it's like how do you call it, Russian roulette? God knows I pulled that trigger."

T-Bone was quiet for awhile. "I love my girl," he said. "I want to do right by her."

Another minute of quiet.

"Way I figure it? She might not *be* mine, but I took her to raise or rather my parents did and she wouldn't have any people at all if I didn't step up. It's not like I'm good at stepping up, Earl, in fact to tell the truth I have let people go to jail for shit I done myself. That's about as low as you can go in my world."

Yep. Earl would know something about that. Here he was listening to T-Bone when he should be home. But he knew he would be home soon. Tom would turn up. His people would go his bail. His daddy hadn't been to see him. Moon and Sleep and B.C. were his real people. They were the ones keeping him alive in here. Why was he here again? He kept asking Arthur. Finally Arthur had said, Listen, Earl. It's a song as old as a hymn and as hummable: they're going to go after you hard because your daddy is no-count and your mama, like so many mamas I come across in my line of work, is both left to do everything by your no-count daddy and typically protective of him. And this Adelaide Morgan? She comes from money. Her people don't think they are better than y'all, they *know* it. Only thing you got going for you is you're white. If you weren't white, they'd have found a way to send you up already. They don't have a goddamn thing on you other than the blood in the trunk and she hasn't turned up yet. Some places that would not be enough to hold you but guess what? This is East Texas. They do about what they want with the law when a fancy doctor's daughter goes missing and the last person to see her can't account for the forty-eight hours after he last saw her."

Blood in the trunk? Vaguely Earl remembered the vehicle. It was blue. Leif kept it clean in the manner of pretty boys, who spend all of their Sunday afternoons waxing and vacuuming their vehicles. He remembered the smell of Armor All on the dash. He remembered Leif giving him the keys and saying be careful with my ride. Then Tina sticking her hand out the window, letting the breeze bat it back and forth. Twisting the dial to find something decent to listen to on the radio. Leaving the keys under the mat for Tina when he set off for the lake-pond-pool. But blood? He never even opened the trunk.

"So if I could account for those two days they would let me go?"

"You'd have to do more than account. You'd have to have some proof. An alibi, Earl."

T-Bone said now, "Maybe you can go see Gaby when you get out, Earl. You'd like her, she's just as sweet . . ."

"Concan," said Earl.

"It's on the Frio. Maybe y'all can float the river."

"The Rio Frio. I've heard of it," said Earl.

"Why don't you tell me a story, Earl," said T-Bone.

T-Bone had talked himself to near tears. Earl could smell him now and his sweat was pure fear. His words were damp with held back tears. Old T-Bone. Don't ever tell nobody I told you all this, he would have said if he could have. Don't let anyone know you seen me go soft. But he didn't have to say any of this because Earl heard it and he smelled it. It hung in the air. It rose to the top of the cell, a cloud, and Earl breathed it because he had no choice.

So Earl whispered some words to T-Bone. He knew he could not tell him anything that would ease his fear or make him smell any better. He knew it would be better not to say, things are going to be okay, you'll get to see your daughter again soon. He knew better than to say, Gaby is yours, because Earl had his doubts. He was touched that T-Bone would love this little girl so hard because he loved her Mexican mama and that even after the mama disappeared, he would keep the girl to raise. Or his parents. Earl thought about T-Bone's parents. Maybe this was the one thing T-Bone had given them that they could celebrate. They could shower this little girl with love which they had also shown their errant junky son until that love got stretched so thin because T-Bone could not keep from fucking up. Now they had Gaby and she was innocent and sweet and she was theirs.

The only story Earl could think of to tell T-Bone was what went on down in Austin. All other stories had gone out of his head, even (tragically) *His Life and Times*. The only parts he remembered were the parts at Angola and this made him wonder if Arthur wasn't right when he said that Lead Belly was not a great role model. He only wanted Arthur to be right about a couple of things—the kind of biscuit Earl favored from Sunrise and whatever it was he needed to ascertain to get Earl out.

Earl told the story of What Happened in Austin to T-Bone, as much as he remembered. He remembered more as he whispered it in the cell that reeked of fear and of not-knowing.

"I was with this guy, Tom. We'd been up for two days doing crystal and coke. I never have done anything more than smoke some of my brother's shitty dirt weed. But I guess I took to it, that powder. Especially the crystal. I felt like I could stick my foot in a campfire and my foot would clap thunder and douse the fire with flood. I felt like a midnight train barreling through sleepy towns, all twinkling lights and that's it, so fast was I barreling. I felt like I could do no wrong and no wrong would ever come to me so long as I kept the tank topped off with a here and there pretty much continuous line of that crystal and some coke to boost it and oh yeah there was good weed and hash oil to calm me down.

"We had met these girls at this crazy swimming pool that was more like a pond and we partied with them for a while until one got tired and went home and the other two got into a fight. Something to do with pizzas. I remember we were in the kitchen at Tom's place, standing around listening to *Houses of the Holy*, you know that song "No Quarter," it lasts about an hour, and pizza slices were flying past me and then the girls were on each other down on the floor which was greasy from pepperoni juice. So Tom kicked them out."

"This dude Tom, he's from Austin?"

"Nah. I don't where he's from. He never said."

"I thought I might know him. I know some Toms."

"Beats me. Tom's all I know."

"I used to party down in Austin. Whereabouts were y'all throwing down?"

"You ever been to the Continental?"

"Sure," said T-Bone.

"We passed by there on the way to Tom's house. It was up the hill from there, off that main drag. That's all I remember."

"You and Tom, y'all did these girls?"

"We did them both and then we watched them do each other."

"Earl my man!" said T-Bone. "I'll be wanting some skinny on that."

But Earl knew better than to tell T-Bone more because in his mind what he had done with his Highnesses and what he had done with Tom were all mixed up. It was like trying to unkink the phone cord that connected his mother to her sisters in Bossier City. Sometimes Earl thought that the cord was however many miles it was from Stovall to Bossier City. Off on its own it snaked through the woods and the swamps and pastures and somehow no farmer had sliced his mother's private line while out disking his field, no wild animal had picked it apart allowing his mother's words to rise up and mix with the mist in the mornings in that boggy neck of the woods.

"Tom got tired of those girls messing up his kitchen so he made them leave. We cleaned up. I mopped the floor. I have never mopped before. I really got into it."

Earl liked it because it was not like sweeping the floor. When you swept a floor there was always some little line of dust you could not force into the pan. Earl would end up sweeping the stubborn line beneath a piece of furniture or an appliance. Under the rug was too cliché.

"After they left, we did more crystal. That stuff makes you horny."

"Do tell," said T-Bone.

"Anyway we went and got Tina from Richie's place."

"Who is Tina?"

"Not who she claimed to be."

"Sounds like my old lady. Who did she claim to be?"

"Tina," said Earl. "Last time I had seen her before I went off with Tom, she was with this dude Richie. We were supposed to go see her mother in the hospital, but it turned out her mother wasn't in any hospital. What I have learned from other people, not Tina herself, is that her mother is some real estate lady in Houston."

Earl was quiet for a bit. "I guess you could say Tina used me."

"Bitches are bad for that," said T-Bone.

Earl thought about it some. "Nah," he said. "Not all of them. But I went and told Tom about how she'd asked me to drive her down to Austin to see her mother and then asked me to stop by this dude Richie's house first and there was a party going on. We were in the kitchen getting high and she disappeared. I went upstairs and found her in bed with Richie."

"Getting it on?"

"I mean, I guess that's what you could call it."

"So y'all went in and got her?"

"Tom went in. I sat in the car. I couldn't face her once we found Richie's house. Maybe I was scared? Nah, I wasn't scared of anything. I was just too fucked up on that powder and hadn't had any sleep in two days nor much to eat besides pizza and I decided I would just sit in the car and wait. Tom went in. He was gone for a while. He came out with Tina. Not her real name. They were laughing like they'd known each other for a long time. Tom's a real charmer with the ladies. Tina got in the car and looked at me and said "Hey, You," as if she'd not used me or fucked Richie right in front of me.

"That must of pissed you off big time, man."

"Hard to say what I was feeling," said Earl, but it was much harder to remember what happened. Did he go in and get Tina or did Tom? Did they go together? Either way, he wasn't lying when he told T-Bone it was hard to say what he was feeling because people did not understand him when he tried. He would say he felt like pedal steel and draw blank faces. He'd say he felt like a midnight train with two lights on behind and the red light was his mind and they would just study his mouth. He'd say he felt like a frog kick. Good at turnstiles. I am a love letter blown out of a sweetheart's hand into the gutter and the wind that blew me had the bad breath of crawlspace.

"Then Tom told us to follow him back to his place in the car I'd borrowed from my cousin, but I was too fucked up to see straight. I couldn't have walked to the end of the street, much less driven. So Tina drove. I didn't even know she had her license."

Earl stopped talking. He waited for T-Bone to respond. He heard sounds from other cells and, somewhere beyond the door that separated them from the guards, a radio playing. T-Bone was quiet but Earl could hear him listening. You don't have to see people's faces to know if they are listening. A certain kind of silence can tell you if you're being heard and even if what you are saying is sticking in the mind of the listener.

"We stopped off at this one place so Tom could conduct a transaction and it was up on a hill above town and the sun was going down behind that tower where that Marine shot all those people. The tower was all lit up and I remember thinking how fucked it was that it was both beautiful and the scene of so many people dying. That's the kind of thing you get all caught up in thinking when there's more drugs running through you than blood."

"I hear that," said T-Bone.

"Back at Tom's we were sitting on the couch drinking beer and listening to *The Low Spark of High Heeled Boys* and then Tom started messing around with Tina, trying to take her halter top off. She looked at me, but I shrugged. After catching her with Richie, I didn't think I had any say in what she did or who she did it with. I remembered thinking how much I hated Richie when I found her upstairs with him, but somehow her doing it with a guy she knew and had probably done it with before was different than her doing it with Tom. When the goods wore off, I did not know what I was still doing there or why Tina was there but then I took some more and the saxophone solo on 'Low Spark' replaced whatever I was thinking. My thoughts were notes and they were held long and low by the guy on the saxophone."

T-Bone said, "Man, that's heavy right there, Earl."

"Tom said he had a waterbed did she want to see and Tina said she had always wanted to do it on one. It was dark in the bedroom, but Tom turned on a light. It cast blue shadows across the wall. The blue light was my baby. When Tina saw the two of us naked though she got a little bit nervous but Tom asked her did she want a lewd and she said sure. He pulled some out of a box up under his bed and I took one too. I had only had my first lewd the day before and I liked it so when Tom was kissing Tina I acted like I was reaching for my beer and I found the box which was a separate box from the other goods, the coke and the crystal. I swallowed another one. Tom got on top of her, and I just watched and after a while she wanted me. Her eyes were all glassy and she had her mouth open and she was drooling a little, and I thought either she is really getting off or she is pretending. Tina was good at pretending."

"Was?"

"Yeah she was. Because who she had become, I did not know. She wasn't the girl I met in the woods. The old Tina, she was long gone."

"Damn, son," said T-Bone. "I never figured this was the story you were going to tell."

"I can tell another one," Earl said, even though he didn't know another one.

"No way. You got me all stoked down here. What happened next?"

Earl didn't remember much after that because the lewds slowed him down. But the lewd hit Tina hard. She fell over on him but she kept moving up and down. Just a slow grind and it felt a little better to Earl. It felt like the right rhythm at the right time, like they'd found their groove. They kissed and their kisses took Earl back to sunning turtles lifting their sleepy heads to watch, no longer indifferent to their love.

Earl drifted. He wasn't asleep but he was floating out toward elsewhere. It felt like he was the only one in the room, though Tina was still in bed with him, and so was Tom. But Tina was no longer on top of him. She was lying beside him, and Tom was on top of her. Then Tom had turned her around and was behind her. He was trying to get her up on her knees but she'd gone limp from the lewds.

Earl was afloat. He had this line from a song by the Who in his head, "the way the beach is kissed by the sea." Tom kept trying to pull Tina up on her knees. But she too was afloat. Tina and Earl, kissed by waves. Then washed up side by side on the wet sucking sand. The shells tinkling like a bracelet of charms. A washing-over peace until Tina started crying. It hurts, she said. Just give it a minute, said Tom, and the hurt will pass. It'll feel great, right Earl? See, Tom told Tina. You can trust old Earl. He'll tell you the truth.

Come on, Clothesline, we'll be your clothespins. Then Tom said he'd go easy and the girls were suctioned up beside him kissing him and if he cried out or said stop, it went in their mouths and maybe down into their lungs. He knew he had not gone along with it just like it was a line or a lewd or Tom leaning him against the tree off a path that led to the Pedernales River. But now a wave came and lifted him up. The water floated back out to sea, and he went right along.

Stop, Tina was saying. She was crying. Earl heard the hurt in her voice as he washed up on the beach again. He half rose up from the sand to see Tom behind Tina. Tom had his hands around her waist holding her up. Tina began to scream. Put your hand over her mouth, Tom said to Earl. The goddamn neighbors will call the fucking cops if she don't shut up. But Earl did not move. He was lying on the sand. Tina screamed louder. Tom was yelling at her to shut up and at Earl to shut her up. Tom grabbed a lamp off the bedside table. He hit her in the back of the head with the lamp. She turned her head to look at Earl. Tom hit her again and harder. Blood was all over Earl. Tina was lying limp next to him and Tom was sitting on the edge of the bed holding the lamp and looking at Earl.

"He was going to kill me next," Earl said, and this is when he realized he'd been talking, not just remembering, that he was there and only there.

10.

IN THE MORNING they came for T-Bone. Earl had not been to sleep. He was awake and alone with the story he had told T-Bone. T-Bone had asked for a story and Earl had started talking. He was thinking the story was made up. Or that maybe it started out true, because he remembered going to get Tina and bringing her back to Tom's, but everything after? All of it he remembered as he talked.

Over the sawmill snores he heard Tina's screams. And he would hear them for the rest of his life, in loudspeakers, in the clanging shut of doors, even in the flush of a toilet. A flushing toilet had always seemed polyphonic to Earl, but it became over the years a horrid screechy tuning-up middle-school orchestra. And in the wrong notes, the flats and sharps, the shrill violin and flat clap of cymbal, he heard the screams of Tina.

In phones, in birdsong, in wind through trees, in sacred, failsafe pedal steel.

When they came for T-Bone, he had not spoken to Earl though Earl could tell by his breathing that he too was awake all night. Was he afraid of Earl? Now that Earl had told him a story in return for T-Bone's tale of his love for that little girl who, chances were, was not even his? Earl wanted to say something to T-Bone, just to test whether or not he believed his story. Maybe he just thought Earl was just making stuff up. Earl wasn't sure he wasn't.

The C.O. came and called T-Bone's real name. It was Dwight Corn. Hell, no wonder "T-Bone."

Earl leaned over and looked down as T-Bone got dressed. He wanted to wish him good luck (though he wasn't even sure what for since he'd never asked him what he was in for), but T-Bone wouldn't look at him.

"Well," said Earl, as T-Bone walked out of the cell. T-Bone kept moving. He acted like Earl was the water spot on the ceiling, like he had not shared a cell with him for the last three weeks.

Then Earl was alone. No one brought his breakfast. He was hungry. He got up and used the toilet and for the first time in three weeks he had a satisfying time of it. He was loud and long on the toilet and glad T-Bone was gone because good God the stink. It was like the stink of the vomit that came out of him in Tom's backyard. He remembered then that Tom, instead of killing Earl, put down the bloody lamp and said, "I'm going to shower, care to join?"

Earl couldn't look at him.

"No? Okay cool, I'll keep it running for ya."

Earl lay there beside Tina. Blood in his eyebrows, drying and caking. He tasted her blood as it was all over his face. He was frozen until he heard the water running. Then he stroked

Tina's cheek and did not look at what the lamp had done to the back of her head.

Tom came back with his long hair wet and neatly combed. "You're up, man. Better hurry if you want hot water."

Earl got up quietly. He wanted to be respectful to Tina and not disturb her sleep. She would wake up while he was in the shower, and he'd take her to the hospital. They would bandage her up and then they would go to the police or maybe Earl would drive them straight back to Stovall.

Tom sat naked on the edge of the bed with a mirror, a razor, a dollar bill, and a pile of powder. As Earl walked past him, he looked Earl up and down and smiled.

Finally, the C.O. came and called his name. He had gotten back in bed and was staring at the ceiling. He was exhausted but not sleepy. He was as frozen as he'd been with Tina lying alongside him, now that he remembered Tina lying alongside him.

"Get up before I come in there and yank your ass down off that bunk."

The C.O. was usually pretty nice to Earl. Now he wouldn't even respond to Earl's pleasantries. He took Earl to the room where he usually met Arthur. Earl's hunger came back. But Arthur wasn't there, and neither was any biscuit. The cop who used to go with Arthur's sister sat at the table. He appeared more pumped up than when Earl saw him last. He smiled at Earl like he was glad to lay eyes on him. Even on no sleep and pushing through the troubling fog of disturbing memories that he thought he might have just imagined, Earl knew that a grin on this man's face was a bad sign.

He needed to show up now. He willed himself to be there and there. The red light that was his mind had switched off. That meant the midnight train rolling by was black in the night. All the crossings were unsafe until the sky turned purple. That would take hours, days. Years of darkness, broken red light, blank mind, and Earl a sitting duck in front of a grinning cop.

"Well, Earl," said the cop. "How you feeling?"

Earl didn't say anything, so the cop said, "Need me to speak up?" But he always spoke up because he thought it made him more manly. Also, his voice was naturally pitched toward ceiling or sky.

"I don't sleep too good in here. Not at all last night," said Earl.

"So I heard."

Earl was about to ask who he might have heard that from when the red light of his mind blinked on faintly, then fully, followed by a flush all over his body.

"He never did have any little girl named Gaby," said Earl.

"Do what now?"

"Dwight fucking T-Bone Corn," said Earl.

The cop shrugged, as if he'd never heard the name.

"I want Arthur in here."

"Arthur? I called him already. Left him a message, told him to be here at nine. I guess we could wait awhile. You ever laid eyes on Arthur before ten a.m.?"

"There are no clocks in this place."

"Observant of you. Turns out you observed more than you've let on. No, I take that back, see, because I always had you pegged as an observer. Nothing gets past you, does it Earl?

You sit back and take it all in. It's all up in here"—he pointed to his temple with his finger, a gesture Earl remembered him favoring in their first meeting—"filed away for a rainy day."

"There aren't any windows in this place either. Could be sleeting for all I know."

"You know it ain't sleeting, Earl. You know what day it is and what month. You know it's hot out. You thirsty? Want a Pepsi while we wait for Arthur? I called and told him he needed to come over here, but he's probably stopped off at Sunrise. Sometimes Arthur's all about Arthur."

"I'll take a Pepsi," said Earl. Arthur often forgot to bring him a Pepsi or he drank it himself.

The cop went to the door and cracked it and nearly screamed in his smoke-alarm-done-gone-off pitch, "Bring us two Pepsis and call Arthur again," then closed it and then opened it again and said, "Lots of ice." He closed it again and sat down. Earl was listening. He didn't hear anyone on the other side of the door.

The cop sat down and said, "I got that right, Earl? Lots of ice?"

Earl shrugged.

"Let's talk some. It'll take 'em a while to get our drinks."

Earl said, "I believe I ought to . . ."

"Ought to? Little late for ought to."

Earl did not know why this crushed him, the cop talking about how late he was with what he ought to have done. Usually he paid no mind to this cop. He felt mad at himself and at Arthur, who was probably sitting in the parking lot finishing his breakfast. He was not mad at T-Bone because he knew enough to know T-Bone would get his down the road.

Earl ought to have kept his mouth shut. But like the cop said, now it was a little late for "ought to." No reason why he should wait for fucking Arthur. T-Bone had told them all his story.

"I'll talk," said Earl.

"You don't want to wait for Arthur?"

"Why should I?"

"He's your lawyer, son."

"You're not my goddamn daddy and if he was my lawyer wouldn't he be here? Also, what is it going to change, him being here?"

"That's a legal question," said the cop. "Beyond my pay grade. You'd have to ask . . ."

"It is something you need me to sign?"

The cop looked nervous. He usually had imposing posture, but now he slumped back in the plastic chair.

"All you got to do is say you waive your right to counsel when I start the tape."

"Start the fucking thing, then."

"This is Phillip Bondurant talking to Earl Boudreaux. It's April 27, 1974. The time is eight thirty-two a.m."

He pushed Pause and said to Earl, "Now you say your name and affirm that you have refused the right to have counsel present during this interview."

"Affirm, ascertain, whatever the fuck," said Earl. "Push the button."

"This is Earl Boudreaux and I hereby affirm that my right to have my counsel present during this interview is waived. Now I guess you want me to tell you what happened after Tom killed Tina? I guess you know what happened before, since I told that to my cell mate and he obviously told you. After Tom killed Tina with the lamp, he snorted some crystal. Then he took a shower. I stayed with Tina. I kept thinking she'd wake up. Her blood was all over me. Tom came back in the room and said he left the water running. I stayed in Tom's shower for a long time. The hot water went away. I shivered when it got cold but there was too much blood. Tom's one washcloth was so ragged that it was as coarse as a brush. I scrubbed my scalp and the blood turned the water red. I got out finally and wiped the steam off the mirror above the sink and got the washcloth from the shower and soaped it up good and scrubbed my eyebrows and forehead until they were raw. I heard Tom cussing and I locked the bathroom door. It sounded like he was moving stuff. I stayed in there until I heard the door close. Then I waited for a while. I don't know how long. Obviously I have a problem telling time. I went into the bedroom and all the sheets were off the bed. Tina was gone. There was blood on the mattress. The lamp was also gone. I looked around the room to see if I had left anything in there. I couldn't find one of my shoes. I got down on the floor and found it up under the bed beside the shoebox where Tom kept his goods. I was down there anyway, so I helped myself to a baggie of the crystal because see I had to get home and I knew it would keep me from getting sleepy. Someday I was going to sleep again. Also I had borrowed my cousin's car and I was a day late returning it, I thought, though it turned out as y'all know I was over two days late but that's not why y'all got me in here. I went outside and sat in a lawn chair. It was hot and I was sweating because I had done some of the goods in the kitchen. A little girl came out of the house next door. She went to play on her swing set. She waved at me and I waved back. The little girl opened her mouth to say something maybe hello and Tina's scream came out of her, and I leaned over and threw up. It lasted a long time. Maybe I don't know five minutes. Until it was only water coming up. The little girl was watching the whole time and it made me so lonesome and sad for her and I thought about all kinds of things that had to do with being little and seeing and hearing things you shouldn't. I thought of my mother on the phone and my father's clean dashboard. I was hungry. I had some money in my shoe. I went into the woods where the people had been standing still as deer for as long as I'd been in town and probably before. I thought they might try and stop me from leaving the scene, but they stood aside. I pushed deeper into those woods because what if Tom came back? He was going to kill me next and especially when he went looking for his goods and found a good chunk of them gone. I was scared I'd run into him so I sat a long time against a tree, until the shadows turned from yellow to gray and I could no longer see the tiny pieces of another world you can see shifting around in light that comes through trees. It was dark then. But Tom didn't know day from night. He liked to sleep in the day. I wasn't safe. I had some money in my shoe though and I was hungry. When it was all the way dark, I would go back to Richie's place to get the Galaxie. I thought I'd stop off at a diner somewhere and get some food, although I also believed I already *had* stopped by a diner because I remembered ordering huevos rancheros and the waitress looked me over and asked me did I have a long night and I told her I didn't have one and she said, oh, there was a night alright. But when would that have happened? In the song 'Sway' by the Rolling Stones they ask the question, Did you ever wake up to find a day that broke up your mind destroyed your notion of circular time. I imagine y'all are wondering what all this had to do with what happened. Everybody keeps asking me where did you go then and how long did that take and what color was this and was it day or night? What I've been trying to tell y'all all along is, I couldn't keep time straight. I had no idea how long we'd been gone from Stovall. I only knew I had to get back there. That's when I remembered us picking up the Galaxie and driving it over to Tom's house, or Tina driving, I was too messed up on the goods. So all I had to do was make it to the Galaxie and hope Tina'd left the keys in there and hope Tom hadn't turned out all the lights and was sitting on his porch with a knife waiting on me. It was a lot to consider, but I felt safe waiting in the woods because I have spent half my life waiting in woods. There was nothing in those woods as bad as what was in that house. I kept watch for a good long time, expecting the lights to come on but they never did. So finally I made my way out of the woods and past the edge where the people stood still. I stopped and looked at them like, What, and they just looked back at me and didn't move.

They knew everything that happened because they had been standing there and heard the screams and besides they had been there forever and knew everything that ever happened. I didn't look at the swing set next door as I crossed the yard because what if that little girl was still there, what if her mother had left her out there all night right next to a house where boys stumbled outside to throw up pizza and beer? God, I hope that's the worst thing that little girl has ever seen since. I came around the front of the house and the Galaxie was parked right along the curb where we'd left it, but the Karmann Ghia was gone. The lights were still out. I got in the Galaxie and started feeling around for the keys under the mat, but they weren't there. I about lost it. I banged my head on the steering wheel and about got out and knocked on somebody's door and told them to call the cops. I was thinking I'd just take off my clothes and run down the road singing some garbage food from a chain store song. Say, 'Baby, Come Back,' or 'I Want to Kiss You All Over.' The cops would show right up. But then I happened to look down and see the keys in the ignition. Tina might of come from Houston but she'd been in Stovall long enough to leave a car unlocked and the keys in it. I started up that car and gave it just enough gas to get past Tom's house and then I realized I did not know how to get home. All I knew was that main drag, Congress. I needed gas so I stopped at a gas station and took my shoes and socks off to retrieve the money I thought I had spent on huevos rancheros and a Goody's Powder. While the fellow was fillin' 'er up I went into the bathroom and locked the door and did more goods. Then I came out and asked directions but the fellow pumping gas didn't speak English good, so

I had to go in and ask his bossman. The bossman started up with all that "this-route-will-save-you-five-minutes" stuff that men of a certain age can't help from doing and I got a little testy maybe, which is not my natural inclination. Just tell me the easiest way to get there, I said. I don't care about five or ten minutes. I was in a hurry to get the hell out of Austin before Tom came after me. I made it to Stovall by midnight. I was just inside the city limits when I got pulled. They claimed I had stolen a car and I admit I argued with them some. But then it turned out I didn't have any driver's license and also I didn't know what day it was because they asked me and I got it wrong. I had not slept, and I was not there. It is a wonder I made it back home but I had the goods, which were long gone by then. That helped me get home but it also made it kind of hard to talk to the police because I wasn't there. I was driving but I was also riding along looking out the window at the ranch houses lit up and the eyes of animals standing in line alongside the ditches watching me like I was a hearse in a funeral bearing the king of all animals which I don't know who that would be. I really was so lonesome I could cry. Okay I believe I was crying. Can you die from dehydration by crying out all your fluids? They said something to me about Tina when I got to the station. I told them she asked me to take her up to see her mother and when we got to Austin, she changed her mind and said let's go to a party at this guy Richie's house. I told them that was the last time I saw her, and I wasn't lying because at the time of my arrest that is all I could remember. If y'all know how memory works you can explain it to me, but I am telling y'all, what I told the cops when they pulled me over was what I knew at the time. I told them I was planning on going by this Richie's house to see if she wanted a ride back to Stovall, but I knew what her answer would be considering how the last time I had seen her she had been all tangled up naked with Richie. Also I did not see how it was my job anymore to make sure she got home. Maybe I said all this already, y'all got it on tape. I don't know. Everything would have been fine had I just gone home right after I came up on Tina and Richie spread across that mattress. Everything would have been okay had I not gone to that pond they call a pool. I did not kill Tina and I am sorry for what happened to her. I didn't kill her though. How could I have saved her? Well, how? Stick my head out and let the lamp crush my skull instead of hers? I wish I would have now. I know y'all don't care what I wish I would of done. I know it's too late for 'ought to.' Y'all want me to say I helped him. I did not help him. I was scared he was going to kill me too and I'm still scared he is going to find me and kill me. He is not right, that guy. They claim I am off, but that dude is so off it's like there is no night or day or moon or sun in his sky. No people in his world, just things to fuck. I didn't help him, but it's true that I did not report him because I don't know why. I guess because I was so messed up on that powder. I didn't realize we were in Austin, Texas. I don't think I was there even if I knew I was there. But *there* there? Not like y'all want me to say I was. I did not know Tina had another name and a mama not in an insane asylum until I heard it from you. I know that does not justify what happened to her. I know I ought to have reported it. But when I got back here and they pulled me over and said Leif had reported his car stolen two days earlier I told them Leif needed a new watch. I did not know what day it was. It's all on some tape somewhere if y'all want to check it. It might seem to y'all like I'm lying, but I swear it all came back to me in chunks and as soon I would remember part of it I would go to doubting it because other chunks were missing so how it could be real, a little part of a thing? I have never done more than smoke my brother's headache dirt weed and drink some beer and maybe some wine and once some vodka before I went to Austin. I wish he had never come up to me and offered me those goods. I am not blaming the goods for what happened, but I am blaming them for me doubting what happened because it was the goods that cut up everything into chunks and then gave it back to me a little at a time over the next few weeks and it was like I had suffered a concussion. That is all I have to say, except I am sorry for what happened and I wish I had never agreed to take Tina up to Austin to see her mama in the state hospital for the mentally insane."

II.

ARTHUR CAME IN just after Earl had finished talking into the tape machine. They heard him out in the hallway. Trash-talking. His hoarse laughter echoed down the hall. He might have been telling a joke. Phillip just shook his head. He wasn't nervous anymore.

"Arthur always did have shitty timing," he said.

Then Arthur came in and pointed to the tape machine and said to Phillip, "That thing better not be warm." Without even looking at Earl, he slid him a Pepsi. It wasn't the Pepsi that got to Earl. It wasn't that it had so much ice, like he liked it. It was the way Arthur slid it across the desk without looking at Earl. He knew who Earl was and what he needed.

Phillip pushed Play. He paused the tape after Earl said, "After Tom killed Tina with the lamp, he snorted some crystal."

"What the holy fuck, Phillip?" said Arthur.

"You'll be wanting to hear the rest of it I guess."

"I'll be wanting you to get out and leave me alone with my client."

"May be he's not your client no more," said Phillip.

Arthur said, "You either leave or find us another room."

"Fine," said Phillip. "I got plenty to do now." He reached for the tape machine, but Arthur said, "Leave it. I'll be wanting to hear the rest of it."

Phillip shrugged and left the room. Arthur said to Earl, "I guess he trusts me not to destroy the tape. Or the entire machine. Well, that's one thing. One kind of surprising thing, actually. How's your drink?"

Earl said "Good." He had not waited for Arthur, and he had told it all to the machine, which even Phillip the cop seemed to think was maybe not a good idea, but Arthur didn't seem mad. Why wasn't he mad? Was it because he'd come to count on Earl to act odd? Because he had no faith that Earl would do the right thing?

"Enough ice for you?"

"Yep."

"Well, let's see what we got," said Arthur, and he pushed Play. He ignored the food he'd brought and sat back in his chair and looked at a spot above Earl's head. A couple times he winced. Once he stopped the tape and pushed Rewind and let it play over and then did the same thing. When it got to where Earl described him and Tom and Tina in the bedroom, Arthur started rubbing his eyes. Earl had seen tired-out babies do this, but not grown lawyers.

When it was over Arthur said to Earl, "I need to find out what your cellmate told them. It'll take me awhile. They'll take you back to your cell now. Keep your chin up. I'll be back tomorrow. We can talk about what you actually said to that cellmate of yours and if there was some translating going on, which there usually is. We've got to figure out what to do now. So you sit tight."

For most of the day and night Earl lay in bed thinking about how much he loved Pepsi-flavored ice. He could nearly live off it. It was a thing he'd dreamed about during the past few weeks, but he could not bring himself to take a sip while Arthur was listening to him tell what happened on the tape machine. He could hear the ice melting above the sound of his voice on the tape. The melting ice was more silence than noise and Earl thought of the silence his mother had once tried to get him to hear, which was nothing more, really, than the noise of the world having left her behind while she talked on the telephone and did not leave Earl's daddy nor tend too much to the care and well-being of her children.

The next day the C.O. came for him before 10 a.m. Arthur brought him a biscuit but no Pepsi. Was he punishing him for waiving his counsel or had he noticed that Earl did not touch yesterday's Pepsi, just watched the waxy cup sweat out on the metal table.

"We're not going to talk about why you decided to talk yesterday before I arrived. I believe I know the answer anyway, knowing you the little that I do. I believe I understand how you felt. But I need to know if there's anything Phillip said to you that made you want to start talking before I got there."

Earl thought back over the morning before. It was hard to remember much besides the cup sliding toward him across the table.

"He asked me how did I sleep the night before and I said not good and he said, Yeah, I heard. And that's when I figured it out. Because T-Bone, see, they came for him that morning first thing and he never has come back. So that's when I knew and Arthur, I would have waited but at the time—"

"It's okay," said Arthur. "He ought not to have said anything to you before I got there but he'll claim I was late which I was, and as for the remark about him hearing you didn't sleep good, he'll deny it and it'll be his word against yours and we're not even going to talk about all that, nothing we can do to change it."

"What are we going to talk about?" said Earl.

Arthur said, "Let's talk about something you brought up in your confession. Let's talk about how memory works."

"It's going to be you doing all the talking," said Earl.

"I do have some things to say on the subject, only because in your case it's going to be more than pertinent. First, while I have always admired, in general, your knowledge of music and your ability to work a song into normal conversation, I can't say it was the best time for you to go off about circular time and how you go back and forth and in and out and all that. Number two, I'm just going to point out that you don't have to take enough drugs in two days to keep you high for a month for things to come back to you in what you described in your statement as 'chunks.' Have you ever heard of repressed memories?"

"No," said Earl. His mother sent her memories through phone lines. They were alive and present so long as a storm did not knock out the phone. His father was a memory Earl would not mind repressing.

"Say someone did something awful and you were a witness to it. Say the person it was done to was someone you were close to. You block it from your mind because it's just too awful. It's called trauma. What you underwent, watching Tom kill Tina right in front of you? That was traumatic."

Did Arthur believe him or was he just being paid to take Earl's side? Earl didn't much care for the fact that you could pay people to pretend to believe you were telling the truth, especially because he was fucking telling the truth.

"One of several problems here, Earl," said Arthur, "and this is worse than all that stuff about circular time because they can't hold that against you if they don't understand it, is that they've got you on tape claiming it's the drugs that made you not remember things until they came back to you. And any jury—"

"I know all that, we talked about it already, it's not a defense."

"But we discussed this before you went on the record with it. Can you see the pickle, Earl? I would have argued that you blocked out what happened due to psychological duress. Your brain could not get itself to process what went down. But the prosecutor's going to quote you saying it's the drugs that made you not remember it or remember it little by little because it's right there for them to play on tape."

"Could it not have been both?" Earl asked, but Arthur ignored him.

"Another thing, and this is unfortunate. This fellow Corn, your cellmate, who by the way's got to be getting something out of this and when I find out what, I'll do my best to discredit him, anyway, he claimed you knew where Tom lived. But I asked you to tell me everything you knew about Tom thinking we might get to him before—"

"I did not kill her, Arthur." Earl started to cry. He hadn't cried since he drove home from Austin and he'd cried the whole way even when he stopped to sample more goods. Now his crying came in heaves, bent him over the table. He thought he'd cried out all the water in his body and then he found more.

Arthur waited for him to stop. It seemed like two days. Then he was sniffling like he had a cold and Arthur handed him a napkin that said *Sunrise Biscuits Get Them at the Crack*.

"I believe you, Earl," Arthur said.

"Because they're paying you to?"

"They haven't paid me in a while, actually. I have not been able to reach your people for a few days now."

Earl thought of his mother with the phone cord in her hands. She liked to twist the kinks between her fingers while she talked with one hand and in the other was her cigarette. Sometimes he spied on her while she talked. She stared off down in the woods toward Shreveport as if she could see which sister she was talking to. Or she looked at her cigarette as if it were growing out of her hand. Or she stared into her lap. Once she caught Earl looking at her through the trees. She held up the hand that held the cigarette and smiled. Her hand smoked at him and he ran away.

"Try her sisters. Call them all because she can only talk to one at a time."

"I'm not worried about the money, Earl. Shall we proceed?"

"I didn't kill her. I won't lie, I was mad at her, though. She used me. Plus she cheated on me."

"Which gives you a motive. But even if you didn't touch her except the way you described touching her to that Horn fellow, it doesn't much matter. They got you confessing to being a witness to her murder. You claim you were high and the other guy did it. You also claim the other guy was raping her. And she was telling him to stop and he didn't and you didn't do anything to stop him."

"I wasn't there," said Earl. He was and he was not.

"Austin PD's been all over that house since Phillip left this room yesterday. Found your fingerprints are all over that bed. Your hair is in the shower."

"They found Tom?"

"Found his house. He and his Karmann Ghia and his goods are gone. But not her blood. It looks like at some point he came back to get his car. You didn't hear him come back to the house to get his vehicle?"

"I was hiding in those woods," said Earl. In the pines in the pines where the sun don't shine.

"Back to what you did not do. You're the only one in custody for killing this girl and you admit to not stopping him from raping her and you're going to have to hear all about what you told this Dwight Corn and what you wrote down repeated in a courtroom with what I can guarantee will not be a jury of your peers. Her parents are going to be sitting there staring at you. They are going to hear how y'all gave that girl drugs and took turns with her. And they are going to hire a lawyer from

Houston and he's going to come up here and say, sure, she's been in a little trouble, got caught shoplifting, skipped school a few too many times, might have smoked some grass but she would never touch hard drugs nor do the sorts of things you're saying she did."

"Tina?"

"No, not Tina. Goddamn it, Earl. They don't know anyone named Tina. Adelaide Morgan. Forget Tina. She's Adelaide now. Has been ever since she disappeared and will always be now that she's been murdered."

Earl was silent. So was the jailhouse, for once, and the world beyond it. He heard nothing and it made him start up with the sobbing again.

"Go ahead and get it out. Since you're seventeen, under Texas law you can be tried as an adult. You'll probably be transferred out of the jail to a real prison. Hopefully it will be one close by so I can get by to see you because I guarantee you the DA and whatever lawyer they hire is going to drag this out as long as they can. If you got crying to do, go on ahead and get it done here. You don't want to be crying after you leave this room."

Earl nodded.

"The charge now is murder one. And kidnapping and rape. We plead accessory to murder and rape because they have no body and—"

"I never raped anybody."

Arthur looked at that spot above the wall he'd studied while the tape was playing. Then he slowly lowered his gaze to Earl.

"I'm going to have to ask you something now and it's

important. When you were with her, before Tom got with her and before he hit her, did you finish inside of her? Because if they *do* happen to find her body . . ."

"I didn't," said Earl, starting to cry again. "I couldn't. I didn't."

"Well, I hate to say this, but that's good to hear. They can't make the rape stick without evidence, and they will have a hard time proving murder without some proof you were the one who hit her with the lamp. Did you touch that lamp?"

Earl thought about it. He remembered when Teresa first led him into the room. Tom was in bed naked, and it was dusk but still enough sunlight streaming through the blind slats to see body parts and lines on the mirror and the joint they passed. It was never dark in that room because night never came. The waitress at the diner claimed there was a night but not up the hill at Tom's house.

"If that lamp was to turn up with your fingerprints . . ." Arthur was saying.

"Tom is the one who hit her."

"But if you even switched it on, Earl, they would claim y'all took turns with the lamp just like you took turns with her."

"Where is my father?"

"Let's stay focused here. There's going to be an arraignment now that they've filed new charges. I've sent my girl out to buy you some nicer clothes. My advice is we plea out. We go to trial without a body and with proof that Dwight Corn is getting something out of snitching and it's his word against yours. He's not an upstanding citizen by a long shot. Maybe there is some chance. Fucking Phil ought not to have said anything to you before I got there, especially that line about how he heard you'd not slept good. It's not going to get that tape thrown out, but I'll go after him anyway. It can't hurt. But I'm sorry to say, in this county? With her cancer doctor daddy and her River Oaks real estate mama sitting in the front row? And the details of what y'all did those two days coming out?"

Arthur rifled through his heirloom briefcase and pulled out a legal pad.

"Also according to T-Bone Corn, he claimed Tom said to the girl before he raped her, "Just give it a minute and it will feel great, Earl knows exactly how it feels, don't you, Earl, and Horn claims you said, Yep, that's right. Only hurts at first and then it feels great. Which, goddamn, Earl."

"But I never said all that. I might have said it hurts but the rest of it T-Bone made up."

"It doesn't matter if it's verbatim, Earl. If they were to bring it up, I'd object. But the jury's going to hear it before I get the chance to object."

"How much time, Arthur?" said Earl.

Arthur sighed. "It won't be short, even with a plea. Even without evidence they could send you away for a good long while. Let's not worry about numbers right now."

Earl had no love for math, but he found shocking the rest of his years would be calculated in numbers. He knew they had taken away the death penalty the year before, but he had a sudden fear of them bringing it back just for him. He saw the lights in a farmhouse across a cornfield from the prison flicker. That flicker was Earl: all he is or was or would be to the old couple who lived for decades within sight of the prison because the land was cheap. So used to the momentary dimming of an overhead kitchen light, the slowing of a ceiling fan, they hardly noticed. He'd be a stutter step, a record that skipped only once. Earl the wrong note. Hey Earl, you're nothing but a hiccup.

Arthur was saying how there was an APB out on Tom. Earl tried to hate Tom, but it wasn't Tom's fault that Earl stuck around partaking of the goods. Time collapsed. Earl wasn't in charge of Time. Neither was Tom. Tom would have done what he'd done to some other girl, but he didn't, he did it to Tina. He would not have ever laid eyes on Tina had not Earl said, Let's go get her. Earl hated Earl.

Arthur was saying how Tom might be in Mexico by now, if he's half Mexican he's bound to have people there.

"I only said he had dark skin. I might have said he looked Mexican but that don't make him Mexican."

Earl's people on his daddy's side were olive-skinned as gypsies. Fifteen minutes of direct sun in March and they were base-tanned for the Texas summer. Some white people were just not as white as others. He was going to say this to Arthur but maybe Tom *was* in Mexico for all Earl knew.

He imagined a life without woods or eaves. No pedal steel winging in from the high lonesome.

"I don't even have my license yet," he told Arthur.

"Never stopped you from driving."

Arthur talked to him like he was his daddy, so Arthur was his daddy. He imagined the dash of his car. Maybe Arthur had some secrets, but he was late to everything, which somehow to Earl meant probably not any secrets.

"Are you married?" he asked Arthur.

"No."

"Any kids?

"Where are you going with this, Earl?"

"What would you say to me if I were your blood?"

"What I told you we'll do. I'm going to do everything I can to get you off. But you have to understand where we are."

"Texas."

"Not only. Texas is bad enough if you fuck up. I had a kid get sent up for two joints, three years medium security. But Stovall, man, people here are filled with hate."

"Before you told me I'm lucky to be white. But I believe I am the kind of white that don't matter."

"That's a fact. But don't go feeling sorry for yourself because your parents didn't have the means to send you to one of those segregationist academies. If you were Black or Mexican, they might not even wait for a trial."

"What? String me up in the courthouse square?"

"Wasn't that long ago shit like that happened around here."

Arthur had his arms crossed. He was looking at Earl with a mix of pity and impatience. Sometimes he seemed angry at Earl for getting mixed up in this mess and for mixing him up in it. Other times it was more like he saw Earl as a victim and an idiot both.

"You ever met her aunt?" said Earl.

"Whose?"

Tina, Earl almost said but he caught himself and said the name she was going by now.

"Seen her around."

"Tina said she was a lesbian Methodist."

"Methodists come in all stripes. But I don't know the woman. Just because she never married don't make her a lesbian. Why are we talking about her?"

"She fixed up Tina's room really nice. It was all frilly. She probably thought they'd spend their nights watching *Green Acres* and Gilligan and *Mod Squad* on the couch eating popcorn."

"Are you worried about the aunt, Earl?"

"Yes," he said. But he was worried more about himself. Everything had come back to him and he had told it all and now it was the truth. It didn't matter that Earl wasn't there. He could not claim such. He was not allowed to even mention it. All he was allowed to say—and believe—was what he had told Arthur and Dwight Corn and Phil the cop. Somebody somewhere was transcribing it at this very moment. They were leaving out everything good that ever happened to Earl, the blown-up love notes, the shadows of branches upside the wormy chestnut shed and the night swimming and of course the pedal steel. What they were writing down right now was *Clothesline: His Life and Times.*

PART TWO

Cliffside, Oregon, 2018

1.

IN THE IN-BETWEEN—FOR after his release that is what Earl preferred to call his years inside—Arthur brought him paperback books to read until he didn't. Earl wrote Arthur letters anyway. He listed the things he'd purchased from the commissary and also the books he had read. One thing about Arthur that Earl appreciated was that he claimed to be allergic to plot summary, an allergy Earl shared. Instead of saying what happened in the book Earl would judge its quality depending on whether or not it made him want to (a) gargle salt water, (b) dissolve in his bunk into a puddle of salt water, or (c) . . . well, (c) just depended on properties mysterious and unpredictable, which is to say (c) meant pedal steel.

Earl could only talk about books for so long because, besides the ones Arthur sent, which he read and then read again, there wasn't much else available. He wrote about food. He had never given any thought to what he put in his mouth other than how insulted he was by ants on a log. How, he asked

Arthur, did his mother learn to cook chicken tetrazzini and why? Also beef Stroganoff. Things with the name of a meat followed by a foreign word.

Another thing he put in a letter to Arthur: why do people say, "Just don't think about it?" when it only makes "it" all you can think of. Also, Arthur: Is it possible to not think? He had read in a book about Transcendental Meditation. Seemed to Earl something you had to learn how to do and, if so, you had to think about whether you were doing it right or wrong.

Everything he tried to put in a letter to Arthur went back to What Happened. His thoughts went there because thoughts went wherever. They might start with chicken tetrazzini but they would dead-end in a dark room with a waterbed, a lamp, blood.

He tried to write to Arthur about the music they both loved, but music was lost to him now—less the notes themselves, the melodies that played sometimes unsummoned in his head, than lyrics. Lyrics were words meant to describe memories. Earl could not think of a single song he loved that was not about memory.

So many subjects were off limits. Out of bounds. Before, his thoughts had no limits or boundaries. Though the words—limits, *bounds*—weren't right. You ain't right, his brothers used to say to him all the time. Not just his brothers. Girls on the bus. They meant not right in the head, but Earl interpreted it as just plain wrong. Everything he did or said was plain wrong.

All that stuff that used to fill up his head, what was it for? Take the eaves: why were they more beautiful to him than a jet liner in the sky leaving a plume of fake cloud and carrying people to places he would never see. For instance, Old Mexico, since there was a New Mexico. Take the Band-Aid at the bottom of the pool: Why were things other people saw but let pass right on by so important to him? Other people talked about what they saw and it was mostly car wrecks they had witnessed, or snakes they had encountered. The snakes other people saw was something Earl might talk to Arthur about in his letters to be something besides plain wrong. Because he would never, not ever, be right.

His letters rolled like a stray ball out onto the street. Out of bounds, off limits. So he would X out the wrong words and start with some new ones. But words were not new because they were everyone else's. You couldn't have your own, you had to share. And like the words of his songs, the words he wrote down were all about memory.

Sometimes Earl would start out talking about his job in the sewing room, or how he was teaching himself to speak Spanish, but he'd end up crossing it out. In the in-between, he could not talk about the in-between, and he did not think Arthur cared to hear about it. He knew how bad Arthur felt about the way things had gone, but sometimes it seemed to Earl that Arthur just did not like to lose. Arthur's letters in the beginning were mostly about the appeals he was working on, but Earl would skip right over that and wade down to where Arthur talked about his life before he knew Earl, which is what Earl asked him to talk about in one of his first letters. Earl never said don't write about an appeal or building a case or finding new evidence because it was rude to tell someone what to say. He didn't hardly know what to say. I can sew a mean hem. I can say "pass the fish" in Spanish.

He'd cross it all out in favor of questions. Why are refrigerators so loud, he wrote to Arthur. What are the names of some birds you like? Tell me again what are the types of columns. Arthur wrote back and said there was Corinthian and Ironic. There are some more kinds, wrote Arthur, but I forgot them if I ever learned them. He did not ask Earl why he needed to know about columns. He understood why Earl was asking about birds and columns.

Then—Earl could not say when exactly, because unlike in the movies about prison, he did not cross the numbers off a calendar—there were no replies from Arthur. One of Earl's letters was returned to him with a stamp listing reasons for its possible return. A sloppy X beside "Deceased." A strange way to learn of someone's death but no stranger than Earl deserved. Who even knew Arthur visited Earl? He was in another part of the state by then, a seven-hour drive from Stovall, and every time Arthur had come Earl had thought it might be the last.

Earl worried that Arthur's death was of the all-alone-and-off-by-himself sort. He never did get married. The only folks he had looking after him were the secretary in his law office and a sister he liked who lived in Chicago. The sister who used to go with the cop Arthur didn't get along with. Earl knew a lot about Arthur's life because Arthur had indulged him and did not talk about anything that would lead Earl to have to think about the place where he would live longer than anywhere else in his life.

He was eighteen by the time they sentenced and processed him. He could not claim his development had been arrested, though the notion that he'd had to grow up quick wasn't quite true, given that the grown men he spent his days with consumed themselves with things that other men—men in the world, men *of* the world—had put aside. But what did Earl know of men of the world? He had lived his entire adult life with men who would do anything, schemers and liars who created a world inside that to them replicated their life before, and yet everything about it was desperate and upside down. Their currency was not coin or bill but packets of dried soup and muscle relaxants. Their "girls" had cocks. Earl understood now how his allowing time and space to unfold in two spheres had led to his downfall.

One last letter from Arthur came when Earl was released. Along with new clothes, a bus ticket, and his wages from forty-four years of labor in the Texas Department of Correction, Earl was handed a yellowed envelope in larger manila one. He recognized Arthur's scrawl. There was no date.

Dear Earl

Must be the biscuits did my heart the way it's done and it's done, Earl. I'm about done.

I'm writing you from the hospital down in Houston. I'm up on the 14th floor. I can see all the superhighways and inner and outer beltways with the million cars and trucks driving round the city like they all got stuck in these circles or are afraid to come into the city proper.

It's nicer here than you'd think. Or than I thought. But I'm not writing on behalf of the Houston Chamber of Commerce.

I've had a lot of clients, Earl. Stovall—and East Texas in general—is fertile ground for a lawyer like me. Too many no-counts to count. No end to the preyed-upon, the disenfranchised, the don't-have-a-bootstrap-to-pull-up-on. Not telling you anything you don't already know but you and your tribe fit several of the above categories. All those years of coming to visit you, bringing you paperbacks to read, talking about Muscle Shoals and Jimmy Webb and how Rod Stewart started out so good and turned out so schmaltzy—we never once talked about your family. I mean to say your family of origin as I believe you found another family with those characters who at least had your back when you were in County. That did not seem like a wise choice at the time, you hanging out with that crew, but it made sense the more I got to know your real family, by which I mean your mother—I never met your daddy.

They got me on some drugs now. Not the kind that led to you being where you are. More the sleepy rather than the stay-up kind, the stuff that kills the pain. I had a heart attack in line at Sunrise. Laugh all you want, it's funny to me too now, the fact that I'd be waiting on the thing that put me under *when* I about went under.

Anyway, your family, or rather your mother: She ought to have done more for you, Earl. Every time I drove out there, she was on the phone, talking to God knows who, and when she saw me pull up (if she was outside, which she almost always was, if it was wet out or cold she was sitting on that saggy porch, smoking) she'd hold up a finger to signal Hold Up a Minute and then Take Five. She ought to have been paying more mind to you.

One thing I have seen over and again in my line of work is people having babies who have no business having babies. I got a quarrel with Biology or God, one. I don't know quite who to pick it with because here I am about to Goddamn die, and it seems risky to pick a fight with God and silly to worry with Biology. I finally did give up the Scotch and the Pall Malls and I even went to some of those fellowship meetings for a while, though I drove sixty miles to attend them so I wouldn't run into any of my clients the court had ordered to attend. Those fellows in that ship said when it comes to a higher power it doesn't have to be God, it can be anything, a tree, the universe, so I made mine a biscuit. (I know you'd like that detail, Earl, out of everyone I know.) My beef with the Biscuit is this business of making the end result of fucking be something a good half of the people doing the fucking are not qualified to attend to. Time and again I have represented someone who either had no business having a child or was a child born to folks who had no business having children. In some ways the Chinese might be right to limit everyone to two kids, though I don't think that would work in Texas. Plus, for a good quarter of the population, two equals two too many.

It has taken me a day to write all this and I'm not half done. And no end, Earl, to the cars circling Houston. Now they all got their lights on. It's night and the overpasses and flyovers are invisible, so it looks like spaceships circling the city. It's no wonder they put NASA here because Houston is not unlike outer space.

I guess the fact that I could start out talking about your family and end up in Outer Space is why I am writing to you now, Earl. I had a lot of clients, but none of them were anything like you. I am going to put aside for now the crime of which you were accused and for which you are serving what is to my mind an unjust period of time even for the state of Texas, though I'll get to that before long.

Truth is, I'm not a very good lawyer. I was good at volume—I could handle more cases at once than anyone else in East Texas—but credit for that's due more to my secretary than any genius on my part. I will say that I worked harder on your case than any other comes to mind. Maybe not at first, but when we got into the appeals. Maybe that doesn't speak well of me, that I got more energy as your case seemed more and more doomed, but there it is. And here's the truth: your case wasn't nearly as important to me as you were—are, I mean to say, because I'm still here above Houston, watching it like it's a movie or some kind of ride at a theme park, and I expect this letter to find you when you walk out a free man, I expect it to find you when you need it most.

That thing you said about Adelaide Morgan, how she made you feel like you were there and not there? I told you not to repeat that for obvious reasons that I explained at the time: it made you sound like a sociopath. Someone who can be in a room committing a crime, a crime they were right to call heinous, and also feel like he wasn't in that room: I don't know, Earl. Those psychological terms are so elastic these days. They don't mean much. I heard a fellow say not long ago that a part of him wanted a drink and another didn't, therefore he felt schizophrenic. I'm no doctor but I'm pretty sure that's not what it means to be a schizophrenic. I'm pretty sure that any jury in Stovall or even Texas would not have known back then to call your state of mind dissociative, but I didn't want to risk it. All it takes is one smarty pants to turn a jury.

But I have been thinking about what you said ever since you said it. I made you swear not to say something in court that really, when it comes down to it, I've felt most of my life. I'd be willing to put money on the fact that we're not the only ones feeling it. I'm thinking maybe it's just the nature of existence, what you described. The way you talked about it? You made it sound like a kind of freedom. Like all your life you'd been looking for someone to both set you free and keep you close. Well, who wouldn't want that?

Now about your crime.

You probably don't want to hear about it. But I'm the one who's about done, so I get to decide what to talk about, unfortunately for you.

What happened to that girl was awful. Made even more awful by the fact that we never located a body. It's hard on the family when there *is* a body. Seems so much harder when there's not.

You know where I stand on what happened. I've made that clear in our visits, and I won't waste paper repeating myself or trying to make you feel bad for not helping her or calling the cops right off, since we can't change what you didn't do. I always thought we'd find that Tom fellow. I figured he'd turn up in jail one day, confess it all to his cellmate. But I'm thinking he made it across the border. He was smart enough to use your car to dispose of the body and not leave a single print, and he was smart enough to get rid of his car. He's smart enough to get across the border. I imagine he's dead. I imagine you sometimes wish he were. I would have said at one point that things would have been fine for you had you not run into that Adelaide in the woods, but you always maintained y'all had some good times and I believe you.

I would say your luck changed when you met Tom at the pool. I believe something awful happened to you too that night. The "goods" as you called them were no excuse for what you did, but you weren't used to all that. Even though you came up rough, when I first met you,

you weren't anything like those brothers of yours. You were a dreamy kid but not lost in the way of so many I had to deal with over the years. You might not have known where you were going—who does at that age?—but you weren't lying or cheating your way there. You gave the impression of being along for the ride, though you were looking out the window the whole time. Most people are more about studying themselves in the mirror. Like that fellow Tom.

What I am trying to say is this: even though no one was holding a gun to your head, making you do the things you did—like what you did with Tom, and I want you to know again that I never judged you for it—I believe you might have been taken advantage of. Just a bit. I wasn't there so I don't know, but some of what you told me suggested it. Sure, you might have gone that way naturally, and that's none of mine. But I don't believe your choice would have gone the way it did if your head was clear.

It saddens me that we live in a world that equates sexual preference with moral depravity. I believe that is why you are still in there, because of what you told your cellmate about you and Tom. Didn't matter that my objection was sustained; it was out there. Jury heard it. Judge heard it. Of course, the state would never come out and say that had a thing to do with it. But they knew that all they needed to do was put it out there.

I still can't claim to understand how memory works.

I still don't understand why things came back to you the way they did, why you told a bit of it and then some more and then the worst thing. So I went for the obvious. You probably figured out that my claiming you were in shock was right out of the defense lawyer's playbook. Everybody in that courtroom would have been shocked had I not claimed you were in shock.

It's not like you understand it all yourself, so why should I get to? I guess because I grew to care about you, Earl. And I feel like I failed you. I've made a little money over the years. I have no one really to leave it to but my nephews but I'm not inclined to fund their video game habits and also my sister divorced that meathead she met down at Sam Houston State and married her high school boyfriend. You will remember him by the name of Phillip. Anyway, I want you to have it. It's not a fortune by today's standards, but it's enough to get you started when you get out of there. It's in the First Farmers Trust, in Stovall. All you have to do when you get out is go see Annie Peoples and show her your discharge papers and she'll see to it. If for some reason she's not there anymore, her replacement will know what to do.

I wish I had more to give you. I wish I'd given you more. If I were the Biscuit, I'd see to it that your days from here on are full and rich and sunny. I know how you love to be outside. Maybe you can get a job on a ranch. Go be a cowboy. Hold your head up, Earl. Make good use of the time you got left. Eat right. If you're reading this, you made it through many hard years in a dark place. Now you got to get thinking about someday soon, because things won't just get better. Think about someday, and think about that day coming soon.

I know you'll be reading this, Earl. I know you'll make it out of there. And I hope you live long enough to find some music you like and throw yourself into some ocean. (Best avoid the Gulf, it's muddy and weedy and I never did trust those derricks not to leak.)

I hope you'll meet someone to wake up alongside. Should that person steal the covers, I know you would, in the words of your dubious role model, shiver the night through rather than wake them up, because that's the kind of person you are. No matter what you did one day back in 1973, and no matter what you've gone through since, I believe you're still that person. Stolen covers are something you're happy to overlook. Just make sure that cover thief is worth your forgiveness.

Arthur

Was it the tinted windows of the bus that gave the outskirts of Stovall the air of evacuation? The parking lots of abandoned businesses were ruptured by weed and sapling. Some of the vacant buildings had housed concerns Earl realized had been eclipsed by technology: the old icehouse, the cold storage. He passed Ash Warren's Feed and Seed, where his mother took him and his brothers to buy overalls, briefly a fad in the early seventies when everyone went to fiddler's conventions, not for the music. It was flanked by a Walmart and something called

Bed Bath & Beyond, which sounded to Earl like the title of a porno.

Annie Peoples was still alive. She was old, though, a wrinkled woman with a wet voice. Earl figured she knew everything about him and what he'd done but she acted as if he was just another customer come to cash a check. He told her his name and she nodded and disappeared for a good five minutes, during which Earl felt stared at, though he never once looked up from the beat green carpet beneath her desk.

"Here it is," she said, handing him an envelope. Inside was a check for $150,000. Annie Peoples shed her mask to watch him as he looked at the figures typed out by some kind of machine in the line next to his name.

She asked him if he would be wanting to set up a checking or savings account.

"Is that what people do?"

"I don't get this sort of thing every day," said Annie Peoples. She wouldn't look him in the eye, but she wasn't unkind, exactly. Just distant again. "If you're planning on staying here, I'd say . . ."

"I'm not," said Earl, and Annie Peoples looked relieved.

"Your best bet would be to get yourself an account set up when you get to wherever you're going," she said. "These days most people use something called a debit card. It's something you can use at the grocery store, plus you can pay your bills with it."

Debit sounded too much like "debt" to Earl. He must have looked worried, because Annie Peoples said, "Don't tell my boss, but I'm old-fashioned when it comes to money. When I was traveling, I used to ask for Traveler's Checks."

She explained how Traveler's Checks worked. Earl didn't quite follow, but he liked thinking of himself as a traveler.

"Whatever you think best," said Earl.

"It's going to take me awhile to get this together," she said. "Why don't you come back in a couple of hours."

"Can you give me some of it right now? I need to make some purchases."

Annie Peoples studied his prison jeans and sweatshirt. She looked at the bag he was carrying, full of Arthur's letters and his diplomas. She bent down under her desk and pulled out a pocketbook. Then she handed him fifty dollars.

"I can't take your money," said Earl.

"I know you're good for it. You're going to need a suitcase to carry all this in. If I were you, I'd go down to the Goodwill. You can get some clothes there too if you can find any to fit. My husband buys all his clothes down there. His entire wardrobe is valued at thirty-seven dollars."

Earl nodded. He wasn't sure if she was bragging or joking. But he followed her advice and found an old suitcase there and some clothes that fit. He went to another store for underwear and socks. Wearing someone's cast-off shirts was one thing—he'd done it when he was growing up and also in the in-between—but he needn't save money on clothes that touched any place where he was likely to catch a disease.

The clothes smelled musty. Earl found a laundromat and watched bored women feed dollar bills into a machine that turned them into quarters. You bought little boxes of detergent that reminded Earl of the miniature loaves of bread they used to toss off floats at the Christmas parade. The women stared at their telephones and yelled at their children. Earl watched the clothes spin, thinking of what Arthur said in his letter about how some people ought not to have kids.

If he had a kid, he would teach him to play harmonica in the woods. Earl would put some Spanish moss on his head and tell the boy all about the live-on-television wedding of Tiny Tim and Miss Vicki. He sure wouldn't waste any time on skipping rocks across a pond. He would take him to the office supply store and let him buy the most expensive pencils they carried. He might get some spray paint and write his boy's name on a train car while the boy slept in his own bed with a wagon-wheel headboard. They could build something together. Earl had picked up some pretty good woodworking skills in the in-between. They could build a teepee with a turnstile. At some point the boy would get tired of him and Earl would understand that better than the boy himself.

By nightfall he was on a bus to Dallas. In Stovall he'd felt the smallness of his past, shrunken and paint-peeling. He'd made mythological forest out of piney woods thinned from logging and lightning strike. The center of town was dead. Around it they had built an ugly thriving circle of the type Arthur described high above Houston from his deathbed. Earl wondered why they didn't just rip out the rotten core and put all these flat buildings closer to where people lived. It reminded him of how his parents used to put new appliances atop old dead ones.

Earl hardly gave a thought to going out to visit his house. He had called his mother a couple times from prison. The third time was the charm. No, I'm afraid not, said his mother when the recorded voice asked if she would accept a collect call from an inmate in the Texas Department of Correction.

He imagined the family compound. Rusting cars tilting on flattened tires. Televisions with broken screens stacked to the saggy ceiling. The wormy chestnut shed a weedy pile of rotting wood. The porch where his mother dialed her sisters caved in on the concrete slab.

In prison, Earl had passed most of his hours reading. He remembered almost everything he'd read there because the things that happened in books were far preferable than the boredom of prison. "Raggedy as a bowl of cole slaw": as a boy, he had read this line in Louis Armstrong's biography. Satchmo could have been talking about the young Earl. He'd been thin once, and almost tall. Now he was stooped and creaky and preceded in the world by his belly. Had he come upon a turnstile he could push through Look Ma no hands. He would not still consider himself good at turnstiles.

After Arthur died, Earl was at the mercy of the prison library. All the books there were donated and deemed safe. Most were Christian-themed. Earl could not be choosy. He sought out the oddest books on the cart, one of which was *A Pictorial History of Seattle*. What was this book doing in a maximum security prison in the Texas panhandle? Why, it was put there for Earl. He studied the pictures of Seattle in its earliest days, the muddy streets of the original skid row, the Victorian mansions of the lumber barons. There were many shots of Mt. Rainier looming over the cityscape, most featuring the Space Needle and other remnants of the 1962 World's Fair. The photos switched from stark black and white to blooming color in the 1950s. He studied the conifers and the ferns found in the Arboretum. Images of this strange city, so foreign-looking to a boy out of Louisiana by way of East Texas, had soothed and enticed Earl.

And so in Dallas, he purchased a bus ticket to Seattle. He spent days staring out grimy windows at the no-good-for-him country. Cornfields raspy in the wind, bloodred mouths of woods beyond fields. Stay out of those woods, Earl. Logs littered the floor of the forest. He'd been sitting on one, reading *His Life and Times*, when along came Tina, not her real name.

Earl sought alleyways with rusty fire escapes, city blocks cornered by bodega or bar. Old women pushing collapsible grocery carts. Kids playing in the gush of fire hydrants. He knew his notion of city life was culled from books and movies he'd seen over forty years ago, but he was set on finding a room high up in some building where he might watch the ferries moving across the Sound to the many islands mapped out in the *Pictorial History*.

On his way from Portland to Seattle, the bus stopped briefly in a socked-in town built on hills above the Columbia, near where the river blended with the Pacific. Earl had been sleeping. The hiss of the brakes and the sound of an announcement woke him. He rubbed the window glass clear with his sleeve to stare at the streets. Windows of stores and houses were lit against the cold rolling fog. For a few seconds the entire city disappeared in a cloud, only to emerge in edges and blurry haloed light. A high bridge spanned the river, most of it enshrouded, though even in the mist Earl could see the headlights of travelers.

Earl was sitting behind the driver. He tapped him on the shoulder.

"What town is this?"

"Cliffside."

"Washington?"

"Oregon." The driver pointed to the other side of the wide river. "Washington's other side of the bridge."

Earl sat back in his seat for thirty seconds before retrieving his suitcase from the rack above him.

"This ain't your stop, chief," said the driver.

But Earl was a free man. For years he'd adhered to orders and regimen. He'd not known until this misty town told him so that he could get off wherever he wanted. Seattle wasn't going anywhere.

Earl went into the terminal and out onto the street.

Down along the river road, he found a room at a motel called the Lamplighter with a good view of the suspension bridge. He sat in front of the picture window and watched for hours the lights of Washington State blinking on the far bank. The room was five times the size of the largest cell he'd shared. He had his own bath with a tub.

He took long walks through wet streets, listening to the cry of gulls and the bleating horns of tugs and barges. Back at the motel, damp from mist and drizzle, he ran a bath. Slowly did he lower himself into the tub. He'd never taken a bath in his life. There sat Earl, his head against the wall, his spirit rising, leaving behind his body, which he'd just as soon be shy of. He tried not to look down at the tip of his penis bobbing in the manner of seagrass swayed by current, or the scars from various beatings, the burn marks from lit cigarettes on his forearms, reminder of his first days inside, before he learned how to save himself from their savagery.

In the days following, if he had any schedule it was this: bed, bath, beyond. Beyond was where his body went after rising from the bath. You can focus on the beyond. The beyond is not the future. It is Earl's treasured eaves flooding back in bathwater, the blurring where house becomes sky, earth becomes horizon, cloud becomes bridge, Earl becomes elsewhere.

Through the walls the noise was near constant: television and crying children and couples having sex. He didn't mind it because he was used to noise. Often he fell asleep with the television on. He remembered staying up late to watch *Shock Theater* with his brothers and waking on a pallet of couch cushion and ratty afghan on the floor to a screen filled with fuzzy snow. Now there were shows on all night. The world did not stop. A grocery store down the street never closed. Earl went down there at 3 a.m. and bought an apple. The apple was organic, which meant—Earl wasn't sure what it meant. He had a long list of questions to ask Arthur, and this was one of them. Also all the new words and many questions about the large orange president whose English wasn't all that good, though as far as Earl could understand, the president was an American.

There was a theater downtown and Earl went to every movie they showed. He was not disinterested in the dramatic moments, the scenes where characters screamed, slammed doors, floored cars, but he always looked at what the camera captured beyond the action: light falling like a half-drawn curtain in backyards where lovers met to conceal their passion from others. Parking meters and traffic lights and storefronts viewed from the window of a car. Rings on the fingers of women holding their hands over their eyes to hide tears. Bubbles disrupting the glassiness of ponds into which bodies are tossed.

Where had all the combs gone? When he'd gone in, everyone carried a comb in their back pocket. Black people had fancier combs, with fists for handles. Picks, they were called. Earl had had wavy hair to his shoulders, and it was quick to tangle, so he'd gotten a fist pick to put in his pocket and work out the tangles of his hair and also the bits of seed and twig that sifted down from the trees in the forest. His brothers made fun of his fist pick. Soul Brother Number One they called him. Earl didn't care. He stayed in the pines where the sun don't shine shiver the whole night through.

The world had not stopped, though at night, or rather in the early morning, from 3 to 5 a.m., the all-night grocery store played songs mostly from his era over loudspeakers as the workers restocked the shelves. Once he heard a Joni Mitchell song he remembered loving in secret, for Joni Mitchell was not someone he could admit to liking back in the day. It was quiet in the store but for the sound of stockers stamping prices on merchandise. Earl froze to listen: "Send me somebody who's strong and somewhat sincere," sang Joni Mitchell, "With the millions of lost and lonely ones I called out to be released."

Earl had not cried since he'd been in the room with Arthur before his trial. Now in the toiletry aisle, tears dripped in the manner of the slow daily drizzle of his adopted hometown.

2.

YEARS AGO, EARL remembered seeing that painting *Nighthawks* in a book and thinking, as he had done with "Ruby Tuesday" and *Christina's World* and a lot of other things, that he'd been born knowing it. Well of course the diner is peopled with the lost and lonely ones. So was the grocery store, which he preferred to visit at 3 a.m. Most of the stockers and some of the shoppers wore headphones. Even the folks not wearing headphones did not seem to see him. Was he invisible because of his age or because of what he'd done? Or was it this town, so different from the small town of his youth, where everyone had stopped him as he prowled the outskirts, asking his business, or hitting him up for money: Hey, ho, Earl, let me hold a case quarter so I can get me something to drink?

Though sometimes the night clerk at the Lamplighter engaged Earl on the subject of weather. He was often outside smoking when Earl returned from his wee-hour shopping trips.

He never asked Earl why he went shopping in the middle of the night. He must have looked at Earl and seen the solitary diner with his back to the plateglass window in *Nighthawks*.

There was also a cashier at the grocery store who sometimes spoke to Earl. Once Earl had bought a small sewing kit: a needle, some thread, some buttons in a plastic casing.

"You sew?" The woman was middle-aged, but tattoos rose up her neck from the smock she wore over her street clothes.

Earl had sewn most everything there was to sew in a prison: uniforms, curtains, the gowns worn in the infirmary. He used machines, as they weren't trusted with needles, but he'd been years without buttons (or zippers or shoelaces for that matter) and all of a sudden, he was buying shirts from Goodwill that were forever missing buttons.

"I'm about to find out," he said.

"My daddy fished," the woman said. "He grew up mending nets and sails. He was good with a needle and thread. That was back when this was a fishing town. Anyway, I admire a man who's not afraid to sew on a button."

Earl flushed. He had not had a compliment in so long it felt like he'd been punched. But he did not know what to say next, except "Yes," when the woman asked if he wanted his receipt.

Earl had been in town a couple of weeks when he discovered the indoor swimming pool. It was built onto the side of the city recreation center, its sides and roof made of glass like a greenhouse. He stopped to watch the children playing around the slide, the adults swimming laps on one side of the pool, and what seemed to be a team practicing on the other. Young swimmers bent over on platforms, their arms in front of their heads, slipping into the water at the sound of a whistle. Their entry into the water left hardly a bubble. Past the flags dipping over the pool, they emerged on their sides, sleek as torpedoes. He saw men his age crossing the pool with long, limber strokes, their faces turned to the pool bottom, their heels breaking slightly the surface behind them. He could watch for hours, and he did, as he used to watch the shadowy branches claw the side of the shed back home.

In the in-between—sleeping, walking to chow, sewing hems on hospital gowns, biting a bedsheet to keep from screaming; day or night, waking, dreaming—Earl had thought often of the lake in Austin they called a pool. It was hard to imagine the place without thinking of His Highnesses and Tom, of course, but there had been a blissful few minutes when he had sculled around on the bottom of the pool, looking up at swimmers slicing through water wavy with sunlight. He'd often imagined himself moving through water with the same streamlined and buoyant grace as those he came to watch daily in the Rec Center pool. It became his attic eaves, his pedal steel. Now, lured by the orderly disturbance of the blue box of water by arms and legs, the Rec Center pool went from being a pause on his daily walks to being his destination.

Earl was standing outside the pool one day when a woman came around the corner of the building. It was raining moderately. Like most of the residents of Cliffside, she didn't seem to care for raincoats or umbrellas. She was a thin woman with hacked-off hair, passing into middle age with no signs of putting up a fight—strands of gray in her hair, no makeup to hide the darkening of eye sockets.

"Can I help you?"

Earl smiled at her while contemplating her question. So rote was this phrase on the outside, so rare to him in the in-between (no C.O. ever wanted to help anyone; they were there to tell you where to go and what you did wrong) that he understood its emptiness and yet, still: every time he heard it, he could not help but take it literally. People wanted to do things for him. They wanted Earl to be settled, content, comfortable, challenged, engaged. They knew nothing about him, is why. If they knew the first thing about him, they would not ask how they might go about assisting him in accomplishing his long-dormant desires.

"I like to watch them swim."

The woman pointed at the junior swim team practicing, preadolescents taking up all but two of the lanes.

"'Them?'"

Then Earl understood. He had seen how child molesters were treated inside. To be mistaken for one, now, when he'd only come to see arms and legs—any size, any age—disrupt the placid blue square, was horrifying. He felt his face burning. He worried she'd notice the flushing and interpret it as guilt. Would he ever not worry over guilt? He had cradled Tina's bloody head and stroked her hair. He still heard the shower running. Tom singing over the sound of the water pelting the plastic curtain. The James Gang, "Walk Away."

"Not just the ones in there now," he said. "Anybody. I just like to watch people swim."

Her look was a summing up. On what was she basing her judgment? His clothes? They were wet and ill-fitting from the Goodwill where he often saw travelers. She thought he was a traveler. As soon as he realized this, she confirmed it.

"Are you from around here?"

"Texas, but I live here now."

"What part of town?"

"By the river," he said, which was vague, since half the town had some view of the river. He wondered what difference it made to her, where he lived. He thought, for the first time in decades, of the compound outside Stovall where his family had circled their train of trailers and vehicles around a shabby farmhouse with various deteriorating outbuildings. He wondered if there was something about him that still suggested outskirt, if the boundary of a city really was a limit for those consigned to settle beyond it.

"Well, I can't have you standing out here every day. We have had complaints."

Earl said, "Oh?" He was surprised; he'd thought himself invisible.

"From the staff. Also some parents."

But not the swimmers. They couldn't see Earl because they stared at the black lines on the bottom of the pool. Sometimes they stopped at the end of the lane for a sip of water or to grab some strange implement that they put between their legs or to grab a piece of what looked to be Styrofoam to extend in front of them while they kicked back and forth across the pool. But they couldn't see outside.

"If you are a resident, you can come inside and swim," she said.

"It's free?"

"You need to buy a punch card. Or a day pass, but a card is cheaper."

"Are you the manager?"

"Aquatic director."

"So you teach swimming?"

"Used to. Now I hire others to teach. Why?"

"I can't swim," said Earl. "I mean, I can, but not like that." He nodded toward the pool. "I am good enough to where I won't drown and I float okay or did when I was a kid—I have not been swimming in over forty years—but it's not pretty."

"We teach lessons," she said.

"To grown men?"

"To anyone who has the money."

She thought he was a traveler. Maybe he was. He lived in a motel room. He shopped when the world slept. Walked the backstreets and downtown alleys all day long, staring down at the concrete, rain or shine, and it was mostly rain. He loved the rain for it was finally water and a gift from a sky that in forty-four years he'd only seen a square of, the sky that loomed like a dropped ceiling over all the prison yards. Diced sky, contained as he and the men around him were contained. Sometimes a sliver of sky appeared through a window, but sky should not be slivered, diced, or contained.

"All you need is a driver's license showing your local address."

"I don't drive."

"We'll take a utility bill."

He was thinking of the sky again, of how close and gray and heavy were the clouds that blocked the sky most of the days. After all those years of seeing only patches of sky, it seemed strange to him to settle in a place where clouds sometimes lowered themselves onto the town itself. The sky was a memory then. Yet he didn't mind the mist. It enveloped him, hid him from the rest of the world. Why did he deserve the sort of sky he'd seen in West Texas and Arizona and New Mexico on his way out here? The sky was one of the things he had forfeited when he failed to save Tina's life and his own. The sky and a utility bill.

"I'm staying with relatives," he said.

She studied him again. She was a studier in the tradition of the cop who had married Arthur's sister. Earl had forgotten his name, which was a good thing. Whatever his name was, he'd studied Earl to ascertain who he really was. This woman appeared to know who he was, if not what he'd done or what he'd let happen. Arthur said the drugs were no excuse, but was it not pertinent that Earl had never taken drugs in his life besides smoking his brothers' headache-inducing dirt weed? He had stayed up for days. Arthur tried to argue that Earl's judgment was impaired from lack of sleep, but Earl saw one old woman on the jury, a white woman who looked like she might have attended the Methodist church with Tina's lesbian aunt, shake her head in obvious disgust. He saw the way it was going and lapsed into what Arthur called disassociation, his fancy term for "here and not here." Prison had only exacerbated this tendency: why be present for prison? His sole escape was to be elsewhere, and so he'd been elsewhere everywhere but in the cafeteria, the yard, the shower—places where he was most likely to be assaulted. He was assaulted a few times, until he accepted the protection of a man named Mattox. Mattox shot a highway patrolman after robbing a liquor store. At least that was what others claimed. Mattox said only that he was in Del Rio at the time they had him killing some son of a bitch in Eagle Pass.

Innocent is not the same as not guilty, Your Honor. I am guilty because I let myself drift off like an unleashed balloon. I floated above Austin, high as the tower where the former Marine shot all those people, one of them pregnant according to Tina. Tom killed her but I watched. True enough, I was out of my mind from all the goods and sleep-deprived, and yet all I am guilty of is hovering. I remained untethered. I ought to have been in that room with Tina, protecting her, instead of floating above.

"That's fine," said the aquatic director. "Just put down the name and address of your relatives. We'll get you in the water. But in the meantime, I can't have you standing out here staring anymore. Either you come in and swim or keep walking."

Earl thanked her and kept on walking, all the while thinking: keep walking? Was she calling him out? She knew he wasn't staying with relatives. He didn't have any relatives and somehow she sensed it. She smelled the Goodwill still lingering on his clothes, the back-alley dumpster juice he sometimes stepped in when he forgot to look down, the sulfuric stench of that inlet of river where he often sat upon slick rocks to watch the barges. She smelled passing barge. Also prison, the trapped odors of which often woke him nights in the Lamplighter, which is why he preferred to sleep in the daytime. It was quiet then, the only sound coming from the Guatemalan women who cleaned the rooms. He heard their carts wheeling into the rooms, and the telenovelas blaring on the television while they worked. Sometimes he left the Spanish-speaking channel on when he went out, along with a couple of dollars. He'd heard from the night manager that the cleaning ladies sent most of their salary home to relatives in Guatemala.

Why had Arthur saved all his money and left it for Earl? Did he feel as if he'd failed Earl? In his letter he claimed he'd grown to care about him. During their visits, Arthur never let on that he felt especially guilty for not doing more for Earl, nor did he ever say he cared one way or the other about him, though Earl thought now how he sometimes drove five or six hours to visit. Earl recalled Arthur's response when he arrived at the jail to find out Earl had waived his counsel and told it all to the thick-necked cop. Maybe he's not your client no more, said the cop. But Arthur never once said to Earl, Are you still my client?

Sometimes Earl talked himself into thinking that Arthur left him the money because there was no one else. He had a sister in Chicago he got on pretty good with, but Arthur said she was as rich as Ross Perot, whoever that was. Probably some Stovall big shot. Earl and Arthur traveled in different circles. Arthur in his letter started out talking about Earl's people and ended up in outer space. Your mother ought to have done more for you, Earl, wrote Arthur. She ought to have been paying more mind.

Earl didn't quite get what his mother could have done but, as Arthur suggested, hang up the phone every once in a while. Would that have prevented him from borrowing Leif's car and driving Tina up to see her mother in the state insane asylum? Say his mother had spent her days keeping track of Earl and his brothers, talking to them instead of to her sisters over in Bossier City. Would that have kept him home?

He doubted it. Also he felt as if thinking about such was about as helpful as riding a rocket around in outer space. He was born to be here and also elsewhere.

Earl let himself into his room. It was just getting dark out, four o'clock in the afternoon, fog rolling in and out, the rain still steady. He was soaked but water was a gift from a sky he'd been denied. He looked around his room. Even with Arthur's money, Earl knew he'd have to get a job soon. Life had gotten pricey. A pack of cigarettes now cost about what a tank of gas did when he went in. Earl did not smoke or drink, he was rightly terrified of drugs, and he didn't care to eat out. Mostly he ate as he had in the in-between: heated-up ramen, Hungry Man soup, and bologna sandwiches. He was thinking he might like a kitchen. A place to cook real food. He had a hotplate and a refrigerator so small it fit beneath a table. He filled it with milk, juice, cheese. His mother's one consistent dish—the meat-and-foreign-word meals were rare—was something called Welsh rabbit. He would like a real kitchen so he might cook up some Welsh rabbit. Also he could get himself a utility bill. You need one to learn to swim.

3.

BECAUSE HE HAD no idea how to go about finding a place to stay, Earl went to the public library. On the bus from San Francisco to Portland, a traveler had told Earl that if you needed something, you went to the library and instead of looking through the books or newspapers threaded into wooden racks, you looked at a machine.

"Where did all the newspapers go?" Earl asked.

"Into the machines," said the traveler.

The library in Cliffside was filled with women and young children, who played in set-off rooms vibrantly painted and cushioned with pillows. There were a few rows of books everyone bypassed for the machines.

How had he learned that the line of computers was called a bank? From listening. He listened for the names of things and found that they were old words. It was called recycling. You could no longer pick up bottles from ditches and turn them in for money because of this recycling. There were special blue containers to put them in and it was good for the earth and bad for the winos and the travelers and kids who had never heard of an allowance. Earl didn't see the sense in learning *all* the new words. Likely they would pass from Planet Earth in a matter of decades, as had fist combs.

There was a sign by each machine that said, "Please keep food and drink away from the monitor." He assumed that *monitor* was the name of the machine. The term put him at ease. If there was one thing he was used to, it was being monitored.

For a half hour he browsed the stacks. When he saw that the young librarian was not busy, he approached her and said, "Hello, I would like help monitoring for lodging."

"I'm sorry?" The librarian phrased it as a question.

"You needn't be," said Earl. Why would she be sorry? And why would she seem unsure if she were sorry or not? She wore a small diamond on her right nostril, impossible not to stare at, but Earl did not stare because he had seen so few women for forty-four years and then they were everywhere and because so many barely covered themselves, at least in Texas and on cross-country buses, he was extra careful not to stare. Here in Oregon, where the sun only emerged sometimes late in the day to backlight banks of clouds, and where it was always windy and often chilly, it was rare to see flesh. When it did appear, it was most often covered in ink, and not just on the young people.

"I'm afraid I didn't understand you," she was saying. "What do you need?"

Well, *there* is a question. What do I need? There was desire and there was need. He had learned to pare need down to not much of nothing and to squelch desire entirely.

"I need a place to live," he said. "Somewhere that has utilities."

"Utilities?"

"I need them printed out on a bill so I can go swimming. Also I would like a stove to cook Welsh rabbit."

"I see," she said, looking him over, making her calculations, divining, by something he said or the way he said it, where he'd spent the last four decades. Everyone saw it. Most noticed it immediately. For all those years he had been a number and they'd stamped it on his forehead like all the ink he saw spreading up from collars and out of cuffs.

"This way," said the librarian. She was much shorter than Earl but wore high-heeled boots that raised her considerably. Her hair was not a color he could name. She had a discerning manner, which he preferred over aloof. Maybe she was doing her job, leading an ex-con to a monitor, but she did not seem judgmental in the least.

They came to a line of computers. She was telling him how to log in. On a log in the forest he sat reading *His Life and Times*.

The librarian was typing words into a box on the monitor. Would he be required to type? He had been taking a typing class before he got arrested. During the first week of class, he had been taking a test and hit the wrong key and spelled his name Earp. The teacher, who was both funny and mean (a winning combination to Earl's mind; he could forgive meanness if it made him laugh) had called out "Earp" when handing the tests back, leaving his classmates to call him Wyatt and Gunslinger until he disappeared and turned up in jail, a bona fide outlaw.

"Here is the link for local real-estate listings," she said. Words he knew come back around again. Link had nothing to do with sausage.

"Where are you from?"

"Louisiana," said Earl.

"I thought I detected an accent."

That would be because no one out here had one except the Guatemalan women who cleaned the rooms at the Lamplighter.

He wanted to ask the librarian where she was from, but it seemed too forward. He would have to look her in the eye, which so far he had avoided.

"New Orleans?"

"Shreveport," said Earl.

"I guess that's like assuming everyone in Oregon lives in Portland. Of course, most do these days. I confess I know nothing about the rest of Louisiana. What is Shreveport like?"

There are phone lines snaking away from it through patchy piney woods, beneath swamps, buried just deep enough in the furrows of fields that farmers cannot sever them when they plow or disk. You can follow these lines straight to Texas in the manner of beer cans and underpants littering stray paths into the forest.

"It's got a river," said Earl, "but nothing like that one."

He inclined his shoulder in the direction of the mighty Columbia, which far below them raced toward the ocean.

"That is a good river as rivers go," said the librarian. "Can I ask you a question?"

Earl nodded. He had never been asked such a question. Where he was from, people just up and asked.

"What is 'Welsh rabbit'?"

"My mother used to cook it for us. It was one of the few things she knew how to cook besides corn on the cob and watermelon. We ate a lot of watermelon."

"What's in it, Welsh rabbit?"

"Oh. I think cheese and some sort of seasoning. Maybe ketchup? You melt it on bread."

"So no rabbit?"

"Oh, no. I don't know why they call it that. I guess we could look it up on the monitor."

"Now that you know how, you can look anything up. But back to the task at hand. You want a place so you can cook a grilled cheese sandwich and get utilities."

"That's right," said Earl. It wasn't exactly a grilled cheese but close enough.

"Where do you live now if you don't mind me asking?"

"The Lamplighter. It's nice. I have a big room with a view of the bridge."

She stared at him closely and for so long that Earl grew nervous. Was she thinking hard on a subject of great import, or had she figured out his history? Earl's forehead grew cool with sweat. Cliffside was not a sweaty place. After what seemed like a minute, she said, "Hold on."

What was there to hold on to? Not the past. Not the library, which did not seem to much care about books. Yet he was accustomed to doing what he was told.

She returned with a piece of paper, upon which was written a name and an address.

"My mother has a garage apartment. She's looking for a tenant. It's furnished."

"And it has utilities?"

"All mod cons," said the librarian in an accent he recognized as fake British. Then she said in her normal no-accent English, "I can't promise anything. She's picky about who she lets live there. But I have a feeling she would like you."

"Why?"

"Well, to be honest, and I mean this in a good way, strange things come out of your mouth. Even stranger things come out of hers."

"Are y'all close?"

"Depends on the day. She has a lot of passions. I should warn you that she sometimes sees people as projects."

Earl had no idea what this meant. It sounded wrong to him, akin to seeing women as objects, which he had recently learned was wrong, since this was not something people talked about in 1974. But he liked the librarian. He suspected she was closer to her mother than she let on, due to some sort of young-adult code he understood from his own youth, even though he was close to neither of his parents. Had he been, though, he didn't think he would have outright revealed it.

"I would like to thank you," said Earl.

The librarian smiled, as if he had said something strange.

Earl was resigned to everything out of his mouth seeming strange.

"You're welcome. Again, no promises. It's her decision. Go see her. I'd give you her number but she's not much for answering phones."

"She must not have any sisters."

"I'm sorry?"

"You needn't be."

"Okay, well. I have to get back to work. My name's Jade, by the way."

"Earl."

"Good luck, Earl. You might compliment her on her so-called garden. You'll probably find her at work in it. She calls it an English garden but what it is, as you'll soon see, is a wild tangle."

The house was almost to the top of a steep street above town. Though it needed a paint job, the house had once been grand. Three stories of intricate scrollwork in the gables, a latticed porch. Earl remembered a couple of houses like this in Stovall, gingerbread houses, the kids called them, all of them owned by widows. He wondered if Jade's mother was a widow.

As for the English garden, had Jade not told him it was a garden, he'd have seen only wild tangle. She *had* told him it was a garden and he saw only wild tangle.

Earl opened the squeaky front gate and a woman rose from the bushes. She wore tight-fitting pants of the sort he'd seen on joggers and a sweatshirt that read PEPPERDINE. Earl had no idea what was a pepperdine.

Her hair was long and graying, pulled back beneath a visor. She wore athletic shoes and pink gardening gloves.

"You must be Earl," she said. "Jade told me you were coming. Alana," she said, taking off her gardening glove and holding out her hand.

Earl had never shaken the hand of a woman. He had not shaken anyone's hand in so long that it felt like a custom from another culture. He remembered the endless handshakes he shared with Moon and Sleep and Cheese. He smiled remembering the elaborate sliding of palms, knocking of elbows, pinky curls. Alana smiled back at him.

Her hand was soft for someone who worked a wild tangle. Oh, gloves. The things his father kept in his glove compartment.

"Are you on foot, then?"

"I don't drive," said Earl.

"Good for you. Too many cars in the world. I park in the garage so if you did have a car you'd have to park on the street, which would mean getting wet most days, but if you choose to live in this town, wet ought not bother you. Living in Cliffside is basically like living in a car wash. I hate it when I say 'basically.' It's a tic and it means nothing. It's like booze. Empty calories. Some words are empty calories, I guess. Others are nutrient rich. Well, let's take a look at the apartment, shall we? What do you do for fun?"

Earl had not heard anyone talk so much in years. Maybe since he'd been Clothesline. But she wasn't "tweaking," as he'd learned to call it in the in-between. She was just voicing every thought she had. What if he did this? He might have been put in jail well before he ever met Tina. The thoughts in his head, the things he saw—they scared other people in the way school nurses and cuckoo clocks scared Tina. He would not even know how to put them into words. Some were songs. Others debris falling from trees. Phone lines snaking beneath bayous. Complicated handshakes on street corners. A Band-Aid floating among clouds above a pool.

"I take walks. I'm about to start taking swimming lessons."

"With Tamara at the Rec Center? She's the best. She taught me to swim. I didn't learn until I was in my thirties. Lived by the water all my life. I had slight aquaphobia. Chalk it up to Mary Jo Kopechne–in-the-Chappaquiddick nightmares. Only Tamara could have gotten me to get my head wet. She could teach an animal to swim."

"Don't most of them swim naturally?" He responded to the last thing she said because it was the only thing he understood.

"Nothing swims naturally except creatures of the sea. Man was not built to swim. Actually, when I say man, I don't mean mankind. I mean males. Women are more buoyant. More body fat. But you know all this."

"Not really," he said, though he was thinking it might be better to just agree with her. To say yes when he meant I don't know what you are talking about.

"Well, no matter. Swimming is really about breathing. And fear. Everything is about breathing and fear."

Earl tried to think of things that were not about breathing or fear. He would have liked more time to consider it, but they had climbed the stairs attached to the garage and entered the apartment.

The floors were dark wood and sloped in the main room,

which was small but furnished with a couch and a desk and a television. Most of the furnishings seemed cast-off, dated, but comforting to Earl as they reminded him of before. There was a small kitchen with a stove and a full-sized refrigerator, a tub in the bathroom, a tiny bedroom filled mostly with a bed, a chest of drawers, and a bedside table upon which sat a lamp with a wooden base so similar to the one Tom had used on Tina that Earl almost decided to stay in the Lamplighter. But the front room had huge windows overlooking the river, Washington State blinking beyond. He could switch the lamp out for a smaller one. Or he could just live with it, turn it on and off every night and know that he'd never touched the one it reminded him of.

"It's nice," said Earl.

"Of course, you can move things around. There were some things on the walls, but the last tenant took them down and I haven't gotten around to putting them up again. I love the phrase 'gotten around to.' It suggests life is round instead of the tedious linear notion that most people subscribe to. Maybe you think of time like that. I suspect if you don't own a car, you are not of the linear school. Somehow the two seem related. Where do you work?"

"At the moment I am taking some time off. I have some savings."

"Well, you should hold on to that."

Why should Earl be shocked when he expected it the whole time? Still, he could hear his surprise when he said, "You don't want to rent to me?"

"Why would you say that?"

"You said I ought to hold on to my savings."

"Well not *all* of it. A person's got to live. What I meant was, you don't want to run down your savings. Did you know that the average American has approximately four hundred dollars in their savings account? I read that in the paper. I still read the paper. Do you?"

"I thought it was all on the monitors now."

"The monitors?"

"The computers. Like in the library."

"You sound about as tech-savvy as me. Though as a rule I believe it's incumbent on us to adapt to technology. All my friends depend entirely on their grandchildren to help them with their phones. Newspapers are still printed. I get the *New York Times* on Sundays and the *Cliffside Advance* when I can find it in the garden. The paperboy has a mean slider. I could never not take the paper. When you get to a certain age you are meant to claim you read the obituaries first, but if someone I know dies, I don't need to read the paper to find out. Though I do love obituaries, mostly for what they choose to include. Every time I read one, I wonder what they chose *not* to include. I have told Jade that when I die, I want my obituary to include everything I did wrong. 'In fifth grade Alana Nystrom made out with her best friend's boyfriend behind the bowling alley. In the sixth grade she stole a copy of the final exam in Algebra II and sold it to her classmates and kept her mouth shut when the principal blamed William Strom despite his pointing the finger at the deceased,' etc. And I am fond of the euphemisms people come up with for 'up and died.' 'Succumbed,' 'slipped away,' 'departed,' 'gone home,' 'entered eternal rest.' 'Passed away' of course. 'Lost his or her battle with' x, y, or z. Actually only x. No survivor is going to print that their dearly departed lost his battle with alcoholism. Jade's father has been losing that battle for forty years, though he still feels he is fit to serve. The *Advance* is mostly given to stories about the rising crime rate. Do you like crime shows?"

Earl was winded just listening. He wasn't uninterested, though. She could teach him things, stuff he'd missed in the in-between. He'd have to sift through her words, but wasn't that true of everyone, even those like he'd become who say as little as possible?

Earl did not think he would care for crime shows.

"I don't watch much television," he said. "I keep it on all night, but I hardly ever look at it."

"That's a male thing. Falling asleep to late-night television. I don't think it's very good for your health. But I'm not a doctor. How old are you?"

"Old," said Earl, which made her laugh.

"Good answer. I'll try it. I need a new response to the question. Not that anyone ever outright asks it. It was rude of me to ask you, but sometimes I say whatever I'm thinking and then remember things like manners after the fact. I often say I am mid-century modern, since that's all the rage now. Jade and her husband bought one of those hideous and I quote 'mid-century modern' eight-foot-long stereo cabinets, do you remember them? Longer than a canoe. Took up half the living room."

Earl did remember them. Tina's supposedly lesbian

Methodist aunt had one. When she was at work and they skipped school, they played 45s on the long stereo. Ike and Tina Turner's "Proud Mary." Sometimes when they grew tired of "Proud Mary," they flipped to the B side, "Funkier than a Mosquito's Tweeter." Often they sucked on Atomic FireBalls while dancing around the room. Every time he heard "Proud Mary," his tongue burned.

"Of course, in those days no one did any living in a living room," Alana was saying. "We weren't allowed to go in ours. Basically empty calories, our living room. The carpet was white as were the couches, so my mother covered them in plastic. There was a plastic runner leading from the door to the den. It had these sort of cleats on it so that it would adhere to the carpet. I liked to put my arm under it and get one of my siblings to step on it. The pain was a confirmation of much inner strife. It felt delicious. Where are you from?"

"Louisiana, but I have spent most of my life in Texas."

"Texas is an enigma to me. It doesn't come across well in the media."

"There's a lot of crime, I guess," said Earl because she seemed attuned to crime.

"I was thinking more about your politics."

"Oh," said Earl.

"But speaking of crime, it does seem that for many years they led the country in executions."

Earl didn't realize people were keeping count. It seemed an odd thing to track. And too close to that image of the old couple living across from the prison on cheap land, their lights dimming and their clocks blinking every time someone got the chair.

"Though maybe that was Florida," she said. "I believe there are some similarities between the two?"

All Earl knew of Florida was a photograph of the Fountain of Youth he'd seen in the *World Book* once. It looked like an abandoned half-dug well. Its surroundings resembled a truly wild English garden. Maybe it was so magical it needed to be camouflaged.

"I have a friend who travels to Texas. She is a birder. Did you see many varieties of birds growing up there?"

"Mostly grackles. But maybe there's more. Tell the truth, I only looked up at the sky at dusk. The rest of the time I looked down at the ground."

"And why is that?"

"To see where I was going."

"Well that's sensible. Was the terrain rocky and dusty?"

Earl remembered the view from the window at James Lynaugh Unit in Fort Stockton. He spent five years there toward the end. High desert, the Texas that people assumed all of Texas resembled.

"No. There are four or five Texases."

"By which you mean?" By which he meant he wasn't sure how they had arrived at the geographical regions of Texas.

"You got East Texas, which is basically Louisiana. That's where I come from. Then you got South Texas, which is like Mexico. And the panhandle, it's like Oklahoma."

"So what part of Texas is like Texas?"

"West Texas is the Texas y'all think of when someone says Texas. Though it's not much different from eastern New Mexico."

"You make me want to visit the place. I can't say I have ever uttered the phrase 'I would like to go to Texas' before. You should have gone to work for the state tourism bureau."

"I've done my time with the state of Texas," said Earl.

"Oh, you worked for the state? Alana works for the city, which is similar in that the benefits are good."

Earl tried to think of a benefit from the in-between. Maybe "expect nothing." If that was a benefit he'd broken it already, because he wanted to live in this apartment.

Something about Alana—the strange things that came out of her mouth, the ease with which Earl fell into conversation with her—reminded him of Tina. Tina, also, had been known to talk a streak. Her mind did not follow any straight lines. Earl would read aloud from *His Life and Times,* and she would bring up a Brazilian soccer player. Or a Leon Russell concert in Houston.

"Do you like Leon Russell?" Earl asked Alana.

She sang the first lines of "A Song for You." Alana's voice was high and hoarse and warbly, and singing Leon Russell cracked her up. Earl laughed too.

"I haven't thought about that song in years."

"How much is the rent?"

"Oh," she said. "Right."

His abrupt shifting of the subject was rude, and she seemed deflated by it, but Earl was enjoying himself too much. He was thinking, while Alana sang "A Song for You," of Tina singing

"Delta Lady" in the woods and of Arthur talking about the Tulsa Sound. Any more of this and he would be pancaked on the floor, awash with pedal steel. In the in-between he had not let himself go back to the forest, nor anything that happened between when Tina showed up until he was sentenced. Had he allowed himself to think about it, or talk about it with Arthur, who never brought it up, he'd have died. He hated prison but he did not feel like he deserved to die.

"How does eight hundred sound? Utilities included."

"I need a utility bill."

"Why?"

"So I can get into the swimming pool."

"Hmmm," she said. "The thing is, it's all on one bill. I've always included utilities. I've never had anyone asked to have the bill put in their name. Can you not show your voter registration?"

Earl knew he wasn't allowed to vote.

"I've not gotten around to all that. I just moved up here."

"Well it's easy. I take people down to get registered all the time. We need all the help we can get, even in supposedly blue Oregon."

"I'm not that political," he said.

"I'll pretend I didn't hear that."

"Do I have to be political to rent from you?"

"No," she said. "But let me ask you a question."

This wasn't the same as her daughter asking permission to ask a question, but it was still unnerving to Earl, who nodded okay to Alana.

"Did you vote for the current president?"

"The burnt-orange fellow?" said Earl.

"A charitable descriptor."

"No," said Earl.

"Okay, we're good," said Alana. "Though I have more to say on this subject. Let me see about getting the power bill in your name. If there is a fee involved, I will of course pass that on to you."

"Of course," said Earl.

"When would you like to move in?"

"Tomorrow."

"Oh dear. I'll need to check your references, but I guess I could do that this afternoon."

"Of course," said Earl. Back to the Lamplighter. Or maybe push on to Seattle, since he could not go back to the library or take swimming lessons. Arthur was long gone. Who else could attest to his character? He had maintained forty-four years of good behavior in the in-between, not that it helped, due to Tina's parents, and after they died, her sister showing up at every parole hearing to argue against his release. Maybe he could put her off. Claim he was having trouble finding addresses. He didn't want to lie. But he wanted this place. He liked Cliffside. He liked listening to Alana talk. It was not unlike rolling, rolling, rolling on the river.

"And it will take me at least a day to clean the place."

"Okay," he said. He could stay at the Lamplighter a day or two longer. Stall her on the reference front. He didn't tell her she needn't clean on his account. He was used to cells lousy with roaches. It being Texas, the roaches were appropriately gargantuan. He had been glad when they finally transferred him to Fort Stockton as he did not mind the tarantulas that somehow penetrated the walls of the prison. Some of his fellow inmates got themselves bitten on purpose. Anything to get to the infirmary, which they treated like a vacation, plus there were drugs there, though not one of them got away with stealing anything. They came back sullen and sober, their spider bites red, swollen, and innocuous.

4.

ALANA SAID THERE was no hurry on checking his references and offered to help him move, but Earl did not need a car to haul his suitcase and backpack up the hill. He said goodbye to the desk clerk and gave each of the Guatemalan housekeepers ten dollars. He had never let them know that he had learned Spanish in the in-between. He had lots of time, plus half of the inmates were Hispanic and he wanted to know what they were saying. It was more about survival than cultural refinement. Like learning a martial art, but with badly rolled *R*s.

Alana was out when he arrived, but she had left the keys on the counter alongside a fresh cherry pie. Earl was more interested in the keys. To carry keys, your own keys to your own place, a place you could access anytime and that you never had to share, felt finally like freedom. He'd had keys to his room at the Lamplighter, but he'd known he would not stay there forever. The transience, which at first had attracted him—for he had thrived on unpredictability and an absence of regimen—had begun to wear on him. The in-between would never fade, but it had dimmed a bit. Earl wanted to endure silence and stillness of the sort he'd found once in the attic eaves. Or when Alana stopped talking, though he liked to hear her talk. He thought of others he'd known who talked nonstop. The difference, as far as he could tell, was that they were interested only in themselves. Alana's monologues almost always ended with a question for him.

Earl went into his new room and lay down and went to sleep. When he woke it was dark and he was in the pines. Along came his mother. She sat beside him against a tree. He marked his place in *His Life and Times*. She said things about Tina. He asked her if she were going to leave his father. Listen, she said, and he heard nothing, then falling trees, traffic, drums.

Remember this, said his mother, and Earl had remembered it. But now he heard different things: the intermittent noises of a small town at night. A siren. A barge on the river bleating its horn. Dogs barking, the beep of a backing-up garbage truck. Bass-thump of rap music from a passing car. Earl got up and stood by the window, eating cherry pie while listening to the mostly silent night.

He remembered the references. He needed to have an excuse at the ready, but he was not accustomed to making excuses. Was he that way before the in-between? Maybe he had tried to use the goods as an excuse, if not for what happened then his choppy memory of it. Even before Arthur called him on it, he knew better.

But Earl did not need an excuse because Alana either forgot about it or grew so used to him that she decided she did not need anyone to attest to his character. Some might have called this a lucky break. Earl did not believe in luck, but he believed in the patchiness of memory, though if he believed in such, he had to worry that one day she would remember.

His worry was not what kept him up nights. He still preferred the all-night grocery store, the downtown sidewalks empty of people, the possums and raccoons darting down alleys or into storm drains when he approached.

He started spending his days at the library, reading at the newspapers on the monitors. He took some delight in reading the obituaries, looking as Alana did for the things not included. He tried to determine what the writer of the obituary suggested by these omissions. He stared hard at the space between sentences, the margins, the indentions between paragraphs.

He sometimes took notes in the event that Alana should bring up an obituary she'd read. If Jade was not busy, she might come over and talk for a bit. Small talk about the new apartment, usually, or the garden Jade seemed to hold in suspicion if not disdain. Earl was polite and formal, and it took him awhile to understand that his manner incited Jade to ask more questions. She was not by nature an intrusive sort, which suggested to Earl that she took after her father, about whom nothing had been said but that he was a bad drunk.

"Jade says you are an enigma," Alana said to him that first week when he encountered her in the garden.

"Well, you said Texas is an enigma and I do come from Texas," he said.

"I don't think Texas is an enigma to Jade. She has spent some time in Austin. She even thought of moving there. She loved everything about it but the heat. Is it as wonderful as they claim?"

"I've only been there once."

"And? It didn't wow you?"

Oh but it wowed me at first, Earl remembered. I went here and there. Tom leaned me upside a tree in the woods near a waterfall. He went to town on me and then we went to a bar on the outskirts of town, a bar overlooking the river called a lake with a jukebox stacked with sweet pedal steel. Tom referred to the regulars lining the bar as cedar choppers and said the music sucked. We went on to the next transaction. Goods exchanged for cash. Tom kept the cash and shared the goods. At the edge of Tom's backyard, in the shadow of a wood, people stood still as deer as I threw up for hours. Next door, a child watched from the second rung of a tiny sliding board. I have never forgotten her. Where is she now and how did she escape that backyard littered with sun-bleached toys, within spitting distance of a drug-dealing murderer?

Then Earl came back into the conversation.

"I'm wondering when I might get that utility bill."

"I guess it didn't wow you. The bill might be a problem. If you're itching to get in the pool, I can call Tamara and explain the situation. This is a small town. We all know each other. The proper channels are easily circumvented."

"That is awfully kind of you."

Alana laughed.

"You are awfully polite. It seems that you were raised right, as we used to say. It's a little shocking sometimes. Like you walked out of an earlier time. Most men around here are a little rough around the edges. Like, for instance, the one I married."

"He live around here still?"

"Haven't seen him in a while. That usually means he's down in Portland or somewhere else where he has some long-suffering woman fooled. Or not fooled. When he's around he's either bothering Jade or he's barking up my tree. He's always a few dollars short. Once he was the loveliest man. There is loveliness in him still. I have to believe that because he is the father of my only child. But he feels like everything he had was taken away from him. He's stuck. I really hate to say this, but it baffles me how long he has been wallowing in this rut of victimhood and self-loathing. I could not continue if I was as consumed with bitterness as he. I would jump off the bridge. But why am I telling you all this? You don't need to hear about my abusive alcoholic ex. Nearly every woman's got one, if you read the advice columns, which I do, as religiously as the obituaries. The advice is always obvious when it's not outright wrong. I suppose I read them to feel some moral superiority. I don't know why I read them. Thank goodness I have never been interested in astrology. I do like the crossword but lately the music references escape me. I have to call Jade at work and ask her the first name of a singer named Bieber. She has asked me not to call her at work for such trivialities but finishing a crossword, especially when there's only a word or two left, is a dire emergency. I would call 911 if I didn't think they'd recognize my voice. You can't just get to that point in a puzzle and let it sit there on the kitchen table and go about your Thursday. You could, but have you ever gone on a trip and thought maybe you left the coffeemaker on and worried over it for hours until you either turned around and came home or called your neighbor and ask them to check on it?"

"Not really," said Earl, but he knew well the worry that something bad was looming. Like, for instance, Alana one day remembering the references he'd never provided.

"Well, let me just warn you that you might get a call from me down the road asking you to check the coffeepot. I promise not to bother you about the crossword, though I have a feeling you know more than you are letting on."

"Likely I know less."

"That you make that claim suggests you know more. Let me call Tamara. I assume you own a swimsuit?"

Earl had never needed one. In the oily ponds and slow rivers of East Texas, he and Tina had skinny-dipped. At the pool where he'd met Your Highnesses and, fatefully, Tom, he'd swum in his underwear.

"No."

"Fred Meyer's is the ticket. I'll drive you over there this afternoon."

"I can walk."

"Nonsense. It's over in Warrenton. Ten miles on 101. You'd be walloped by a Winnebago. I have to stop at the Tractor Supply out that way anyway. You can help me load up some potting soil and a few flagstones for a path I'm making, after we find you a suit."

Earl said he did not want to put her out, but she ignored him and was punching numbers into her phone. She asked to speak to Tamara. It was then that Earl remembered he'd told the aquatic director, who he assumed was this Tamara, that he was staying with relatives.

It was too late to stop her. And to stop her he would have to inform her of his lie. She would learn who he was and what he'd done. Earl would never learn to swim, at least not in Cliffside. Forget the Welsh rabbit he had planned to make for Jade and Alana when he got settled in his new digs.

Earl was taking his clothes out of the bureau and stuffing them into his suitcase when Alana knocked on the door.

"We're all set," she said. "Tamara's not teaching many lessons these days, but she agreed to make an exception if you don't mind waiting until six when she gets off. Some years ago, Tamara's partner was in a jam. I helped her out. It was a far bigger deal to them than it was to me."

She was looking around the room.

"You don't have much stuff. I can lend you some art to hang on the walls. Oh, but maybe you prefer it spartan. Jade proclaims herself a minimalist. Goes with her mid-century modern aesthetic, I guess. Did you meet her boyfriend? Kaiser? Well, he's wonderful. I will never tell Jade how much I love him because I fear it might backfire. Do you have children?"

"No."

"Ever been married?"

"Nope."

"Jade would be appalled by my prying. She thinks I have no boundaries. That is why I would never tell her how much I like Kaiser."

"Jade asks me questions," said Earl. "I see her at the library sometimes."

"Does she ask about your romantic history?"

"Mostly she asks about your garden."

"Which she dismisses as a thicket. She and Kaiser live on a farm. Organic, sustainable. They take it all very seriously. They grow things in rows. They are forever weeding. I am against weeding and would be even if my back could take it. Fortunately, I don't have to worry about watering. It bothers Jade that I prefer to let nature act naturally. Surely there was a sweetheart or two along the way?"

"Yep," said Earl. *The blue light was my baby.*

"Tragic breakup?"

Earl knew that was not exactly the term for it, but he nodded, lest she quizzed him on it.

"Well, we all have them. I lived down in Humboldt for most of my twenties, in a tree house with a pot farmer named Jeb. Turned out he had a woman in every other tree. Not literally, but he certainly did not believe in monogamy. I suppose if he's still alive he is polyamorous. That's all well and good if you have a lot of energy and are emotionally superficial but it's not for this old-fashioned gal. I met Jade's father on a trip back to Portland, where I grew up. He was working on his doctorate in psychology at Portland State. We met in the nonfiction section at Powell's. We got in an argument about Pauline Kael. He invited me to finish it over a Widmer hefeweizen at the bar at the Heathman. A Portland cliché. Winston—that's his name—was brooding and darkly handsome. Possibly the worst combination ever. I thought he was my Mr. Rochester. I mean, I'd been living in a tree with a closet polygamist for three years, stoned the whole time. One could argue that my social cues were skewed. Are you still unpacking?"

Earl did not understand half of what she said—what was *polyamorous* and who was Mr. Rochester—but he wasn't about to ask, because Alana had spied his suitcase on the bed, half full of clothes.

"Just reorganizing."

"You travel light."

Did this mean she thought he was a traveler?

"Well, it's none of my business. I've intruded enough. Though perhaps some other time you might tell me about this tragic breakup. I have this theory that your molecular structure is rearranged by bad breakups. Certainly it affects your breathing. We need to get going if you are going to help me at the nursery and make your swim lesson."

"I'll be down in a second."

Alana left. Earl went to the window and stared at the river. It was a sunny day in Cliffside. Light hit the highest girders of the bridge. He watched the seagulls swarming over what he knew to be the parking lot of the all-night grocery store. Tamara would be the one to catch him in his lie. She seemed far more formidable than Alana. But she was also indebted to Alana. This might mean she'd give him a break, though it could also mean she would be overprotective of Alana, suspicious enough to rat him out.

He heard Alana's ancient Volvo start up, the engine rattling in the manner of diesels. Well at least he would have swim trunks for Seattle, where he would find a place with a tiny kitchen, a motor court that did not ask for references.

But he loved his apartment. He wasn't going to lose it, surely, over a nervous, spur-of-the-moment lie? He'd lain beside Tina while her head was smashed by the base of a lamp. He hadn't smashed it. He'd done nothing to save her, true, but he had paid for it, paid double. They'd had him up for murder, but he never murdered anyone.

He only wanted to learn to move through the water like a wave. He wanted a place to make Welsh rabbit for Alana and Jade and even Jade's newfangled farmer boyfriend. He remembered another dish his mother made them: Stay-Abed Stew. Big chunks of beef and potatoes and onions and carrots simmered in tomato soup. He could fairly smell it simmering on a rare cold day in Stovall.

Alana was waiting for him. When was the last time Earl had anyone waiting on him? He retrieved some traveler's checks from his hiding place and climbed into the rattling old Volvo.

At the department store, Earl told Alana she could wait in the car, but she insisted on coming in. She knew where the swim gear was, led him right to the rack.

"What size?"

He'd worn a small in orange jumpsuit when he went in, and a large when he went out.

"I guess a large?" he said, and she handed him several suits of the slick sort he'd seen bicyclists wear as they moved in packs along the river road. Skintight lurid stripes.

"I was thinking the kind with pockets and a drawstring," he said. He'd never owned a pair, but he'd seen other boys wear them to the Stovall parks and rec pool, from which he had been banned for life because his brothers trashed the locker room and Earl was guilty by blood.

"Might as well tie a parachute to your feet. You can't properly swim in those things."

"I can't properly swim at all," he said.

"A few hours with Tamara and you'll be Michael Phelps."

"Who?"

She laughed. "It's so refreshing to be around someone that is more clueless about popular culture than I am. Really, it's as if you've spent the last twenty years on a desert island."

"I do love *Robinson Crusoe*," said Earl. Arthur had sent it to him. He read it until it disintegrated.

"Not surprising. You seem nothing if not the self-sufficient sort. But I believe *Robinson Crusoe* might be one of those books which have been deemed a kind of imperialist fairy tale."

Earl was lost. He took the swimsuits into the dressing room. He could barely pull them on over his legs. They pinched his waist and pushed out his belly. Forty-four years of prison grub, supplemented by ramen and peanut butter crackers. Once he'd been skinny. Tina lay against him by the oily waters of the pond and counted his ribs. He sat straight as a sapling, and she lay between his legs, which fanned out like cypress roots along the sand. He'd long ago taught himself to tolerate hunger. His mother rarely cooked. When she arrived back at the compound from her weekly Thursday afternoon trip to the grocery store, Earl's brothers appeared out of nowhere to help her unload the bags. They pilfered all of the good stuff—Strawberry Pop-Tarts,

Barbecued Fritos, Lucky Charms—leaving Earl only ants on a log for a snack, which meant he went without, because really? Ants on a log?

"How's it going in there?" Alana called. He could hear her chatting with what seemed to be a teenaged clerk, some young boy who probably thought they were together. Easy assumption. They were close to the same age, judging by her musical tastes. Earl could have a child the age of Jade.

Earl chose the least garish suit, a royal blue one that came to his knees. He handed it to the teenaged clerk along with a few traveler's checks, which, predictably, the boy had never seen before. A manager was paged on a loudspeaker. Alana, thankfully, had wandered off and did not have to witness Earl explaining to the not-much-younger-than-him manager how a traveler's check worked.

At the Tractor Supply they ran into Kaiser, Jade's boyfriend. He was buying fence posts. He looked like he'd been wandering the streets of Austin back when Earl took Tina up to see her mother in the state insane asylum. Shoulder-length blond hair tied back in a ponytail. Overalls and scuffed work boots. A hound dog sporting a bandana around his neck followed him around the store. His manner was peaceful easy. He had a nice wide smile.

"Been hearing a lot about you," Kaiser said to Earl.

Earl said, "Oh?"

"All good, brother," said Kaiser, clapping him on the shoulder, winking at Alana. Where was he in the world? How could such an ordinary occurrence seem miraculous? Running into Kaiser at the Tractor Supply felt magical, even though Earl had grown up in a town half the size of Cliffside and believed nothing happened for any reason. He believed only in water, pedal steel, train whistles, barge horns, lonesome whippoorwills. The morning mist that draped Cliffside. But here was Kaiser, with his crooked smile and his organic chitchat.

"Having fun with Alana?" She had wandered off with the dog to find her potting soil.

"She brought me over here to buy a swimsuit. I'm going to learn how to swim. I mean, I'm going to learn proper. I know how, I just want to get better at it."

"Right on," said Kaiser. "I grew up here, surrounded by water, and I can just past dogpaddle. So what else are you up to besides swimming lessons? Alana got you helping out in the garden?"

"Not really. I'm helping her pick up some paving stones."

"Drives Jade nuts, Alana's garden."

"Why?"

Kaiser shrugged. "Jade likes things tidied up. That's not Alana's bag. I guess Jade's dad was like that at one point. God knows he's not tidy these days."

"See a lot of him?"

"He was by the house a couple weeks ago. We ended up having to call the cops on him, man. Don't tell Alana, okay? Jade doesn't like to talk to her mom about her crazy-ass dad."

"What did he do?"

"He wanted us to put him up in this barn we turned into a guest cottage. But we've been renting it out for the dough. He told Jade if she loved him, she'd kick out the guests because he had no place to go and he was going to get paid soon for some job or other. When Jade refused, he drove his car through the garden. That's what I'm doing up here today. He took out half of the fencing. Plus ruined a quarter acre of produce. He was all fucked up, man."

"They put him in jail?"

"He left before the cops arrived. I talked Jade out of pressing charges. It's only plants. They'll grow back. And dealing with him when he got out? It wouldn't be worth the money we lost. Anyway, enough about him. Jade says all he wants is attention, so let's talk about you. If Alana's not claimed you for her garden, maybe you can stop by and help me out sometime? If you're into it, I mean. I can use the help. I had some Hispanic guys stop through for a few weeks, but now they've gone to Wenatchee to pick apples. I can't pay much but I can keep you busy. I'm only asking because Jade said she thought you might be looking for something."

Earl did not recall mentioning such to Jade. Maybe she thought he came to the library to read the want ads. Alana had told him he needed to save his savings. Hadn't Arthur urged him in his letter to find work outside? Go be a cowboy, he'd said. There were no ranches in this part of Oregon so a farm would have to do.

"I could use the money," said Earl. "And something to do all day."

"Sweet," said Kaiser.

"What's so sweet?" said Alana, who had joined them.

"Earl's going to help me out on the farm."

"Not before he helps me load these pavers."

"I know better than to poach your help, Alana," said the

smiley Kaiser. "In fact, I'll help you with the pavers. I'm in no hurry."

He called his hound dog, who had wandered off to sniff at fertilizer. The dog's name was Waylon. Straight off the streets of early seventies Austin, this kid. The part of it Earl had seen before he stepped into the locker room of the pond they called a pool.

5.

EARL GOT TO the pool around five-thirty. Alana had told him he would need goggles and lent him a pair, though it turned out he did not need them for this first lesson, which was all about fear and breathing.

His fear was that Tamara would confront him about his lie. Which she did, straight off.

"Still staying with a relative?"

Earl had eaten meals beside men who shot up street corners. Their stray bullets had pierced windows and killed sleeping toddlers. And now this woman's question made him hyperventilate. In the in-between, nothing scared him because he thought there'd never be an after. Fear came from having so much, suddenly, to lose.

Earl didn't see how she could teach him to swim if the sight of her deprived him of oxygen.

"Doesn't matter," she said before he could answer. "Alana's rec trumps your lie. Plus I knew you weren't a child molester. No child molester is going to come every day to stare at the pool for a half hour. I had to check you out after the complaints, though."

"I get that," said Earl.

"It wasn't any parents, actually. It was one of my lifeguards. She said you were skeevy."

"I don't know what that means but I don't think it's me."

"No. You seem more spacey than skeevy."

All these new words. They'd never made it to Stovall. Or maybe they came after he left. He'd missed so much, going in so young: some nutjob shooting John Lennon, Stevie Ray going down in a chopper. Those planes flying straight into skyscrapers. A few wars. Come to think of it he didn't miss any good stuff.

Tamara sold him a punch card. He had cashed a few traveler's checks at the bank, as they seemed to confuse people and he did not want Tamara further confused. She showed him to the men's locker room and told him to meet her on deck by the training pool.

The locker room was filled with teenagers, worked up after swim team practice. They were loud and sloppy. All the benches were covered with gear, wet towels, suits. Earl undressed in a corner, invisible to them. Being invisible seemed especially advantageous now, given how uncomfortable he was in the suit Alana had talked him into buying. He had lost a bit of his prison paunch walking the hills of Cliffside, but he was a fifty-eight-year-old man with a fifty-eight-year-old body. The suit made him feel ridiculous.

And he was fearful. Not of the water, but of doing something new. Though in a sense, everything he'd done since he'd gotten out was new. He'd had to learn how to wash clothes in a laundromat, buy a bus ticket, rent a hotel room, use a monitor. None of these things had he dreamed about, awake or sleeping, as he had pushing through water without effort or even much of a splash. So much of Austin was long lost to him, but he remembered the sight of swimmers sliding across the surface of the pool that was a pond with the same eerie detail as the girl on the swing set, the people at the edge of the woods, the voice of Merry Clayton rising in Tom's dark-in-the-daytime bedroom.

"Nice Jammers," said Alana. She was still in her street clothes.

"You're not getting in?"

"I don't need to."

She sat him down on some bleachers and quizzed him about his prior swimming experience. He couldn't remember when he'd learned to swim or who taught him but whoever it was did not know what they were doing, for he swam with his head out of the water like a dog.

"Did you learn in a pool or a pond?" The only pool he'd ever seen besides the Stovall parks and rec pool was a pond. Or a lake. Someone had the strange idea to pour concrete around it and call it a pool, but it was and was not a pool.

"Pond, I guess," he said.

"You don't remember?"

Earl had no idea how memory worked. Why did he remember the swimmers gliding above him when he could only rarely remember his father's face?

"Not really."

"Well, it doesn't matter. Let's go over the strokes."

They got up and stood by the pool. She had him move his arms. At one point she came around behind him to correct the angle of his elbow. Her touch was both confident and careless, without hesitation and with more force than he expected. Earl wondered if she liked women.

After thirty minutes of this, she had him get in the "training" pool. The water came to his waist. Tamara had him hold on to the side of the pool, extend his legs out, and kick.

She mimicked a scissors with her hands. "Harder and lighter," she said. "Relax your ankles. Let them flop. And kick from your core."

"My what?"

"Your stomach muscles," she said.

Then it was over. She went over what they would do next lesson as Earl dried himself with Alana's towel. Then she nodded at his tattoo.

"Where did you do your bit?"

Earl never took his shirt off in front of others. Because he'd had the tattoo for so many years, he no longer saw it.

"Paper clip and ink from a pen, right? Holds up pretty well for makeshift. I've seen far worse."

Mattox had given it to him. A dagger on his right rib cage. "I catch you with anyone else and you'll get a real one of these in the same place," he'd said.

"My dad's doing fifteen-to-thirty down at Salem," she said. "Boosting cars. He actually thought of himself as a car dealer. Had a card printed up. Of course, when I was nineteen, I had to go and marry a drug dealer. He owed a lot of money and disappeared. I mean *disappeared* disappeared, not lost. Now I'm married to an addict. Steph."

She was married to a woman? Earl was still adjusting to the news that grass was legal. In county, awaiting trial in 1974, he met a kid who was serving three years for two joints. Now, according to Kaiser, you walked into a store, a regular storefront with plate glass windows and parking spaces right in front, not some Quonset hut on the outskirts of town, and said to the clerk, I need something that's going to make me clean the house and be able to listen to classical music while I'm dusting and pick out the oboe, that's very important, and the clerk would slap a bag on the counter and ring you up.

Seemed to Earl like there was less and less to sneak around about. Still and always were the ways to lie and cheat. But now you could outright marry someone of your own sex and didn't have to hover in a culvert to get high. The two weren't the same—he understood that having to hide who you loved was not the same as carrying around a vial of Visine to clear your eyes before you went to class—but his experience with Tom was so linked to the goods that it seemed furtive, something he got away with, even though it had, according to Arthur, extended his sentence.

Earl also knew that he had liked some of what he'd done with Tom. Then there was the part he had not enjoyed, the part he was not sure he'd agreed to. Did he cry "No" or "Stop" into the mouths of Tina and Marcia? That he still did not know what he said or whether anyone heard him confused him even more, since everything else had come back to him in time, most of it so clearly that he could not disremember it.

Forty-four years gone and he still didn't understand what people now called their sexuality. He'd read an article in a magazine that explained that sexuality was only a concept, fluid in nature. He wished Arthur was around to hear this. He imagined what Arthur would say: try telling *that* to a jury not of your peers in Stovall, Texas.

Earl remembered Tina's aunt. Maybe she actually had been a lesbian. Tina never offered up any proof except that she wasn't married, which did not make you what they now were calling gay. She was surely dead, and if she was alive now and in her prime, Earl doubted she'd have sat in the pew of the Stovall Methodist church with her wife. Cliffside was a small town, but it was a world away from the Stovall Earl had known. This gay marriage deal struck Earl as more of a local option thing, like integration, or blue laws.

"Steph got sober in prison," Tamara was saying. "Prison saved her life, really. She never could have afforded rehab. When she got out, Alana got her a job and paid for her to go to a counselor. She gave her opportunities she never would have had otherwise. So let me tell you something, Earl. I'm not stupid enough to ask what you did. I can tell you made the best of your time. Otherwise you would be down at Annie's Saloon getting a lap dance, not here taking swimming lessons. But people come out all well-intentioned, don't they? Then they slide. Takes one bad day. Let's say that day comes for you. You know it will. You do one thing that even irritates Alana—I mean so much as leave some of your shit lying out in that garden she loves so much—and I'll come find you."

He pointed to his tattoo. "Same guy did this to me called me his 'prison wife.' When I went in, I was young and dumb and scrawny. I did what I had to or I would have died in there. You're lucky you have someone that *wants* to be your wife."

"I'm not into luck."

"Me neither. I'm talking about being with someone you can trust. I imagine after what Steph has been through, it's hard for her to trust people."

"They have a saying in the meetings she attends: 'Trust is gained in inches and lost in miles.' Might be a cliché—Steph complains about all their slogans being clichés—but it's true. And you're right. She has a hard time with trust. But I don't get how all this is supposed to make me feel better about you living in Alana's apartment. Talk about a trusting soul. I'm thinking she didn't run a background check on you?"

Earl remembered the references Alana had asked for. She hadn't mentioned them again, so he'd assumed she'd forgotten about him. He had never heard of a background check. He thought of his father's false claim to be Acadian. The family compound that sprung up when they moved across the line to Texas. Was this what they meant by background?

"If she did, what she found didn't bother her," said Earl.

"If she did, I'm thinking it would have bothered her enough to mention it."

Earl figured he might as well leave. Change back into his clothes, throw the embarrassing swim suit into the trash, head up the hill to pack his bag.

"She would have told *me* if she knew. She's a principled lady, Alana. She wouldn't have sent you to me if she knew something about you I needed to know. It's not that hard to find out. All she'd have to do is google you."

"I'm not on Google." Jade had taught him all about Google. He used it to look up things he heard that he did not understand. Like *sexuality*, though you had to be careful in the library with words like that.

"You'd be surprised. But back to trust. You lied to me the first time I ever met you. You said you had an excuse, but I never asked you what it was because I understand why you lied. Something about you makes it easy to trust. Maybe that spacey way you have about you."

Earl remembered his brothers, always singing "Ground Control to Major Tom" when he came into the room. He didn't exactly understand how this might allow someone to trust him, but he wasn't going to ask Tamara to elaborate.

"I trust you because Alana called me up to ask if I'd give private lessons to her tenant. She didn't say much about you, but I knew you were the same guy who came around to stare at my swimmers. I know even more about who you are now, but I'm not going to ask you what you did to put you inside for so long. You said you went in when you were young and scrawny and I can tell it hasn't been long since you got out. So it wasn't jaywalking."

"If I was to tell you I didn't do what they sent me up for, would you believe me?"

"No," she said. "Nobody in their right mind would either."

"It's your right not to believe me. I get that. A person can only trust so much. Trusting is not a right, it's a choice. I got more choices now than I've ever had, but my rights are limited. I can't vote. I don't want to run for office, sit on a jury, or buy a gun, but I'd like to be able to vote. I'd like to be able to tell the truth about my past, but in this case the truth seems less like a choice than a right."

"A lot has changed since you went in," Tamara said, "but we still got the Constitution. You have the right to tell anyone anything you want."

"It doesn't feel that way to me, but okay. There's a lot I'm allowed to do but that doesn't square up with what I want to do. I want to learn how to swim. I want to look out the window of my apartment and watch that bridge light up when the fog lifts. I want to listen to Alana talk. I like listening to her talk."

"Well, that's good, because Alana likes to talk."

"I'd never hurt her. I never hurt anyone to begin with. It wasn't like that."

Tamara put up her hands. "Hey, I'm not asking, remember?"

"Well, I'll ask you something. Are we square?"

"Long as you keep your end. You fuck up and there won't be any more lessons or looking out the window or listening to Alana talk."

"I'm not going to fuck nothing up," Earl said. "My end's tight." He stuck his hand out to shake on it. Tamara took his hand but instead of shaking it, she pulled it straight out.

"Extension, Earl," she said. "Extension's the key."

In the hours before dawn, Earl often stood by the window, looking toward the bridge. He could feel the fog beyond the plate glass, though he saw nothing but the aura of a streetlight down the block. But if he stood there long enough (and he could stand there for hours), the clouds would drift off and the world would appear, wet, strange, backlit by an invisible sun, and unobstructed by the tiny crosshatched wires that laced the windows he'd spent years behind. Lights would switch on in bedrooms, bathrooms, kitchens. Vibrantly would shine the red light of his mind. A man might appear, walking his dog, and Earl would note how people walked their dogs in the past tense, as if they'd walked them already. They were already at work, typing into monitors, or talking on telephones, or making loud coffee drinks. They were in another city, in a high-rise hotel, lying in the bed next to lovers who smelled of the free soap and lotion they'd take along when they checked out. Then the dog would quit sniffing a bush and yank the leash, bringing the walker back into the now. That was how time worked for Earl, too. He was tethered to it, but there was so often so much slack on the line.

Midmornings Kaiser came to fetch him for work, but he never knocked on Earl's door. Earl would hear him pull up in his Ford Ranger and know he was inside catching up with Alana, unless Alana was outside in her garden. Alana's garden: Flowers and ornamental shrubs and vegetables and herbs, everything mixed together. After the regimental years of the in-between, Earl found relief in the lack of order, but he could see how Jade, who told him that her favorite part of working at the library was shelving books and often, when they talked, reached over to straighten a magazine rack, would be bothered by it.

As for Kaiser, not much seemed to bother him. He wanted everyone to be happy. He was devoted to Jade and to Alana and especially to Waylon, who accompanied him everywhere, his head out the window, tongue dangling to catch a drop of rain. Earl would hear the ragged idle of the Ranger and then silence and he would come down to find Kaiser drinking coffee with Alana in the kitchen, Alana at the table with the paper spread out in front of her, Waylon at her feet on the floor, Kaiser leaning against the counter in his loose, rangy way, smelling faintly of weed.

The radio would be on in the kitchen, the all-talk station that Alana listened to for news, always bad, of the large orange president. She and Kaiser shared a passionate dislike for the fellow. When Earl had gone in, Jimmy Carter had been in office. He was not popular in Stovall but everyone back home admired Carter's brother Billy, who had his own brand of beer.

"Earl is not registered to vote," Alana told Kaiser one day.

"Earl, my man, we need you. You got to get with the precinct."

"It's on the list," said Earl.

At a certain point Alana would shoo them out of the kitchen, claiming she had somewhere to be, usually a yoga or pottery class, or a political meeting or a swim or the farmer's market or work in her garden.

"Alana keeps busy," Earl said on the way to the farm.

"Always, man. Runs circles around people half her age. You know she used to be a lawyer?"

Earl did not know this, but he wasn't surprised. She was blunt and kind and did not judge. He'd only known one lawyer and to this man he owed everything. He thought of all the talk he'd heard of lawyers in the in-between. They were almost as hated as C.O.'s. How was it he got to know the only two good ones in the country?

They met Jade on the muddy lane leading to the farmhouse. She was on her way to work. Waylon sat up and sang his aria at the sight of her.

"Go shelve those books, baby," Kaiser said. He reached out the window to take her hand. Earl had Waylon by the collar. He was attempting to jump out of the car.

"If only they'd let me shelve all day," said Jade. "Hey there, Earl. Don't let him work you too hard."

Earl was used to working eight-hour stretches for twenty-seven cents an hour, in windowless bunkers thick with floating fiber and the fumes of ancient, dangerous machinery—not to mention the noise, God the constant din of prison, the yelling and the blaring of music and the televisions turned up to talk shows and soap operas to drown out whatever illicit thing was happening on the block. . . .

Earl said he wasn't too worried. He must have said it in a way Jade found humorous, as there was nothing humorous about what he said. But he loved to hear Jade laugh, as her laugh was so like her mother's. He wondered what part of him came from which parent. His mother was a talker, and he was definitely not, though she could, if pressed or tired or attempting to prove a point (which, that day she found him in the woods, was that Tina was not the only woman on earth; though she was, Earl's first and his last), stop to listen. She also said things he remembered. He remembered *her*. His father gave him a radio and taught him words to the unofficial Anthem of Loneliness—midnight train whining low, whippoorwill too blue to fly—but otherwise he was like the dog walkers Earl watched from his window, past tense. He'd always talked to Earl as if he were elsewhere. Maybe this is where Earl got it: always elsewhere. This was his father's gift to him. He would have rather his eyes, or his laugh, or a similarity in the execution of certain letters in a crude cursive.

"No, you don't seem too worried, Earl," said Jade.

Jade and Kaiser said goodbye with their eyes. Kaiser parked the truck in the shed by the barn they rented out to strangers.

"Want some coffee?"

"I'm good," said Earl.

"Back in a sec."

Kaiser returned smelling of weed. Why hide it from Earl? He could care less. No one had ever hit him because they were high. Earl thought he'd smelled it coming from Alana's house a time or two when he'd passed by. A lawyer smoking weed? Why not? She wasn't a lawyer anymore. She took good care of herself, unlike Arthur, who might be alive still if he'd moved to Oregon and started dropping by the dispensary every morning instead of Sunrise.

They got to work, pulling dead runner beans from sticks they'd been tethered to. The vines were crispy and the work was satisfying. Earl wound the vine around his arm to drop in a pile Kaiser claimed he was going to burn off, if ever there was a day without rain.

"How's the swimming going, Earl?"

Earl thought of the moment, a few weeks back, when

Tamara had allowed him to put his face in the water, finally. Blow bubbles, she said. Earl became sunlight streaming through pulled-to blackout curtains. His hair was a nest of writhing eels. Tamara held his legs out lightly as he floated with outstretched arms. Then her touch was gone, and he was suspended, first in the water and then above the clouds that hovered over his new home.

"Good. I'm not going to drown but neither have they called me up asking me to try out for the Olympics."

"You never know, Earl. There have been some who've staged a comeback."

If Kaiser knew what Earl had come from, he wouldn't be using the word *back*. Earl would never go back. He ought not to have been in there for so long in the first place. He yanked hard at the vines, toppling the sticks they'd been tied to.

Kaiser noticed but either he was too high or too nice to say anything.

"Learning to swim is hard when you're old."

"You're not that old, Earl."

"Me? I'm mid-century modern."

"Well, no wonder Jade took to you. She's crazy about that stuff. I bought her an RCA Victor credenza console stereo for Christmas. Found it at a junk store in McMinnville. Spent three months restoring it. We'll go listen to it in a few. You like vinyl?"

"Used to," said Earl. "I got rid of all my records a long time ago."

"My old turntable's just sitting in the barn, man. You're welcome to it. We can go record shopping."

"I'd have to pay you for it," said Earl. He imagined having his own music, in his own apartment. Coming home from swim lessons, putting on a record, pulling his chair up to the window. Reading a book. Cooking a meal. Tired after a few hours of farm work, some laps in the pool, a long walk through the wet streets along the river. If this was the life he deserved, why did it make Earl feel like he was getting away with something?

6.

EARL HAD BEEN in Cliffside for a few months when Alana threw a dinner party. Earl went to the thrift shop to buy a button-down, collared shirt and some pleated grownup khakis, though the other guests—Jade and Kaiser, Tamara and Steph—came dressed as they always did. Alana wore her workout leggings and an oversized sweater, her gray-brown hair pulled back in a ponytail. Kaiser wore his stiff orange pants with many pockets and a hammer loop and his worn hiking boots. Jade wore a tank top, a skirt, and cowboy boots.

It was warm out, and sunny enough to eat on the porch. Everyone had wine but Earl and Steph. He avoided looking at her, but once he caught her eye and he saw in the way she looked at him that Tamara had told her. Well, they were married. Earl had heard married people did not have secrets, that love didn't lie, but he had no evidence of such from his parents.

Alana served fish wrapped in wax paper. Parchment, they called it. You didn't eat the paper. The only thing Earl could compare it to was a tamale, which his mother used to order from Sleepy T's aunt for Christmas. Sleepy T's aunt came from the Mississippi Delta, which Sleepy claimed was tamale central.

Earl was used to canned vegetables he'd eaten not only in the in-between but before. Alana served green beans and squash out of her garden, steamed, she said, which tasted half raw to Earl. Jade brought homemade bread with olives and tomatoes she said the sun had dried. Earl pictured tomatoes pinned to a clothesline, then forced himself to think of them drying by a river on boulders. He did not want to think, ever again, about a clothesline.

After the meal, Alana brought out a salad of just lettuce and dressing. Seemed to Earl she was serving things out of order, but he wasn't about to say anything. Steph and Tamara brought apple pie and ice cream. Earl had never thought to ask what he could bring. He'd never been to a dinner party. A party to Earl did not include food. Sometimes his daddy would grill some barbecued chicken for the drunken crew assembled nights by the shed, but no one came for the chicken.

Kaiser was telling the table about the records he and Earl had picked up on their rainy-day record-shopping sprees. He referred to records as "vinyl," which Earl found confusing, as if they might have started making them out of cardboard.

"Earl's picked up some gems," said Kaiser.

"Lot of stuff I used to own when I was a kid. I was surprised to find those albums still around."

"Everyone our age is cleaning out their basements, I guess," said Alana. "And these kids love the same music we do."

"Not this kid," said Jade.

"I found a Graham Nash record I loved back in the day," said Earl.

"*Songs for Beginners*?" Alana asked.

"I don't remember the title," said Earl, "but it's got that song where he talks about dining at someone's mother's house on whipped cream and wine on a Saturday night."

"'Make me feel good all the time,'" sang Alana.

"Whatever that means," said Jade. She started asking Earl questions about Texas. What part was he from? What was it like growing up there?

"It was right hot."

"Do you still have a lot of friends down there?"

Earl looked at Tamara. He wished she'd look away, but she studied him in the way she watched his rotation from the deck as he moved through the water.

"I haven't been real good at keeping up."

"Are there people you wish you'd kept up with?"

"Well, let's see. I guess Moonwalk, Burnt Cheese, Sleepy T."

Laughter from the entire table. Even Steph, who had surely come across some nick-named types when she was inside, found these names delightful. They made Earl repeat them.

"What about your family?"

"Parents are gone," he said. He did not know whether they were alive or not, but he knew for sure they were gone. "I got two brothers, but we were never close."

"Was your father from Texas?" Jade asked.

"He was Acadian," said Earl, preferring myth over Lawton, Oklahoma.

"Cajun?" said Alana.

Oklahoman who loved Hank Williams was the answer, but he'd gone with his father's lie.

"What's the difference between an Acadian and a Cajun?" Alana asked.

"Sounds like a joke," said Tamara. Earl didn't mind. He'd as soon make a joke about it at this point in the conversation.

"Not a whole lot as far as I can tell. I think Acadian just sounds better."

"What line of work was he in, your father?" said Jade.

"Oh, you know," said Earl. "Little bit of this. For a while, he was a surveyor," he said, remembering his mother once telling him his father had crossed a state line, and a lot of other lines.

"What about your mother? Did she work?"

"She was a telephone operator," said Earl. It wasn't a lie. She could operate a telephone the day long.

"I always wanted to be a telephone operator after I saw Ernestine on *The Muppets*," said Jade.

"Among other anachronisms upon which you set your precocious sights," said Alana.

"Among other who?" Steph said, which made Earl grateful for Steph's presence, for he had no idea what the word meant either.

"Out of place in time," Jade said. To Earl, this explained more than his mother's made-up occupation. It explained his entire life.

Tamara gave Earl homework: a book to read called *Total Immersion*. Earl found it surprisingly beautiful if not sometimes profound. He underlined sentences. "Above the waist, we're mostly volume; the lungs after all are just big bellows." "Press your buoy into the water and the water will press back." "Remember, your body in water is like an unbalanced seesaw, its fulcrum between your waist and your breastbone." He copied out his favorite sentences on Post-it Notes and stuck them on the refrigerator, the medicine cabinet, the plate glass window where he stood watching the world pass by while listening, over and over, to the Byrd's "Lover of the Bayou" and Blind Faith's "Had to Cry Today" on the stereo Kaiser had given him.

Putting the sentences into practice in the water was harder than copying them onto sticky yellow squares, but Tamara taught him to concentrate on one technical adjustment at a time (point of focus, she called it) instead of trying to do everything at once.

He wanted to do everything at once. His impatience only increased after Jade, one day at the library, showed him how to log onto something called YouTube on the monitors, where he could watch hours of little movies demonstrating the finer points of various strokes. Earl took to these movies the way others took to pornography, supposedly available widely and for free now on the monitors, another incredible evolution that had occurred in the in-between. The drive-in out on FM 315 had shown dirty movies after dark. Moon and Sleepy and Burnt Cheese had taken Earl and his brothers to see *Thar She Blows!*. Harpoons were featured. Because it wasn't dirty enough for Moon and them, back to the pines they went when *Deep Throat* and *The Devil in Miss Jones* double-featured for six months. The close-ups of twenty-foot genitals were terrifying enough to stave Earl off sex until here came Tina, walking through the forest.

In the water one day, he tried and nailed one of those fancy somersault turns he'd seen on YouTube. Tamara was not impressed. She said there was time to learn turns and that they weren't there yet. Point of focus. Regimen and order. He hadn't realized till now how much her lessons resembled the in-between, though it took months for him to swim three hundred yards (Tamara taught him to count yards, not laps) without stopping. He wanted to swim a mile without stopping.

"You're doing some things right," said Tamara, her version of praise. "It's funny how those things seem like moves you remember from another life."

"Well, I have had two lives," said Earl, opting not to tell her he'd been studying up on YouTube. "But I didn't know how to do anything in the other one but walk around and look at things."

"Most of us have had two lives," said Tamara. "Doesn't matter if you've done time. There are ways of doing time without getting arrested. Take Alana. She came to me for lessons when she was still married. But you would not have known her, Earl. She was nothing at all like she is now."

"So you knew her husband?"

"Still do. He's in and out of town. I see him around sometimes. Steph sees more of him. He comes to meetings when he's sober. He's gone out again, though. Been out for a while now."

"What was he like back then?"

"Same as now, except better looking. He's always been

charming and smart. But he is one of those who has a special skill at making you feel like it's all your fault. I grew up with a man like him. I guess there's an official medical term for it or whatever. Those terms don't do much good if you ask me."

Earl remembered the part in Arthur's last letter where he talked of this very thing. Elastic, he called the terms.

"Did he beat her?"

"Words are his weapons. As far as I know. She was taking lessons when they were at their worst. I saw her every week in a swimsuit. Seems like I'd have seen some evidence if he was laying hands on her."

Early on, Earl had caught Tamara staring at the scars on his forearm.

He was still awaiting trial when it happened. Three older guys in for holding up a Harley dealership held him down and burned him with cigarettes.

Earl thought about Mattox's bulk pushing him into his bunk, grinding his face in a pillow. He smelled of the foul hooch he made in his toilet. He hated Mattox. He had never hated anyone. He did not hate Tom because according to the court, Earl had made Tom up. He disappeared in his Karmann Ghia off of what the district attorney called the face of the earth. Earl tried to remember to ask Arthur what the world's face looked like. They found Tom's house and his fingerprints and even his goods, but since it was only Earl telling everyone that Tom did it, Tom was a ghost. Ghost hate was just smoke blown into the mist Earl knew was waiting for him outside of the rec center. Mattox was the one who taught him how to hate.

"You with me, Earl?"

"I want to learn the butterfly," said Earl, to get himself off the hate train.

"After you can swim five hundred yards free without stopping. Takes a lot of energy, the fly."

"Do people swim in the river?"

"Not on purpose. There are places way upstream where it's safe. But down here it's way too polluted. And the currents are treacherous. You might end up in Japan."

"I've never been to Japan."

"You might want to take an airplane over there."

"Never been on an airplane."

"It's not all that," said Tamara. "Good place to catch a cold."

"I don't believe in colds."

"What do you believe in?"

"Swimming downhill," said Earl.

"You're all talk, Earl." She pointed to the pace clock. "Two hundred yards of downhill swimming on thirty."

7.

FOR OVER A week it had been pouring. The weather came from Japan, according to Kaiser. Earl was confused by this. The river, should you jump in it, will carry you to Japan, but that's where the weather comes from?

"You can't farm and not know weather," Kaiser told Earl. He had greenhouses and grew hydroponic greens with grow lights, but some days there was not much to do inside. Kaiser picked up Earl for some rainy-day record shopping. They hit all the usual places, mostly thrift shops, junk stores, finally the record shops, which were overpriced but had boxes of cheap records beneath the bins, where Earl found the records he'd listened to in his youth.

In between stops, Kaiser took hits from a tiny pipe.

"Ever smoke dope back in the day?" Kaiser asked Earl.

"Some," said Earl. "Used to steal my brothers' dirt weed."

"Ever get caught?"

"They must have been too fucked up to notice. If they'd

caught me, they would have beat me silly. They were bad for that anyway."

"Were your brothers much older?"

"Two years. Twins."

"Damn. I have two older brothers and they'd pretty much mop the floor with me. But sometimes one would go against the other. I don't imagine that happened much with twins."

"Oh, sometimes they'd fight each other," said Earl. "But when it came to me, they generally agreed."

"Where are your brothers now?" Kaiser said.

"Last I heard, Oklahoma."

Kaiser, even high, knew when to back off. He had a carefree way about him always, but in fact he was a focused and tireless worker and an astute reader of disposition. How he could remain so sharp after so much pot was a mystery to Earl. Maybe he went to the dispensary and ordered up a strain that would allow him a pleasant numbness as well as a heightened perception of the emotions of all those he encountered.

"I need to go let Waylon out. You want to come back to the house and listen to our purchases, or you want to go to yours."

"Mine, I guess. Unless you need my help with something."

"Only thing I might need help with is staying awake so I can have dinner ready for Jade. Good napping weather."

"Sure is," said Earl, who was still maintaining his three to four hours of sleep routine from the in-between. He often took naps when he got home from helping Kaiser.

"Oh hell," Kaiser said when he pulled up in front of the

house. He nodded at a muddy Land Rover parked by the curb. "That's Winston's ride."

"Winston?"

"Jade's dad. Alana's ex."

"Is he not supposed to be here?"

"I think I told you what happened last time he showed up at our place."

"The fence, right?"

"That wasn't the worst of it. Should have heard the things he said to his own daughter. Of course, he was wasted. When he's sober, he's arrogant as hell, but at least he's sociable. He's a mean drunk, though, and he's been on a tear for a good while now. I better go in and check on her."

"Maybe it's better if I go, since he doesn't know me."

"That won't matter if he's drinking."

"I think I can handle it."

"I do need to let the dog out, and Winston's a talker. I appreciate it. You got my number if you need me."

Earl stood in the yard, watching the truck disappear into the mist. When its noisy rattle died down, he stood listening, but heard only soft rain on the hood of cars, the roofs of houses, the leaves of trees, his body. All day the rain had been intermittently heavy and slack. The sudden force of a downpour had excited Earl, who was still, after months in Oregon, a stranger to this much moisture, attracted to its moodiness, the way it made the harshest inside light soothing. But now it was distracting. He had his records stuffed up inside his raincoat and decided to drop them off in the apartment and come back down. He'd left the door open and was putting his records up when he heard shouting.

Earl decided not to knock, given the circumstances. He went around back and entered the house through the porch, which led into the kitchen. There he found them, faced off over the chopping block, Alana and her ex.

"Earl," said Alana, as if nothing were wrong. But she looked both relieved and slightly annoyed. He trusted the relief. He knew her to be willful. He figured she thought she could handle this on her own, as she'd likely been doing for years, according to Kaiser.

"Is this the lodger himself?"

Winston was soaked. His clothes clung to his skin and his hair was matted and dripping. He looked like he'd been standing for hours in the rain. Earl could see the rumored good looks, though they were fading into the ruddy slackness of late middle age. His hair was still thick and because of this he wore it to his collar, as if he were real proud of it. Or maybe he didn't care to spend money on haircuts. He wore jeans, work boots, a corduroy shirt that strained, even untucked, to cover his paunch. His eyes were a bright blue not often found on someone with dark hair and olive skin. He looked to be maybe the same age as Alana but a lot harder rode and forever put up as dripping wet as he was now.

"My name's Earl."

"I'll call you the lodger, since you've taken the rooms that were once my studio."

"That's been years ago, Winston," said Alana. "Fifteen, actually."

"'Time passes slowly when you're lost in a dream,'" sang Winston in a creaky tenor. Earl recognized the song: Dylan, from *New Morning*. He remembered a part of the chorus:

"Ain't no reason to go up, ain't no reason to go down / Ain't no reason to go anywhere."

"Can you still feel my energy up in those rooms?"

Earl had never heard anyone speak of leaving behind their energy, much less in a place. He felt Arthur's energy often, but only because he carried it inside himself. Likewise Tina, though sometimes, wandering around the forest at the edge of town or even walking along the river, her presence came to him, for it was woods where they met, and water where they explored each other's bodies.

"Sometimes I feel kind of anxious," said Earl.

"Stressful job?"

"Not really. I work for Kaiser. He's an easy boss, compared to others I've had."

"Is that how you ended up in my rooms? Kaiser's behind it?"

Earl had few rights, but one of them that he'd been born with, that he'd clung to through everything, was the right not to answer questions he thought were either irrelevant or nobody's business to ask. But this Winston didn't seem the type to allow silence where there might be noise. So Earl said no.

"How do you know Kaiser?" Winston said.

"Through Jade."

"And how do you know my daughter?"

"Enough with the interrogation," said Alana.

"Oh, I don't mind," said Earl, even though he did. He would rather answer silly questions against his will than leave this fellow alone with Alana. He couldn't tell how drunk Winston was, but he could tell by the way his words fell out of his mouth that he was not sober. Also one of his eyes was half-shut and the tail of his shirt had come untucked. It bothered Earl that it was the left eye and the right shirttail.

"I met Jade at the library."

Winston turned to Alana. "Did you check this guy out before you rented him my rooms?"

"Jade referred him. You don't trust your daughter's judgment? He's been a model tenant, by the way. Best I've ever had."

"Where do you come from, model tenant?"

Because he did not want to answer Winston's questions, Earl started to say he was from "all over." He'd heard others say this, though he had no idea what it meant. You had to have been born somewhere. Your people had to come from somewhere. Somewhere there were fields and rivers that called for you, or else a high-rise overlooking a train yard and overpasses, flyovers, billboards, trucks on the highway flashing silver in the setting sun. A city park or a sidewalk was no different from field or forest. You were from there and it was in you.

"I was born in Louisiana. Grew up just across the border in far east Texas."

"So not all over. I thought I detected some cracker in those vowels."

"Jesus, Winston," said Alana. "I don't think that's a thing you can say."

"No, it's okay," said Earl. He was surprised by Alana's thinking her drunk ex-husband, known to plow down his daughter's fence, cared about what you weren't supposed to say.

"So you don't like music?" Earl said. "You just sang a bit of Dylan, but you obviously don't like Dylan."

"What are you talking about? I worship Dylan. I cried when he won the Nobel."

"Without the South, which gave us blues, jazz, country, rockabilly, soul, and rock and roll, there would be no Dylan."

The argument sounded dubious even to Earl, though it came straight out of one of Arthur's letters, which often were more rant than letter. Arthur was talking about how tired he was of defending the place he came from to people who took for granted all the things they loved that would not exist were it not for the South. Music was just one of the examples, and the only one Earl remembered because Arthur and Earl talked a lot about music. Earl remembered Arthur going on about people he called "provincial ignoramuses." Most of them were from Stovall but there were a whole bunch of them in New York and California, according to Arthur.

"Okay, I get it, the South gave us lots of good music," Winston was saying, "but it also gave us racism."

Alana said, "Oh for God's sake."

Earl said, "I grew up in a tiny town. I heard a lot of name-calling. But there were Blacks living beside whites. Black people came to my house. They sat down to eat at our table. Since I've been in Oregon, I've seen maybe a dozen Black people."

"That doesn't mean we'd lynch them if they decided to move here. Or make them drink from a separate water fountain."

Earl smiled. "I believe you're talking about how things were fifty years ago. You claiming nothing's changed, especially if you've never lived there, just makes you sound ignorant."

"Who is this idiot?" Winston asked Alana. "What are you doing here, in this house? Why are you standing here right now?"

"I heard shouting. I came to check on Alana."

"Wait," said Winston. "You two aren't . . ."

"I'm her lodger, to use your term," said Earl, "but I'm also her friend. So no, we're not. But where I come from, you hear someone shouting at your friend, you go check things out."

"What's your last name, Earl? I'll tell you mine if you tell me yours. Mine is Mitchell. Winston Algernon Mitchell. You can look me up. Easy to do these days."

"You don't have to give him your name, or answer his questions," said Alana.

"No, you don't," said Winston. "But I'll find out either way."

"Well, I guess I'll be going," said Earl. "Unless you need me to stay," he said to Alana.

"She didn't need you in the first place. Besides, I'm going myself. I've got homework to do," he said, nodding at Earl.

"Well, it's been a pleasure," said Earl. He walked out into the rain, but instead of going to his apartment he started down the hill to the library. He was thinking he'd better get on the monitor and punch in his name so he could see what lay ahead. Or maybe he ought to just stay here and tell Alana everything. He hesitated in the middle of the road. The rain had been light but fell heavy again. A car came chugging slowly up the hill.

Headlights and noise were all he could make out. He moved out of its way, but not far enough to escape the spray kicked up by its passing. No matter. There was nothing he could do now to protect himself, from the rain or from what Winston would find out about him. Ain't no reason to go up, ain't no reason to go down. Ain't no reason to go anywhere.

8.

AT THE POOL, Tamara kept Earl busy with drills: catch-up, breath/kick/scull, one-arm freestyle, one-arm backstroke, swivel, corkscrew. After thirty minutes of this, Earl asked when he was going to get to swim.

"When I see some focus," said Tamara.

Earl kept quiet. Today he just wanted to swim. He wanted her to let him stay in the water for as long as he could stand. And he could stand to be in the water all night. Tamara would clock out, go home to Steph, fix some dinner, eat in in front of the news, drop Steph off at the Optimist's Club for her eight-o'clock AA meeting, hang out at the bookstore up the street, come back for her, home to bed. She'd be settling into her office in the morning drinking coffee and see, through the window looking out over the pool, Earl, still swimming.

Submerged, he did not think. Or if he thought, it was only what Tamara told him that he ought to focus on: the entry of his hand in the water, his extension, the height of his elbow, his recovery, his rotation. Today his point of focus—what had him so worried that he couldn't lose himself in single-minded pursuit of making Tamara proud, could not submerge himself in the glorious oblivion, was that Winston might find out about him and tell Alana—returned when Tamara said, "That's it for today."

"So no swimming?"

"Drills are swimming."

"You know what I mean."

"You need to show up to swim. You're not here today."

"Trouble sleeping," said Earl.

"You told me before you hardly ever sleep at night."

"Hardly ever and not at all—big difference."

Earl stood in the pool, both hands on the railing of the ladder. He lacked the energy to pull himself out. Tamara sat down on deck, between the railings, her feet on the top rung, facing him.

"Stay in if it makes you feel better. But no swimming."

"It's all I want right now."

"Okay. Good. But why?"

If there was anyone in this town he felt he could trust, it was Tamara, who had sussed out his secret after a glance at the fading dagger still threatening his ribs.

"That guy Winston."

"Fucking Winston makes *me* want to swim all day and I hardly ever get a workout in anymore. So, what? He's been coming around?"

"Yeah. Pretty sure he'll be back."

"Did it get ugly?"

"Never met the guy. Don't know what his ugly looks like. It was a few days ago. Too wet out to work so me and Kaiser went riding around, record shopping. When he dropped me off home, I heard some commotion coming from Alana's. I went to check it out. He was in the kitchen, hollering at her."

"Alana can handle herself."

"Well, that's not all. Winston got all upset about me staying in the apartment. Claimed it was his studio. He asked Alana did she check me out before she rented to me and when she said no, he wanted to know my last name. Said he was going to do some homework on me."

"Winston's known for his big talk. Not so much for his follow-through. Still, I guess you're worried about how Alana would take it if she found out the truth?"

"Well, yeah."

"I told you how she helped Steph. She doesn't judge. She was known for taking on cases no other lawyer will touch unless they were court-appointed. She didn't think too highly of court appointments. She'd help anyone who needed it, whether you had the money or not."

"I knew a lawyer like that."

"Did he judge you?"

"He made it clear how he felt about what I did. He couldn't *not.* That's just who he was. But no. He didn't judge me so much as he saw me for who I was and put what I did in some other part of his brain. His work side I guess you could say. He was the best friend I ever had. He left me money. Not a lot, but enough to live off for a while, until I can get something steadier than helping out Kaiser."

Tamara nodded. "I told you early on I didn't care what you were in for, so long as you were good to Alana. Alana's fond of you, Earl. Alana's complicated, but she presents herself as wide open. She'll talk to just about anyone, as you know. She's trusting but she's not dumb. She's suffered enough to know that people tell you what they want you to hear. But there's something about you that . . . I don't know, Earl. Jade saw it and Jade's less open-minded than her mama. I guess she gets that from her father, who's suspicious of everyone. I can tell you've treated Alana right, and I still don't care what you got sent up for. But if you do want to talk about it . . ."

"I didn't do it."

"Okay," said Tamara. She didn't laugh, as she once said she would if he said he was innocent. She didn't put her hands up in the universal gesture for hold up, now.

"At least I didn't do what they had me up for. This other guy did it. This guy Tom. She was my girlfriend, though. The girl who died. I was seventeen. She was the first girl I'd ever been with. Tom was older. Ten years or so, I can't remember. He was a drug dealer. We were at his place when it happened. I'd never done more than drink a few beers and smoke a little weed. Then I met Tom and he was generous with his product. Coke and hash but it was the crystal, really."

"Meth?"

"I guess. He just called it crystal. Some kind of speed. I

didn't know jack about drugs, but whatever he gave me, I took it. And then some. I was up for two days. Maybe it was three. I lost time. Time got lost. I lost Tina. She got up with some guy she knew from Houston. We were down in Austin and she just up and abandoned me. I was on my own when I met Tom and these three other girls. We ended up back at Tom's place. Man, we got into everything. Tom and me and this girl, I forgot her name, we went off together and then it was Tom and me and these two girls, and then, well, sometimes it was just me and Tom."

He studied Tamara's expression. She seemed unfazed.

"Then me and Tom went to find Tina. We found her with that guy she'd ditched me for. Tina was way more into drugs than I was. Soon as Tom mentioned the goods, she ditched the Houston guy and came with us. We were all sitting on Tom's couch wasted, I remember we were listening to *The Low Spark of High Heeled Boys*. Then the three of us were in bed together. Tom kept feeding both of us coke and meth and then he gave us both a 'lude. I never even heard of 'ludes. I thought it was spelled L-E-W-D until Arthur read my confession and corrected me."

"I know all about a Quaalude," said Tamara. "My ex, the drug dealer, was a good deal older than me. Daddy complex I guess. After he disappeared, I was tossing his stuff and found some of his notebooks from high school. Instead of taking notes he drew pictures of round pills that said Rorer 714 on them. You know, the way boys sit in class and draw pictures of their four-by-fours. Or naked girls. I had to ask my father what they were. Pretty sure they took them off the market a long time ago."

Earl wasn't listening. His point of focus was not on Tamara's ex-husband's high school doodling.

"I don't know any other way to tell the rest than to just say what happened."

"I believe I can handle it."

"First she and Tom went at it. Then she wanted me to join so she climbed on top of me. Then after a while we just drifted off. We were there and not there. Tom never took any 'ludes himself. He was trying to get Tina up on her knees, but she was too limp. So he laid down on top of her and pushed himself in her, but not where she was used to. You know what I mean?"

"Yeah," said Tamara.

"She said it hurt. She told him to stop. She started screaming, telling him no. He told me to shut her up but I couldn't. I always told Arthur I didn't know why I didn't do anything to stop him. I told Arthur I was as terrified of Tom as she was. And I was."

"I never told Arthur this next part. I never told anyone this. It was the look in Tom's eye. He didn't look angry. He just looked like it was a regular Tuesday. He looked at me like, I'm doing this for you, 'cuz. Because I had told him about finding her with Richie. She was screaming and he told me to shut her up, but I was so fucked up, I could not make myself move. I just lay there. So he grabbed a lamp off a bedside table and beat her head with it.

"But he never said he was doing it for you?"

"He didn't have to. I saw it in the way he looked at me. And I guess it doesn't matter. Because I was too fucked up to stop him, she died because of me. And so I felt like I deserved what I got."

"Which was what?" said Tamara.

"Thirty to life."

"And you served how long?"

"Forty-four."

"That's a long bit. You must not have behaved yourself."

"Model citizen. We're talking Texas. And her parents lived forever. Every time I had a parole hearing, they were there to keep me from coming home. They must've died because her sister started coming."

"What about Tom?"

"Tom? Tom disappeared. But first he put Tina in the trunk of my car. I was hiding out in the woods behind his house. He got rid of the body and the lamp, but both our prints were all over the bedroom. I waited until he was gone and then I got out of there. Well, first I took the rest of his crystal. I figured I needed it then more than ever. When I got home, they pulled me, because see, it wasn't even my car. I didn't have my license. My cousin had lent it to me, and he'd reported it stolen because I was a little late getting it back to him. I didn't know until they took me to jail that the trunk was filled with Tina's blood."

"They never found this Tom dude?"

"Arthur—that was my lawyer, he's dead now, everyone's

dead—figured he either made it to Mexico or got killed. Or both. *Disappeared* disappeared, like your ex-husband," Earl said.

"So they got you for accessory?"

"Murder one. Also kidnapping, even though she's the one asked me to take her to see her mother in Austin. Arthur wrote me a letter before he died apologizing for not getting me a better deal, but it wasn't his fault. It was more her parents were rich and I come from a long line of dirtbags. Also, it came out in the trial that Tom and I had done some stuff together."

"You mean the drugs?"

"Not that. I already told you. Sex stuff."

"Which had what to do with this girl's death?"

"This was 1973. In Texas. If I was perverted enough to get with Tom, who picked me up at a goddamn swimming pool, I was sick enough to murder my girlfriend. The jury looked at me and figured, he's a queer, he hates women. I did not hate women and I didn't understand how being a queer would make you hate women. I thought it meant you liked men."

"How did the law know what you did with Tom?" Tamara pulled her feet out of the water, moving back on the deck. Why? Was this the point where she changed her mind about him, saw him as others saw him, as he too often saw himself?

"I had a cellmate when they first put me in jail. I got to talking. I was exhausted and scared, and I talked too much. He went straight to his lawyer and told them everything I said so he could cop a plea. But it wasn't like they outright claimed

I killed my girlfriend because I was a faggot and wanted to be with Tom. The prosecutor didn't exactly introduce it as a motive because it wasn't something he could prove. But he made sure to let it slip in court that me and Tom did some stuff together. Arthur objected, but the jury heard."

Earl sank further into the pool. Telling the story made him want to go under and stay there.

"Tom was a fucking psycho. He killed Tina and then got up and did a few lines of coke and invited me to shower with him. Like there wasn't a dead girl in his bed. I heard him in the shower singing some song by the James Gang. The one that goes, "just turn your pretty head and walk away."

Open swim had started. An elderly woman wearing a saggy one-piece suit and a flowered rubber swim cap stood by, waiting to use the wide handicapped-accessible lane where Earl stood clinging to the ladder. Earl climbed out and followed Tamara into her office. He wrapped himself in a towel and sat on a plastic chair.

"I was seventeen, Tamara," he said. "And fucked up out of my mind. But that didn't mean anything to the jury. Hell, it didn't even seem like a defense to *me*. I didn't kill her, but I didn't stop him from doing it."

"Hell yeah, you ought to have stopped him. At the very least you ought to have called the cops as soon as he left the house. You know all this. But that guy, from what it sounds like, was going to kill her anyway. Or you, or some other girl. You fucked up, you know you fucked up, but you didn't kill her. I believe you when you say you didn't kill her."

Lead Belly had astonishing musical ability and they let him out of Angola knowing he'd killed a man, but Earl couldn't play anything but a record. He wasn't even good at turnstiles anymore. He was creek mud.

He looked up at Tamara. "*Why* do you believe me?"

"Because you're no killer."

"That's what Arthur said."

"Arthur sounds like a good lawyer."

"Isn't a good lawyer one that gets you off?" Not that Earl blamed Arthur, who did his best given the time and the place and Earl's coming from a compound of drunk cousins and junked cars, a phone with a busy signal and a clean glove compartment.

"It doesn't sound to me like you wanted to get off," said Tamara. "But maybe I meant Arthur sounds like a good person. Like Alana is a good person. I can't predict what she'd say if she heard what you just told me. But I believe she'd think you did more time than you deserved."

Earl nodded. He'd soaked the chair with his wet suit. He bit the end of a towel. He thought he'd feel better after telling Tamara, but he just felt wet and small and old.

"But Earl," Tamara was saying. "Listen to me, now. You got to tell this to Alana before Winston does. If he goes snooping around, all he's likely to find is what you were charged with and how much time you served. Maybe he'll come across a couple of old news articles, which from what you've told me won't be including your side of the story. Tell Alana what happened just like you told me. Let her decide. Don't let Winston blindside her. It's not his business and it's not his story to tell."

9.

EARL LEFT THE pool and started walking. He walked down to the river, then alongside it. He passed the Lamplighter and thought of how much his life had changed since he'd met, by chance, Jade, Tamara, Alana, Kaiser. Earl didn't believe in fate or luck, but getting off the bus on a hunch when he woke from a half nap into the foggy mystery of Cliffside—what might this be called?

He remembered his earliest days in Cliffside, the late-night walks through empty downtown, trips to the all-night grocery store, the halting conversations with the night-shifters. For a while he hung out beneath the bridge, listening to the rumble of traffic, watching the birds nesting in the girders high above him. What difference did it make that Tamara believed him? Earl had spent decades thinking of himself as a horrible person. It was hard to switch his thinking and also it seemed preferable to the victimhood he encountered in all but a few of the men he knew in the in-between. He'd rather be mad at himself than some rigged system. If you spent all your time blaming everyone else, how could you prepare yourself to die?

One day he sat on a log in the pines. Now here he was on the banks of a river spilling into the Pacific.

Earl missed: *His Life and Times*, Arthur, pedal steel.

He did not miss: *Low Spark of High Heeled Boys*, ants on a log.

He missed the Earl who was surprised by and wary of the red mouths of love singers.

Where was the Earl who could find an abandoned shipyard where tugboats rusted at a tilt, in waist-high sea oats? Sometimes he searched for the cord from his mother's phone, snaking its way beneath bayou and wood, crackling with desperation and desire. He looked for it in the sky sometimes, in the lines sagging between poles climbing the steep streets, as if his mother's words had followed him across the country and like the Wichita Lineman, he could hear them singing in the line.

Could he miss the father he had never known? He was glad his father had given him a transistor radio rather than a generic pocketknife.

Did he miss Time? In his youth it was syncopated, attuned to the rhythm of whatever song was stuck on repeat in his head. So Earl, guided by the rhythm, went here and did this. People popped up and said things out of the corners of their mouths. There were a dozen ways to take everything anyone said. You took it as it came, because one thing did not lead to another. Earl and his people communicated by riff, barb, counterpart, the negative adjectival. Take a basic song structure and wing in, on a westerly breeze, a few bars of pedal steel. There goes your heart, struggling to stay in rhythm and about to bust out all at once.

From his hideaway beneath the bridge, Earl watched a posse of teenagers doing skateboard tricks in the waterfront park. What, for these kids risking concussions on their skateboards, was the equivalent of pedal steel? He'd listened to some of their music. He admired the skill of many rappers but the rest of what he heard on the radio still reminded him of garbage food from a chain store. Earl understood that drummers were always drunk and sometimes did not show up, but why replace them with a machine? And why even write a song without a guitar solo? "Ride Captain Ride" was a throwaway song, memorable only because it involved exactly seventy-three men and a mystery ship, but it had a righteous guitar solo.

Back home he found Alana in the garden. It was dusk and drizzling. She wore jeans, her gardening boots, and a hooded sweatshirt.

"Listen," she said. "About Winston."

"It was no problem," he said. "I hope I didn't intrude."

"What you did was very considerate. But as unhinged as he seems, he's not going to do anything to me or anyone else. He was a good man until he wasn't. I mean, I guess there's still good in him. I don't believe that part of him went away. Do people change? I hope so, but at the same time I just don't know. Our eyesight worsens. We're said to lose an inch or so of height by age sixty. They claim your taste buds change but I still like almonds. I've always liked almonds, my parents should never have introduced me to them because they're not cheap. I will never come around to pickles or pretzels. As for Winston, well—Jade still feels like there's something she can do to help him. They have a term for it, applied broadly and at every opportunity. Enabler. Or maybe it's codependent. No, she's not codependent—-I certainly was, and before it was cool, of course. But she probably enables her father."

"Elastic," said Earl.

"Sorry?"

"I was just thinking of something Arthur said about all these terms they have for describing people's behavior and their mental state and all. He said they were so elastic they didn't really mean anything."

"Arthur sounds perceptive. Was he a relative?"

"Friend. Closest one I've ever had."

"And are you in touch with him still?"

"Arthur's dead. He wrote me a letter from what I guess you'd call his deathbed. A lot of it was descriptions of the superhighways of Houston. The downtown lights. Bridges and overpasses. Something called a flyover."

"He sounds poetical, your Arthur."

"He got that way toward the end, I guess. Just before the biscuits took him out."

"Biscuits?"

"Ham and egg and cheese, every morning of his life. Plus he liked to take a drink."

"Were you classmates in Texas?"

"Well, he definitely schooled me. He was the only teacher I ever trusted."

"Good teachers are rare. I had a couple of good ones and a lot of duds. When I became a lawyer, I learned that most good cops retire after twenty years, when they come into their pension. I decided that all teachers have an expiration date. All of them end up saying the same things to a different audience. They should be forced to retire after twenty years with full benefits for life."

Earl didn't know what benefits were. He knew he had some—Arthur was a benefit to him, as was Alana herself—but he did not think that was what she was talking about. It didn't matter with Alana. There were no turn signals in her conversation. Lawyering, in Earl's opinion, required a logically constructed argument. Maybe she was able to switch it on and off. Like the wildly varied rain of Oregon was Alana's brain. But Arthur had been like that, come to think of it. He could be doing his lawyer talk and swerve off on a side road dead-ending with the Tulsa Sound.

"Do you want to come up and listen to some music later," said Earl. "I just scored a copy of *The Zombies Greatest Hits*."

"'You're not teaching me a new thing,'" sang Alana.

"'Whenever you're ready,'" sang Earl.

Earl climbed the stairs to his apartment. He had to grab the railing, as he was shaky. He was going to tell her. But where to start? When the country love singers opened their red mouths in the shadowy woods? When his mother came upon him in the forest and beseeched him to listen to nothing and he heard, instead of nothing, the wide world. Had he only heeded his mother and not fallen for the first thing that strolled past him in the forest, he might have seen more of that world.

Though he'd seen more of it than he'd thought. He was seeing it now, outside his window, the swooping clouds shrouding the tips of stately conifers. What a privilege it was to reside among the clouds like the monkeys in the treetops of South American rain forests. He knew all about these monkeys because, in the in-between, nature shows were the third most popular viewing fare, after reality shows and soap operas. It made sense that men confined to concrete boxes for the brunt of their lives would want to watch golden-hour shots of backlit giraffes munching leaves in the Serengeti. Earl liked these shows best and had he hated them he would not have said so because the most dangerous thing you could do besides snitch was to change the channel in the common room.

And here he was in the clouds. There were no monkeys, but the Zombies were there, singing "Tell Her No." Here came Alana, clomping up the stairs in her Wellies, filling the air with no's. "Tell her no, no, no."

She was carrying a bottle of wine. Earl found a jelly glass and then apologized.

"Jelly glasses are for wine, not jelly," said Alana. "Besides jelly, what is your favorite food?"

"When I was a kid I was partial to Funyuns."

"You talk a lot about when you were a kid. You must have had a happy childhood. But really, Earl? Funyuns?"

"They taste good when you're shooting pool."

"Let's go shoot pool! Everyone in this town plays pool. I used to meet a lot of my clients at the pool hall. Instead of house calls I made pool hall calls."

"You and Arthur, y'all would have got on."

"I'm sorry I never got to meet him."

"He left me some money. He didn't want it to go to his sister. She married a cop he didn't care for."

"There are cops and then there are cops. I realize one might argue, conversely, there are plumbers and there are plumbers. But I worked with cops, not plumbers. Anyway, back to these Funyuns. How about real food?"

"Welsh rabbit."

"Jade mentioned you were fond of it. I have never had it. Jade explained that it does not involve rabbits."

"Naw, it's mostly cheese toast. I'll fix it for you sometime."

The Zombies sang about the way she walked and the color of her hair. Earl thought again about Tina. If a love song came on the radio, if the singers opened their red mouths and went on about a love that they were going to get to the bottom of or die trying, if there was a she or even if it was a girl singing about a he, Earl pictured Tina. If the singers claimed her voice was soft and cool they were talking about Tina. If they said no one told them about her, the way she lied? Talking about Tina.

"Are you going to join me, or do you always abstain?" said Alana, holding up her glass.

He had not had a drink of alcohol in over forty years. Hooch was plentiful in the in-between but the penalties for drinking or drugging inside were severe and Earl did not feel he deserved numbness.

"I'm good," he said.

"Suit yourself," she said.

The Zombies said what time it was. It was the Time of the Season.

"You know Arthur, he was a lawyer," Earl said.

"I did not know. I thought he was your teacher."

"He was both, I guess."

"Speaks well of him. What sort of lawyer was he?"

"I guess you call it criminal?"

"That was my bailiwick."

"I never asked Arthur this, so I'm going to ask you—"

"Is it difficult to defend someone when I know they have done something despicable?"

Earl said, "You took the words right on out. They had yet to even make it to my mouth."

"Number one question I get asked," Alana said. "After someone cracks a lawyer joke."

"I don't know any lawyer jokes."

"Good. So there's the answer you hear on television. Everyone has the right to a fair trial, etc. You've heard that one, I'm sure."

Not likely on shows about cloud-dwelling monkeys, but Earl nodded anyway.

"That's not wrong. I believe it. But here's the thing I have never admitted. The kind of virtue that comes from taking violent criminals off the streets and putting them in boxes? That is not a virtue I covet. I think it has to do with ambiguity. I knew a few prosecutors who could see beyond guilty or not guilty. But most of them—and a whole lot of judges—really, really want to be right."

"It seems like they ought to change the title of 'judge,'" said Earl. "Since, I mean, we are not meant to judge each other. I think it says that in the Bible."

"Except we do judge. I know I do all the time. When I was working, I came across people I knew needed help, but some of them disgusted me. I judged them even though I suspected that they had been taught to take advantage of everyone and everything."

"Users," said Earl.

"I could write a User's manual," said Alana.

Outside they heard the rattle of Kaiser's truck. It was too late to tell her now. He would have to wait. Time was never so bothersome in the in-between. People thought of life in prison as a ticking clock, everyone scratching out days on the walls of cells like the Count of Monte Cristo or old Robinson Crusoe. Earl saw no need to keep track. A calendar would have compounded the hurt. If he was at all inclined to consider time, it was to remember the music of his youth. Instead of scratching days on the walls of his cell, he wrote out guitar solos on sheets of a sketch pad. Mostly they were jagged but in the case of "While My Guitar Gently Weeps" the notes were curves stretching like hills into the horizon. Mick Taylor's solo in "Time Waits for No One" was a staircase. You got to the top and then started up again. When you reached a landing, down you came.

"Company coming," said Alana. She got up from their perch by the window and went out on the stair landing. "Yoo hoo," he heard her calling. "Come listen to the Zombies with us."

Jade and Kaiser took their shoes off by the door. One did it always at their place and Alana's. It was a Cliffside custom, Earl figured.

Jade said to Alana, "I have been trying you for hours."

"I am gloriously unplugged. You should try it. It's liberating. Like burning your bra."

"Okay, mom," said Jade, eyeing the jelly glass, the level of the wine bottle.

"I wasn't quite old enough to burn my bra. When they were burning them, I wasn't wearing one."

Alana turned to Earl. "Were you old enough to burn your draft card?"

"I just burned bridges," said Earl.

"We mostly burned joints," said Alana.

Kaiser asked Alana if she'd really lived in a tree. He seemed his usual loosely composed and shaggy self, but Jade appeared anxious. Her nose ring was twitching.

"Dad's back," Jade said to her mother. "We need to talk."

Well, that was it. Earl had wasted the time he should have spent telling Alana who he was and what he'd done, instead of talking about Funyuns and teachers and cops. Winston had gone to Jade and Jade had come to warn her mother. Why else would she have been trying to call her mother for hours? Jade had not even glanced at Earl. Therefore she knew everything.

If Alana was going to kick him out, if he were going to lose everything again, he might as well have a drink. Drinking was never the problem. The goods were what he needed to avoid. Alana was not likely to pull out a bag of crystal, or coke, or a Quaalude, which Tamara said were extinct.

Earl poured himself a splash. Pinot Noir it was called. Apparently Oregon was known for it. In the jelly glass it looked a little watery. He tasted it. It put him in the mind of a Worcestershire.

"He was over here the other day," said Alana. "Talking nonsense. He's so much more provincial than he was when I was with him. Or maybe he always was and I just didn't notice. There is a lot you don't notice. Anyway, guess what? We're all going to go shoot some pool at Off Track."

"Awesome," said Jade. "Your old office."

"As I recall, you liked their hot dogs."

"I didn't know any better."

"Maybe they've converted to humane slaughter. Have some wine! Earl, change the record."

"I thought we were going to Off Track," said Jade.

"We're tailgating," said Alana. "I think it is what your generation calls a preparty."

Kaiser said to Earl, "Man, I've never seen you imbibe." Earl shrugged, which he only did if he did not know what to say. He found more jelly glasses and emptied the bottle. It was tasting less like Worcestershire and more like a warmth in the tummy radiating to the head via the extremities. Soon it would reach his tongue. His tongue would thicken but his head would fill with words he needed to get out. His tongue would attempt to prevent this from happening. Words would back up for miles, as if there was a wreck on the highway halting all traffic. I heard the crash on the highway, sang a voice from Earl's youth, one of his father's friends in the yard beside the wormy chestnut shed. But I didn't hear nobody pray.

Earl put on Derek and the Dominos. Alana sang along loudly to the chorus of "Why Does Love Got to Be So Sad?"

Kaiser, who had issues with stillness, drummed wildly on the arm of the couch.

"Do you have anything post 1990?" Jade asked. She did not share her husband's retro taste in music. If her father had told her, if she knew, why was she making a request that would keep them in the company of a convicted murderer? Or maybe she didn't know and Earl could wait and tell Alana after he'd had another drink himself and she'd had more than a few.

"When you were a little girl, you loved Bill Withers," said Alana. She sent Kaiser down to her kitchen for more wine. The valid question of the sadness of love continued to be asked in his absence, both in word and in sound.

Jade said to Alana, "I really need to talk to you."

"Do you want me to leave the room?" Earl asked. He could just walk away from all this. All he needed were his traveler's checks and a change of underwear. In the in-between there was never clean underwear. Now he had gotten used to it, and to clean sheets, and to walking away without anyone shooting at him.

"Of course not," said Alana. But Earl got up and went to his bedroom, for he could see that Jade wanted him to leave the room. Was she looking at him oddly? Was her nose ring really twitching? He left the door ajar and stood frozen by the bed. He could hear Jade lecturing her mother about keeping her telephone with her at all times.

"I just needed some quiet time, Jade," said Alana, the sadness of love in her voice.

"Well quiet time is over, apparently."

Kaiser returned with the wine. Earl came out of his

bedroom. He went into the kitchen and watched Kaiser uncork a bottle of wine. He'd never seen anything so troublesome to open.

"Let's call Tamara and Steph and tell them to meet us at Off Track," said Alana. "Tamara has her own cue stick," Alana told Earl.

"No doubt," said Earl.

"I might have to break the law when I find you," sang Eric Clapton.

"I don't know that a dive bar is a safe space for Steph," said Jade. She was not everyone's mother. Just her mother's mother. And sometimes Earl's mother. And Waylon, of course.

"Where's Waylon?" asked Earl, his thick tongue slowing his already sluggish speech.

But no one answered because Alana was telling a long story about an ex-boyfriend who left his cue stick in the back of a taxi on his way to a Skylab party on the wrong side of Capitol Hill in Seattle. Then she was talking about the day Mount St. Helens blew. Then she was back on the Skylab story. The ex-boyfriend had won a sizeable kitty by correctly guessing that Skylab would land in the Australian outback. Actually, it wasn't a guess, said Alana. She had her hand in it. A huge map of the world had been painted on a basement wall of the house where the party took place. Guests put dollars in a hat and stuck pins in the place where they thought the rocket might plummet. Alana took off her bandana and tied it around her ex-boyfriend's eyes. She guided his pin to a nothingness near Perth. The kitty was enough for her ex to buy himself three new cue sticks to replace the one he'd lost, top of the line, plus a gram of coke. After filling his pockets with dollars and scoring some coke, he called a taxi. Who should show up but the same cabbie, who had secured the cue stick in his trunk for safekeeping. He had planned to return it, he said. The ex-boyfriend was filled with love of his fellow man and buoyed by his good luck (for which Alana got no credit, but she did get to share the coke), he persuaded the cabbie to let them treat him to dinner at the original Ivar's, on the pier.

"This is the dude you lived with in a tree?" Kaiser said.

"Another dude, Kaiser. Not a tree hugger. This one would not humanely slaughter a french fry. Also he was rather dim, since even in my coked-up fog I figured out that the cabbie was never going to return the cue stick."

"How come I've never heard this story?" Jade asked. Earl suspected it might have something to do with the coke snorting. If he had a child, what would he tell it of his past escapades? Surely his father had fallen a time or two into the briar patch that was Lawton, Oklahoma. Otherwise, why claim to be Acadian? This wasn't anything he needed to outright state. Earl gathered it from the cleanliness of his dashboard and from his tales of holding up a transistor radio to his ear under the cover of a blanket at night, protected from the elements outside and inside, music from Matamoras his only solace. Earl had once thought this tale romantic, but now that he was thirty-some odd years older than his father was when he told it, he saw it as midnight train whining low, bird too blue to fly.

But Alana was back to Mount St. Helens, which also involved strategic use of a bandana, this time a wet one to keep from inhaling ash. Another ex-boyfriend was mentioned, as well as a justice of the peace named Vernon Love who rode a Harley. Earl lost the thread while attempting to distinguish between the solos of Allman and Clapton in the soaring outro of "Why Does Love Got to Be So Sad?" Of course a song about the sadness of love must be so beautiful you will flat-out die trying to get to the bottom of it. Alana's Mount St. Helens story now seemed to have moved to Moscow, Idaho. Kaiser asked again if this was the tree house pot-grower dude.

"You are never allowed to ask that question again," Jade said to Kaiser. Then she turned to her mother and said, "Sometimes I get it, why you and dad got together."

"I really don't want to hear about your dad today, Jade," said Alana.

Jade put her hands up in the manner of Tamara when Earl tried to tell her, after that first lesson, that he was innocent. He remembered the story he shared with Tamara while standing waist-deep in the pool. He was wet and tired, and his heart was filled with terror. Kaiser was pouring wine into his glass. Earl's face was toasty. A muscle in his bicep twitched. He began telling Kaiser how *Tres Hombres* was recorded in a studio in Tyler, Texas. This meant nothing to Kaiser, so he explained that Tyler was his choice for where to drop the atom bomb, if they still had such a thing. There are two churches in Tyler for every one hundred people, said Earl. Also it is dry. You mean as opposed to here? Kaiser said. Earl knew nothing of Skylab. He had heard Alana talk before about Mount St. Helens and he had looked up pictures on the monitor of what it looked like after the volcano exploded and to Earl it resembled how Tyler, Texas, ought to look after they drop the bomb on it. No, Earl said to Kaiser, I mean they don't allow alcohol sales. At all? said Kaiser. You have to drive to the next county, Earl told him. Dude, that is messed *up*, Kaiser said. Hold it right there, I got to change the record, said Earl, for even though everyone was talking, he needed music in the background. He put on *Best of Cream*, then came right back to his conversation with the ever-patient Kaiser. I went out with this girl whose best friend was a roadie for ZZ Top, said Earl. Me and this girl were going to get a job at a water park. We were going to get our GEDs and live in an apartment with a balcony in Houston. One day we took off in my cousin Leif's car. Leif was not his real name. He stole it from a teen idol who supposedly stole it from a Viking. There's a history lesson in there somewhere. Anyway, we were going to see this girl's mother, who was locked up in the Texas state hospital for the insane. What happened to this girl, Kaiser said. Someone was climbing the stairs. The door burst open, and Alana hollered Hooray! Tamara stood there, her forever calm self. Alana asked after Steph and Tamara said Steph thought it best to stay home with the dogs. I thought we were going to meet at Off Track, said Jade. I believe a designated driver is in order, said Tamara. She looked at Earl and then into him. She saw alcohol running instead of blood through his veins. She saw his tongue lying like a sleepy toddler inside his mouth. She saw his shame and she saw his memories: strolling about the piney woods of Texas with Tina. Hiking in the hill-country woods, a path above the Pedernales where Tom leaned him against a tree and went straight to town. Tom blew through stop signs and stoplights like an emergency vehicle, lights flashing, siren keening. This train's on its way to Off

Track, Alana was saying and then she was out the door. Earl looked around the room as his apartment emptied of people. Album covers strewn across the floor. Glasses everywhere. On the coffee table four bottles of wine, two of them half full. They left the house wide open with a black disc spinning a song about a white room with black curtains in the station.

10.

OFF TRACK WAS down in the industrial flats south of town, fronting the river, a stretch of warehouse and salvage yard by the piers. Earl knew the place by sight, as during many the late night stroll he had seen, through the socked-in streets, the blinking beer signs in the windows. Tamara drove a truck, so they'd all piled into Alana's Volvo. Order in the court, called Tamara, when a fight broke out about what station to listen to. For a while in the car, Earl came back from also elsewhere. He was in the back seat with Jade and Kaiser. He was aware of Jade and Tamara, of how something had settled in them, a separation. Had someone taken a photo of them that night, Jade and Tamara would be in shadow. Earl had heard Kaiser talk about something called mindfulness. Earl was mindful of the blue bottom of the pool. He would spend an hour there every day for the rest of his life, a vessel, defying the natural inclination of man to sink. He saw himself swimming alongside the car as it coasted down the hill toward the river. Then he was swimming in the river. They would have the pool to themselves. Tamara surely had the keys to the pool on her person. Jade could look out for the rest of them, for Earl knew already that they were working against, instead of with, the water.

But then they were there, inside the bar, and it was dark and smelled of poolroom: chalk, spilled beer, forever odiferous bathrooms, short-order cooking. The music was loud and ugly, but it was drowned out by applause and cheers: Alana! She knew everyone in the place. These are her people, Jade explained to Earl. You mean y'all's kin? Jade smiled for the first and last time that night. No, her clients. She's gotten half of them out of jail. Kept the other half out. Alana went around the horseshoe-shaped bar, hugging everyone. The bartender produced a bottle of wine and poured her a glass. Earl noticed that there were two types in this bar: the obvious regulars, who clapped and cheered at Alana's arrival, and a contingency of younger folks who knew Kaiser and Jade. The younger crowd was mostly male, bearded, flannel-shirted. They don't seem to belong to this bar, said Earl. That's because they're here ironically, said Jade. They think drinking in a "dive" bar, among the people, makes them cool. Earl was confused. Kaiser handed him a tall, sweaty can of Pabst Blue Ribbon. Jade pointed to the can and said, Also ironic. They're really beer snobs, but they want to fit in. What was a beer snob? Earl wanted to understand but Alana was calling everyone over to the corner of the bar, where she had commandeered the jukebox. Some true gems on here if I remember correctly. Jade said she doubted her mother's memory of anything that ever happened here was correct. Earl did not understand why Jade was being so harsh. Get in here and help me pick, said Alana, pulling him to the box. The selection was surprisingly good. Merle Haggard, Waylon Jennings, Bobby Bare. They fed dollar bills into the machine instead of quarters. Earl called out numbers while Jade, who had had only one drink and was still dexterous, punched them in. A-7, E-9, G-12. Someone at the bar called out Bingo! Someone else called "Play something slinky!" Steve Miller's "The Joker" came on, and everyone at the bar (but not the ironic outer fringe, Earl noticed) sang along with the line "Some call me the space cowboy." Then it was "Blue Bayou" and the pedal steel swept over Earl. Alana reached for his hand. He was already swaying so what was the difference? He had not touched a woman since he'd held Tina's bloody head in his hands. Tamara sometimes adjusted his elbow and held him in the water before releasing him into buoyancy but that was work and there was nothing coming off Tamara that reminded Earl of the fact that he had not even embraced a woman in over forty years. Winston had asked if he and Alana were together and he'd quickly said no, but it wasn't because he had never thought about it. If he took her hand and put the other on her shoulder and so much as twirled her around, she would know by his touch the decades of deprivation and also, lurking beneath it, the remnants of desire. She stood waiting for him, among the fishing boats with their sails afloat.

Nothing would happen but a turn around the dance floor. He was not fueled by goods and there was nothing inside of him that had ever wanted to hurt Tina or any woman. The booze had loosened not only his tongue but his body. He felt limber if not liquid. He remembered holding Tina in the black water of a pond, her naked breasts against his chest, her wet hair tossed like seaweed across his shoulder.

Out of the crowd of her admirers came a woman in an ankle-length down jacket, green hair and very few teeth. She grabbed Alana's hand. She was in need of urgent legal counsel it seemed. Kaiser tapped Earl on the shoulder and asked him if he wanted a break. They went outside with a couple of Kaiser's friends. Kaiser pulled out his pipe, packed and passed it. Earl, ashamed of the memory of fucking Tina in an East Texas pond lit only by the moon, did not hesitate when it came his way. After two hits his hearing was extraordinary. He heard sleigh bells, then the flushing of a toilet. The engine of a tugboat chugging to life somewhere upstream. A radio station out of Matamoros, Mexico that his dad listened to under the covers at night. Kaiser introduced his friends and Earl shook their hands. They call me the Clothesline. He pointed to Kaiser. This is my associate, the Clothespin. He hangs with me all the time. He launched into a lecture on the negative adjectival. He had been here before. These people knew and liked him. Where the folks are fun and the world is mine on Blue Bayou. They filed back in the bar to the cowbell intro of "Honky Tonk Women." Alana was huddled in a corner by a pool table with the agitated woman with greenish hair and scant teeth. At the bar Earl ordered a beer and got into a long chin-wag with a regular about Merry Clayton's solo on "Gimme Shelter." The fellow was about Earl's age and knew what he was talking about, though when Earl said that Merry Clayton suffered a miscarriage attempting to hit the highest notes, the fellow, who introduced himself as Buck, said that was bullshit. The true story was that Keith Richards poked her in the ass with a safety pin to make her hit the high notes, which were "rape," Buck said, and "murder."

Merry Clayton was singing in Tom's bedroom. Tina wasn't there yet, but it didn't matter. She was on her way.

Earl went to the bathroom and looked in the cloudy mirror. He was old, drunk, foolish. He was sure Kaiser's friends were making fun of his accent. Where's your Clothesline, Clothespin? they were probably saying to Kaiser whose laughter was not *with* Earl.

He left the bar and started walking. Tamara caught up with him a half-block away. She must have been watching him.

"Where are you off to?"

Earl opened his mouth to tell her, but a train appeared. The blue light was my baby, the red light was my mind. The noise of its passing pushed Pause. Earl's mouth moved and out came nothing. Tamara's mouth moved and nothing. They stood in the wind of the passing train, leaning toward each other, conversing with the sound turned down. Then the train was rocking down the tracks and the silence it left made Earl dizzy.

"Well, you're a grown man," said Tamara. "Just be careful. I need to look after Alana. She rarely gets this wasted. Anything happen to set her off?"

"We listened to the Zombies?" Earl said. He was trying to think what else. He'd always been trying to think what else.

"How long has it been since you've had a drink?" Tamara asked him.

"I can't count that high."

"Well, like I said. You're a grown man."

Earl was an old fool. He was drunk and high and a liar. He pushed away that nagging feeling that most if not all of the words he had unleashed into the world in the last few hours were not the right ones. He remembered his father's friend singing "Wreck on the Highway" all those years ago. "I wish I could change this sad story," the man sang in the high lonesome piney woods. "When whiskey and blood run together" and "I didn't hear nobody pray."

"See you tomorrow, then," Tamara was saying. "If you're feeling up for a swim."

"I'll be up for it. I'd jump in right now if you'd let me in the pool."

"I think it best we wait," said Tamara. "I have to get back in there. I just wanted to make sure you were okay."

"I'm good," said Earl. Was he good? He had been and then he wasn't. What happened to set him off? Buck talking rape and murder? The man was only quoting song lyrics; he had no idea what that song meant to Earl. But it *seemed* like he knew something. Jade knew something she'd been trying to tell Alana all day. Tamara knew because he told her. But the lumberjacks, the girl with green hair: what did everyone know that Earl didn't?

Walking up the hill, Earl composed a letter to Arthur.

> Dear Arthur, hey ho! I'm out here in Oregon and Arthur, I seem to have walked right into something. Again, man! Not nearly as bad as last time. But something feels off. I can't for the life of me figure out what it is. It's not like I've been up to any trouble. I ride around with this kid

on rainy days shopping for records. When it's nice out I help him on his farm. We weed, we build raised beds, we prune. I also help this lady in her garden, Alana, you'd like her, Arthur, she is an ex-lawyer and a good one like you. We went to this bar tonight, not a good move, Arthur, wrong decision, but half the bar was lovin' on Alana from the second she came through the door. She's some kind of local hero. These people, they aren't bad people. They're clean and they grow vegetables and sell them at the farmer's market. They vote. They're my friends. I have friends. The folks are fun and the world is mine on Blue Bayou. Tamara's taught me how to swim. Other than that, I don't know, Arthur. I go to the library and talk to Alana's daughter, Jade. I look things up on the computer, which for a few weeks I thought was called a monitor and in my head, I still call it that. I don't understand the internet thing but everybody I ask says don't worry about it. I've been learning a little about what all happened in the in-between. None of it seems to have been much good. Especially musically. You know these kids today listen to the same stuff we did coming up? That's one thing I've learned that surprised me. A whole lot of what I've learned did not surprise me. The things that come out of people's mouths are what I want to surprise me. In the in-between everyone said the same thing Arthur, and you out of anybody will know what that is: I didn't do it, I was framed, they got the wrong guy, I was in Eagle Pass when that sonofabitch was shot down in Del Rio. I'm innocent. Everyone's innocent. There is

> one guy around here like that. Alana's ex-husband. They say he's trouble but compared to the people I've spent my life with, he just seems like a spoiled drunk. If he were all that bad, they'd have paper out on him, he wouldn't be allowed to just turn up. I'm trying to think what else. How long has it been that I've been trying to think what else? I guess I'm just the same old no-knowing-what-else fool I was last time you saw me.

Cliffside was awake. Cars had their lights on, their wipers timed to intermittent, for the mist came at you sideways, fine as a screen of no-see-ums. Where were people going? Where are you supposed to go? Home to lie on the floor and listen to Santana seemed suddenly a sad destination.

> I reckon I am headed where I am headed, Arthur. That does not mean I subscribe to Luck or its upright lesbian Methodist Aunt, Fate. I would however like to subscribe to the local newspaper. Sometimes I read it in the library. I read about school board meetings and bond referendums for a new water treatment plant. I keep up with the dismal record of the Cliffside High football team.

Earl did not know how to close his letter to Arthur. He was good with the salutation, but he had always been good at getting himself into things. Not to mention Arthur was dead and how do you end a letter to a dead man? He came to a corner market. He went in and bought a six-pack of PBR and a copy of the *Cliffside Advance*. He would take it home and scour the obituaries for what's left of a life scantly summarized, given the dollar charged per word. Once on the monitor he had found Arthur's obituary. It said he was born in 1949 in Stovall, and it said who his parents were. It said he attended UT Austin for his bachelor's and law degrees. That he practiced law in Stovall for thirty-five years. It said nothing of his compassion, his deep-cut knowledge of the Tulsa Sound. No mention of his fatal fondness for a ham egg and cheese at Sunrise. It did not say that, should Arthur be forced to state what higher power he put stock in, it would have been the Biscuit. It did not mention his sly sideways wit, his awful driving. To Earl it was like reading a Stop sign.

Earl made sure to tell the clerk at the corner store that he was buying the PBR un-ironically.

"What about the paper, then?" The clerk pointed to the *Cliffside Advance.*

Earl wanted to engage the clerk on the subject of irony, but some loud boys smelling of tobacco and weed had bunched up behind him, armed with energy drinks and candy bars. Earl turned to look at them. They had the good teeth and smooth skin of the monied, though their pants were droopy and the words out of their mouths were sour and foul. The errant children of good families, decided Earl. The clerk handed him his receipt. Had these spoiled boys not been crowding them, the clerk might have invited Earl back behind the counter and drunk a beer with him while discussing the journalistic merits of the newspaper. This was the disadvantage of shopping before 2 a.m. You are not the only person alive. The service industry is not yet so bored that they would engage an obviously drunk old man on the subject of ironic purchases.

Did we even have irony before? Earl said to Arthur. Sure wasn't present in the in-between.

He stumbled up the hill, swinging the plastic bag of beer, talking to Arthur and sometimes to himself. Behind him someone was talking back. Earl heard footsteps and then a hand on his back, pushing him to the ground. He looked up at the three boys who had been behind him in line at the store.

"Give us the beer," one said.

"And your wallet," said another.

"What about his phone?" the third was saying when Earl stood and swung the six-pack at the boy who asked for the beer. He had seen many times the weapon made from objects placed in socks. These plastic bags were surprisingly strong. He had read about the island they formed somewhere in the Pacific, supposedly the size of Texas and likely to survive the nuclear bomb that would take out Tyler. "Here's your beer." The boy was on his knees. Blood poured from his forehead. He vomited. The other two were too stunned to run so Earl swung at one and said, "Here's my wallet." The third one came alive finally and ran. "Hold up," said Earl, "I don't even own a phone!"

Earl continued up the hill, clutching his bloody bag of unironic beer. If he had a phone, would he call his mother? "Bell South," she might answer in her telephone operator voice. "Give me the party line," Earl might say. "Earl honey, is that you?" she might answer.

Well, they had their reasons for doing me like they did me. If I cared I'd get on the monitor and read their obituaries. Maybe I would write one for her. Cynthia Miller Boudreaux, 1932–2008. What does it matter where she was born, to whom, who she married, why, how many kids she had, when all she did was mostly ignore them? Once she said something to her youngest son, Earl, that stuck with him. Listen, she said, which is something she herself was not quite capable of, or maybe it was hearing that she was no good at. Either way, wherever they buried her, maybe off down in the bayou, phone lines ran above her bones, crackling still with her desperate questions.

The door to Earl's apartment was open. He switched on the light to find the end of the party line. Glasses and bottles on every surface, album covers fanned across the floor. Earl put the beer in the fridge, in the process getting blood all over his hands. His shirt was already speckled with blood from the first boy's head, which he cracked pretty good. What he didn't understand was why the other two stood around waiting to get theirs. Once he was as young as them and as foolish. He went right along with everything and look where it got him? Those boys got off easy compared to what might have happened had they beat him badly instead of vice versa. He barely saw them in the misty shadows, but he saw enough to know they would not survive the places where he'd learned to be there and also elsewhere.

Earl put on *Abraxas*, dropped the needle on "Samba Pa Ti," and turned off the lights. He lay on the floor and looked out the window at the nimbus surrounding a lone streetlight.

The fuzzy guitar solo wound around him like mist. Then came the organ, reminding him of the girl who claimed to love to roller-skate backwards.

He'd opened a beer but he couldn't find it, so he poured wine in a glass and drank from it until he nodded off.

"It can all go to hell in a couple of hours, can't it, Earl," Arthur was saying. He was sitting in the chair where Earl often sat waiting for the sun to emerge and light the tips of the bridge.

"Arthur?" Earl got up and turned on a lamp.

"Who did you kill this time?" said Winston.

II.

"SO WHO IS Arthur?"

Earl could only see the edges of Winston, backlit by the streetlight.

"Why are *you* here?"

"These are my rooms. I might not have lived here for a while but they're still mine."

Earl wasn't about to argue. He'd learned a long time ago that if a man thought something belonged to him, there was no talking him out of it. Earl was going to leave anyway, as soon as he got some sleep and cleaned himself up. If Winston wanted his rooms back, he could have them, but he was going to have to wait.

"Okay, boss. You can have your rooms. But that's not the only reason you're here, is it? What else did you want?"

Winston held up his glass. "I could use more of this."

Earl sat up. The room spun a little, then came rocking to a stop. When he'd left, it had been a white room with black curtains in the station. Now it was dark, the blackness before dawn.

Winston leaned over and plucked a bottle from the coffee table and emptied it into his glass. "Looks like I missed a good party. Well-attended one, too. Lots of glasses and bottles for one man."

"I don't guess you came here for a drink."

"You know what, Earl?" Winston said. "You really should be more accepting of me. All you know about me is what you've heard from Alana. And Jade. Maybe Jade's boyfriend. They have farmers where you come from, I'm sure. You ever met a farmer named Kaiser? Well, maybe a gentleman farmer. Do they have those in the South? I'm sure they do. Maybe that's where the term came from. Here it's pretty rare. Which makes Kaiser a pretty patrician name for someone who raises hydroponic lettuce."

Earl said, "Whatever 'patrician' means."

"At least you're not one of those cats who act above their station by using four-dollar words. And often in the wrong context."

Earl thought of words as money. Alana could cash in and have enough to build an outdoor shower. She was always telling him she wanted one. Earl didn't quite get why, since Cliffside seemed pretty much all the time an outdoor shower.

"'Patrician' means upper class. The name Kaiser suggests a certain social strata."

"Like Winston?"

Winston laughed. "You got me there. My mother's British. She named me after Churchill despite the fact that like ninety percent of babies I did not resemble him. She expected greatness from me. She thought I might be a statesman. She never once criticized anything I did. If I got suspended from school, she went after the assistant principal. Once I got caught shoplifting beer from a Pakistani convenience store and for weeks she went on an anti-Pakistani scree. They're all soulless moneygrubbers, she said. They don't wash."

"All this is supposed to make me accept you?"

"I know it might be hard for you to feel sorry for someone brought up to be prime minister. But it's not unlike someone whose parents completely neglect them. In both cases, the child is invisible. So I would think we would have some common experiences in our upbringing."

"You don't know anything about me." Earl thought about his people. Hell, Arthur knew more about them than Earl did.

"I only know what you did."

He didn't know unless he said it. So Earl wanted to hear him say it.

"What is it I did?"

"Back to your opinion of me. All you've heard is their side. There is always another side. Just like with you. I'm sure your story is not so straightforward. I guess your judgment was clouded. I know how easy it is for that to happen. I've been known to make bad choices when I'm fucked up. But I'm sure that's not news to you."

Earl said, "Until today, I haven't had a drink in forty-four years. Definitely a bad choice. I'm feeling pretty shitty right about now. Be good if you could just leave."

"All that blood on your clothes," said Winston. "Blood

in the kitchen too. On the refrigerator. On a bag lying on the floor. Whose blood, Earl?"

"I was walking home from the store. These kids jumped me. Tried to rob me."

"Is that why the neighborhood is lousy with cops?"

"Wouldn't know. I've been sleeping."

Winston poured more wine.

"Have a drink with me."

"I'm good."

"You're good? Okay, I believe you. You're a good guy. You didn't do what they put you away for. If I believe you, why can't you believe me?"

Earl didn't understand what it was Winston wanted him to believe. That there was another side of him? He hadn't seen it, but he didn't doubt it. Earl had spent decades living with men who had done terrible things and there wasn't a one of them who did not at some point reveal a side of them that they were trying to conceal. Even Mattox, who Earl hated, painted little pictures. The same picture, actually: a farmhouse on a pond. Trees that looked like broccoli in the distance. A horse grazing in a fenced pasture. Over time the horse grew to look like a horse. Earl could see muscles in his flank. He never mentioned it to Mattox but one night when the block was quiet Mattox talked about his grandparents who lived in the country outside of Jasper. He talked about his grandpop taking him fishing. Earl understood this to be the last place Mattox found peace. He returned to it in his mind and on paper, venturing back to it like a pilgrimage, giving shape and dimension to his long-gone innocence.

"Remember the other day when you interrupted me having a conversation with my ex-wife? And I asked were you guys together and you said no?"

"I wouldn't call what y'all were having a conversation."

"You said no too quickly, Earl. It's been a long time since you've been with a woman, right? And Alana is still a beauty. Show me another woman our age who has a flat stomach. I guess it's all that yoga she does. She's always had a nice ass."

"You ought not to talk about her that way," said Earl.

"So you do have the hots for her. Or are you just being a Southern gentleman?"

"We're friends. I told you that in the kitchen."

"Friends with benefits you mean? Alana's always had a weakness for people she feels weren't given a proper chance. That would explain her hanging around Tamara, whose ex-husband used to sell us both coke back in the day. Tamara's dad's in the pokey as we speak. But Alana knew all that up front. She's generous but she's not a fool. Obviously, she hasn't done her homework on you. The only possible reason why is because she's fucking you and she doesn't want to know. But she deserves to know."

"I got no reason to lie to you," Earl said.

"You must be gay then. Is that it?"

"They didn't have that when I was coming up. Or they did, but they had other names for it. Honestly, I never got to figure that part out. You probably think, how could I possibly not know? I always heard you either are or you aren't. I loved a girl once and I loved being with her."

"By being with her, I assume you mean fucking her. Was she the only woman you've ever been with?"

Earl remembered the article he'd read a few weeks earlier in a magazine. It was all about how these days you didn't have to decide. Sexuality, it claimed, was fluid. Made sense to Earl. Over half the body is water. Three quarters of the world. Earlier, in the bar, he'd felt bad for thinking of Tina pressed naked against him in the pond. Well, why? It happened. He'd always felt like he was standing waist-deep in water.

"Since you didn't answer, I'm assuming she was. And when you say you never got to figure it out, are you telling me you've never been with a man?"

"I didn't say that," said Earl. He was not talking to Winston anymore. Winston was speaking and Earl was answering him, but Earl wasn't there. He was pressing his buoy in the water. The water was pressing back.

"Well, I can understand it. Long time to go without a woman. I'd probably do the same if I were out of commission for that long."

But Earl was not there. He still did not understand how he could have thought for years about the things he did with Tina and not once imagined the things he did with Tom. But the body knows more than the mind. He thought often and for years of moving through the water, but once he was in the water, the fear went away and the breathing took over.

He wasn't scared of Winston. He was scared of not breathing, but like he'd told Arthur before he'd even slugged those boys with a bag full of beer, he'd walked right into something.

Again. He ought to finish that letter, but he didn't know how to.

"Well, like I said earlier, people are complicated," Winston said. "I don't go that way myself, but I have my own secrets."

"I just told you, so how can it still be a secret?"

"You've got another secret and it's a big one."

He still hadn't said it. He talked around it, but he hadn't said it.

"Do what you need to do. Just get the fuck out of my house," Earl said.

"*Your* house?"

Earl was tired.

"Okay, Winston. I'll tell you a little something about prison, since you seem to want to talk around it. One of the worst things you can do in there is violate someone else's space. There's no space in there. So people are real protective of what little space they got. Lots of things will get you fucked up in there but getting up in someone's space? That will get you killed."

"You're saying you're going to kill me, too?"

"I never killed anyone."

"Let's have a drink and you can tell me all about what you didn't do."

"I don't want a drink," said Earl. "I want you to go do what you have to do."

"You want me out so bad, go call the cops. Tell them you've got an intruder."

"Even if I didn't just beat the shit out of some kids who

tried to rob me and who according to you already called the cops, I would not call the cops."

"Trust issues?"

"With cops? Yeah, I'd say so. But not with everyone. I trust Alana. I trust your daughter and Kaiser. I trust Tamara."

"Tamara? She's done well for herself. She didn't have much to work with."

"You mean she's not a patrician like you?"

"You ever met that wife of hers? Straight-up white trash."

"Everyone told me you were charming."

"Nice to hear," said Winston, pouring the last of the wine into his glass. "But I don't get why you're so shocked. I'm talking to you like men talk to each other, Earl."

"I've *been* done with how men talk to each other." Earl stood up, wobbling a little. The Clothesline was gone. He wasn't coming back.

"You've *been* done, you say? Okay. I've *been* done with this conversation."

"So one of us has to leave."

"Oh, you can stay," Winston said. "But I don't get why you would. First thing I'm going to do is find Alana and tell her what I know about you. Then I'm going to call the cops and tell them about the blood."

Earl wasn't going to sit down again. He looked beyond Winston, out the window. He saw mist around the streetlight. Soon it would be dawn. The sun would not come up today but there would still be light. Weak and gray but the world would be visible. Earl would be visible.

Winston wasn't anyone. He was Earl's past. He was what

Earl had let happen, and what he'd done, and Earl was a fool to think it wouldn't come back. That it would *disappear* disappear.

He felt the blood caked on his clothes. "I'm going to ask you a favor. Will you give me time to get changed and pack up?"

"Of course. I wouldn't send you out there with the clothes you're wearing. You probably ought to burn them. I'd offer to help, but I'd be tampering with evidence."

Earl said, "There's beer in the fridge. I won't be needing it. Help yourself."

"That's kind, Earl. I'm glad we were able to work things out."

Earl went into the bedroom to pack. He stuffed clothes in his old suitcase he'd bought in Stovall. He stood on top of the bed and retrieved the traveler's checks from a shoebox he'd hidden above a ceiling tile and put them in the suitcase. He unplugged the bedside lamp he'd kept to remind himself of his innocence in another life. He sat on the bed and waited.

All the wine was gone. Earl figured Winston might get thirsty. And he did. Earl heard the refrigerator suck open. He moved quickly and caught Winston bent over, his head in the cold, his hand around a can of beer.

Winston only took two blows to the back of his head. The rest were for others. He hit Mattox twice, because he hated him. Then he hit Tom, even though he did not hate him. He hit him for being a thing he could not hate because everyone claimed he was a ghost, hiding out in Earl's head. People standing still as deer at the edge of the shadowy wood turned to watch. Earl hit them so that they would go away forever. The little girl who lived next to a ghost watched Earl throw up and Earl thought of hitting her if only to save her from a life she did not deserve. But instead, he kept hitting Winston, even though Winston was lying still on the linoleum. He had not been anyone but now he was the person Earl killed.

It was going to get light out soon. Just like in the song his father taught him, the moon just went behind the clouds to hide its face and cry. But the clouds moved and left the moon glowing in a patch of brightening sky.

The lights were off in Alana's house. She would be sleeping by now. Still, he crept lightly through the garden. If you so much as leave your shit lying around out there, I will find you, Tamara had told him, but he wasn't scared of Tamara. It was more a matter of respect.

At an intersection halfway down the hill he spotted from the alleyway two police cruisers, parked facing opposite directions. Lights flashing. Was this a roadblock, or a chin-wag? Probably they were enjoying a biscuit while attempting to ascertain his whereabouts.

He could turn himself in and claim, rightly, that what he'd done to those kids was self-defense. And go back to jail for the rest of his life. Before they even found old Winston.

Fear and breathing: Alana had it right all along. But Earl wasn't scared when he got to the river. Rain in the mountains, maybe snowmelt, churned the waters. Well, no matter: he was going *with* the current. He knew how to breathe in the water.

He stripped off his clothes and tossed them into the river. He tossed his suitcase and watched it bob in the current.

Downstream it hit a rock and Earl worried it was stuck but the river spun it loose and took it away. Earl followed it into the water. In up to his thighs and the cold took his breath away. He stood still for a while, waiting for his breathing to acclimate to the cold. He remembered everything Tamara had taught him, but he knew he had to choose a point of focus. For a second Earl focused on throwing Arthur's life savings in the river, though if the river went to Japan, maybe some needy Japanese person would find it and it would change their life as it had Earl's. Still, watching the suitcase twist in the furious current, he felt bad about it, but Arthur would not want anyone else to have it. Earl was all Arthur had in the end, and now Arthur was all Earl had. Though Earl had found hope in the wet hills of this town. He'd made friends. He remembered the day he arrived on the bus, waking into its misty beauty. This ain't your stop, chief, the bus driver said when Earl got off. Well, it turned out he was half right.

He could have been a bus driver. Drive across the country calling out the names of places while sitting also on a log reading a book in the black-mouthed woods. Take up tickets and listen at the same time to the songs of love singers. Half right and dead wrong. The river that took him when he let go of land would meet the sea and maybe become it. Earl would just as soon it stay both, but it was all water. Water did whatever it wanted, and it never had listened to Earl.

Acknowledgments

APPARENTLY IT TAKES a country: In Texas, Kim Wolfgang, Will Johnson, Laura Furman, Joel Barna, Jimmy McWilliams, Peter Young, Glen Rhoden, Jesse Straus; in North Carolina, James Parker, Travis Mulhauser, Emma Parker, Jesse Moore, Terry Kennedy, Chris Stamey; in Montana, Stewart Parker, John Taliaferro and Malou Flato; in California, Chad Holley; in New York, Jim McHugh, Rebecca Bengal; in Oregon, Kevin Jones; in Washington, Dominic Smith; in Michigan, Andrew Meredith. Thanks and love to all y'all.

Special thanks to Kathy Pories (again, and even moreso this time around) and everyone at Algonquin, and to Joy Harris, who, among dozens of other admirable traits, does not look away.